BOOK OF SHADOWS VOLUME III

THE WOLF SOCIETY

A Novel

MICHAEL PENNING

Copyright © 2022 Michael Penning
All Rights Reserved

This is a work of fiction. Any reference to historical events, real people, or real places are used fictitiously. Other names, characters, places, and events are products of the author's imagination and any resemblance to actual events, places, or persons, living or dead, is entirely coincidental.

No part of this book may be reproduced, or stored in a retrieval system, or transmitted in any form or by any means, electronic, mechanical, photocopying, recording, or otherwise, without express written permission of the publisher.

THE WOLF SOCIETY
First edition. May, 2022
ISBN: 978-1-7771812-9-1 (paperback)
ISBN: 978-1-7771812-8-4 (hardcover)

www.michaelpenning.com

For my daughter,
who brought magic into my life.

Chapter 1

Anna Jacobs was going to kill the man she was dancing with. She wouldn't do it here, not under the brilliant glow of the reception room chandeliers. And she wouldn't do it now, surrounded as she was by the cream of Vermont's genteel society. But within the hour, the beguiling young Southerner with the chestnut curls and whiskey eyes would lie headless at Anna's feet.

"You truly are an elegant dancer." The gentleman pressed his palm into the small of Anna's back and kept her at a decent arm's length as he led her through the intricate steps of the English country dance. If his hand slipped lower, his wrist would brush against the six-inch blade strapped to Anna's slender thigh beneath the folds of her silk ball gown.

"How kind of you to say," Anna replied demurely. "I was raised to be prepared for any situation, including the occasion when a handsome gentleman might ask for the pleasure of a dance."

"Have there been many such occasions?" The man's sly grin revealed two rows of pearly teeth.

"Would it pain you to know there have?"

"Not in the least."

Anna indulged the gentleman's smug confidence with a smile and glanced around the room. The governor's wife had spared no expense on her party in honor of Burlington's celebrated architect and surveyor, John Johnson. They had invited over fifty guests to the governor's mansion to celebrate the inauguration of Johnson's latest accomplishment, the university's new Middle College building.

While the mansion had no formal ballroom, the spacious second-floor reception room had been cleared of furniture to allow space for dancing. A quartet tucked into a corner kept time and tune with a lively medley. Three other couples now shared the floor with Anna and her partner while an assembly of guests in fashionable ball gowns and fine tailcoats stood admiring them from the periphery. The bright lights of the chandeliers glittered off an abundance of fine jewels and gold buttons. To ensure the women wouldn't slip while dancing, the First Lady of Vermont had hired an artist to chalk the polished pine floor with an assortment of fanciful floral patterns, arabesques, and nymphs.

The quartet's song drew to a close and ended the dancing. The bystanders applauded as the couples bowed to each other and left the floor. Soon, the guests would sit to dine and the dancing wouldn't resume until after dinner.

Anna wouldn't get another chance to end the man's life. She had to act now.

"I would enjoy some fresh air before dinner," she said. "Would you be kind enough to accompany me?"

"I know just the place for it." The Southerner flashed a grin and offered her his arm.

Anna swept the room with another glance as he led her toward the door. To avoid attracting unwanted attention, she had chosen an unassuming lilac gown with a fashionable natural waist and a modest neckline that only hinted at the swell of her bosom. But she had still needed to catch the Southerner's eye. For that, she had relied on her own natural beauty. At seventeen, she was in the prime of her womanhood. Her thick, coal-black hair was twisted into a bun and tied with a simple ribbon. Delicate ringlets framed her fine features and angular jaw. Her large blue eyes sparkled like shards of sapphire and her soft lips were rosebuds blossoming from her snowy skin.

Intent as they were on their own conversations, none of the guests seemed to take notice of Anna's departure—except for one woman. She was elegantly dressed and strikingly beautiful, with honey-blonde hair and eyes like a winter sky.

Anna's heart lurched at the sight of her. What was *she* doing here?

There wasn't time to give the woman any more thought; Anna and her companion were already leaving the room behind. Instead of making their way down the curving staircase from the mezzanine floor to the entrance hall, the young man led her down a candlelit corridor that ended at another staircase. Anna quickly understood that it ascended to the squat cupola atop the mansion's roof. The bold Southerner intended to take advantage of the privacy of the rooftop where they would be alone, far above where the other guests would soon gather to dine.

It was the perfect location for a trap.

Anna marveled at her luck and chided herself for not having thought of luring her prey to the quiet spot herself. Her heart quickened in her chest as she climbed the steep and narrow staircase. She had waited weeks for this moment, and her veins now thrummed with the promise of violence.

"What has brought you this far north?" she asked cordially.

"My family has profited considerably from the cotton trade in Charleston, but I have no taste for slavery," the young man drawled. "Timber is where I'll forge my own fortune—and of that, Vermont is plentiful."

Anna knew it was all a lie. This man wasn't who he claimed to be.

But neither was Anna.

The observation room at the top of the stairs was surrounded by arched windows. Anna went to the nearest one and casually scanned the rooftop, making quick mental notes of anything she could use to her advantage. Three storeys up from the estate's sprawling hilltop grounds, the roof was flat and open, with nowhere to hide. A waist-high balustrade ran around its perimeter and the cupola's door was the only way on or off. Days might even go by before anyone discovered the Southerner's corpse. There would be no better place for Anna's bloody task.

The Southerner went to the door and cast it open. In the darkness far below the rooftop, a trail of torches snaked their way up the hill from the burgeoning village of Burlington. A hint of fresh pine from the surrounding forests mingled with the earthy scent of fallen leaves. To the west, the black void of Lake Champlain lay shimmering under the pale light of a moon that was only a sliver shy of full. It was an unseasonably warm night for mid-October, but perched high atop the roof, a stiff breeze still fluttered Anna's dress and twirled the ringlets of her hair. It didn't surprise her when her companion removed his wool tailcoat and wrapped it around her shoulders.

"Where I come from, we'd call this weather positively frigid." He winked and gestured for her to lead the way out to the roof.

Anna realized too late that she had made a mistake in turning her back on the Southerner.

As soon as the door closed behind them, he lunged for her.

The gentleman's grin vanished and his lips peeled back. His teeth gleamed like ivory saw-blades as they snapped and gnashed, intent on ripping Anna's flesh from her bones.

The ferocious savagery of his attack caught Anna by surprise—but not enough to overwhelm a lifetime of training and instinct. She ducked and spun in the same motion, swinging a leg out to swipe at the man's knee as he sprang at her. He tripped and stumbled away as Anna's hand flew to the knife strapped to her leg. It was in her palm in an instant, faster than it took for the man to regain his balance and whirl to face her.

The young Southerner now looked more corpse-like than human as he circled Anna. The whites of his eyes were a hideous shade of red, as if all the blood vessels had burst under the pressure of something straining to get out of his skull. His skin had lost all color and was now a livid bluish-gray. A gleaming line of spit dripped from his curled lips. The vicious snarl of something cruel and rabid twisted from his mouth. His next move came fast as he charged at Anna again, intent on overpowering her with his size and speed.

Anna anticipated the attack and dodged to one side. She brought the knife slicing through the air and caught the creature that used to be the Southerner in the side. The blade sank deep between his ribs as he sailed past her. He let out an enraged cry and whipped out a claw-like hand, seizing Anna's wrist. With inhuman strength, he yanked her from her feet and flung her toward the balustrade at the roof's edge. She hit the stone barrier hard below her waist and windmilled her arms to regain her balance, but her momentum carried her toppling over.

The heart-stopping terror of weightlessness gripped Anna as she tumbled. Her hand shot up and caught the ledge just in time to save herself from free-falling. She clung by one hand with her feet dangling in the air beneath her and glanced down. There was a second roof about thirty feet below her. It was level with the second-storey windows and sheltered the long veranda that wrapped around the mansion's west side.

Anna's breath caught in her throat as her tenuous grip on the roof's ledge slipped. Her muscles burned as she supported all of her weight with the grip of one hand. Her other hand still clutched the knife, but it would leave her defenseless if she dropped it. The smooth soles of her dancing slippers brushed against the wall and left pale streaks of chalk as she scrabbled for traction.

She looked down again. It would be a long drop.

The creature's ghastly face appeared over the balustrade above her. The blood-red whites of his eyes were swollen to the verge of rupturing. A wicked grin spread across his cruel mouth as he reached to grab Anna's wrist, intent on hauling her up so he could finish her.

Anna swung the knife up and sliced through the fleshy undersides of the creature's exposed forearms. Blood showered down on her as he howled in pain and snatched his hands back. The ledge became slick and Anna's grip continued to slip, slip, slip. She clenched her fingers, putting all of her strength into her fingertips as she weighed her options. If she let the creature drag her up, he would have her at a terrible disadvantage as she struggled to fight him from below.

She chose the second option and let go.

A rush of wind billowed her hair and dress as she dropped. The roof below rushed up to meet her with dizzying speed. She hit it and rolled in the same motion to lessen the impact, but a hot jolt of pain still shot up from her ankle as it twisted beneath her. She winced and gasped before snatching the knife from where it had fallen and swinging around.

The creature glowered down at her from the balustrade thirty feet above. Their eyes met for a brief instant and Anna saw the murderous hunger behind them before he spun around and vanished from sight.

Damn! Anna's heart sank. People would die if she let the monster escape. She spun in a circle, looking for a way off the veranda's roof. The drop to the ground below was still another thirty feet, much too high to risk again. Even if her wounded ankle could withstand the fall, how would she slip past the dinner guests now gathered on the first floor?

There was only one other alternative.

Anna ignored the shooting pain in her ankle as she whirled and crashed headlong through one of the large second-storey windows.

Shattered glass rained down upon her. Anna felt the sharp sting of nicks and cuts as she tumbled into a darkened room and scrambled to her feet. There was a moment of blindness before her eyes adjusted and she could make out her surroundings.

She was in one of the mansion's many bedchambers: a nursery that was no longer in use. A cradle and crib stood still and silent in the darkness and an assortment of wooden toys and dolls stared at Anna from their shelves. The muffled sounds of the dinner guests rumbled up through the floorboards beneath Anna's feet. Had anyone heard the window shattering? Or had the din of the party masked the noise? If someone came up to investigate, she would have a hard time explaining herself, dripping blood and brandishing a deadly knife.

Anna couldn't spare a second to worry about it now. She had to find the creature before it was too late. Her ankle was already swelling as she hurried across the room to the door and into the dim corridor beyond. She was back on the mezzanine floor. At the far end of the corridor were the stairs to the cupola. A row of closed doors stretched away to Anna's left. Candles flickered in the wall sconces and sent eerie shadows dancing into the wallpapered corners.

Anna's heart hammered at her ribs and adrenaline slammed through her body as she assessed the situation. Had the creature already gotten past her and escaped to the first floor? Was it still inside the cupola? Or was it waiting to spring at her from behind one of these closed doors?

Anna tightened her grip on the knife and slowly

approached the first door. She paused and pricked her ears, listening for any sounds within.

There was nothing but silence.

But that didn't mean there was no one—or no *thing*—inside.

Anna reached for the knob and turned, readying herself for an attack. The door eased open on squeaky hinges. The bed chamber beyond lay cloaked in darkness. Anna waited a moment, peering into the gloom until she was satisfied the room was empty. The door squeaked shut behind her and she continued on, the wide planks of the floorboards creaking under her slow and wary tread. She crept further down the corridor toward the cupola's staircase.

A trail of blood led from the steps to the door in front of her.

The creature lurked on the other side.

Anna drew a deep breath and swung the door open.

What she saw in the room froze her where she stood.

The creature was there—but he wasn't alone. One of the governor's servants stood bloodied and trembling in his clutches. She was young, perhaps no older than Anna herself. One of the creature's gnarled hands dug into her arm while the other clamped tight over her mouth to keep her from screaming. Her black muslin shift was torn at the shoulder and her eyes were wide and terrified as she pleaded silently for help from across the governor's private library.

A terrible desolation cut through Anna when she saw the bites gouged from the flesh of the girl's neck and shoulder. Blood pulsed from the gaping wounds in time with the beating of her heart. Anna's stomach twisted into a tight knot.

It's too late for her, a voice whispered in her head. *She's already dead on her feet.*

The creature hissed and drooled blood as he kept the maid as a human shield between himself and Anna. Perhaps he thought Anna might misread the girl's wounds and do whatever she could to save her.

It didn't work.

Anna flipped the knife in her hand and flung it hard.

The blade buried deep into the girl's chest. Blood bloomed on the white of her apron and her frightened eyes went very wide, as if cold water had just been thrown in her face. Then the life went out of her and she slumped forward in the creature's grip.

Anna's unexpected gambit caught the monster by surprise. He let the maid's limp body drop to the floor and backed into a corner, blood-red eyes darting everywhere for some way to escape. Books lined the walls from floor to ceiling. Crystal decanters of various liquors sat atop a stately oak sidebar. Kindling and logs awaited lighting in the darkened fireplace.

Anna had all the angles covered. The only way out of the room was through her.

The creature let loose a guttural snarl and charged.

Instead of retreating, Anna dove at the creature as he barreled across the room toward her. Her hand snapped up the iron fireplace poker and in one quick motion, she rammed the sharp point up into the bottom of the creature's jaw. A spray of blood shot from the wound as the creature clutched at his chin and reeled sideways. He staggered and crashed to the floor. His head hit the sidebar on the way down and it snapped to one side with a loud and sickening *crack!* like a chicken bone being broken in two.

Anna stayed on the defensive as the creature lay motionless and bleeding on the expensive rug. His neck was twisted at such a grotesque angle that his very spine had to have snapped.

But that wouldn't be enough. Not for this thing.

Anna kept her palm wrapped around the poker as she went to the sidebar and smashed one of the crystal decanters. She gripped the jagged shard of the decanter's neck and kept her eyes fixed on the creature as she waited, waited, waited, until…

The creature moved.

Anna's pulse raced as he crawled to his knees and drew himself upright. He remained there a moment, blood pouring across the breast of his waistcoat and swaying like a drunk on his feet, before his head swiveled around on his broken neck.

Anna's sharp shard of glass cut through the air and pierced the creature's throat. He thrashed and shrieked as she sawed through flesh and sinew and bone until she had separated the creature's head from his body.

His headless corpse collapsed in a heap at Anna's feet.

She stared down at it a moment, her chest heaving, blood pounding in her ears. The thrilling rush of the kill was exquisite. But as the intensity of the moment faded, Anna's gaze went to where the body of the maid lay crumpled on the floor. Anna crossed the room to kneel beside her.

The dead girl's sightless eyes stared up at her as Anna retrieved her knife. She shuddered to think how long the stark terror frozen into that lifeless stare would haunt her. A dozen thoughts leapt unbidden into Anna's mind: Did the girl have a family? A husband? Children who would weep for their mother and wonder why she had never come home?

Anna sensed another presence in the room. She wasn't alone.

She gripped the knife and revolved around.

The elegant blonde woman from the reception room watched her from the door. Her eyes glittered like chips of ice as she lingered there a moment, surveying the carnage in silence. Her eyes swept from the headless monster to the maid's body and finally to Anna herself.

Anna rose. Her gaze trailed the woman as she entered the room and crossed to the sidebar, where she poured two fingers of whiskey from another crystal decanter. The woman sank into a plush wingback chair and took a long sip. Her cool gaze strayed once more from the dead girl to the decapitated creature and back again. She didn't look at Anna when she spoke, but her voice was heavy with sympathy.

"There was nothing else to be done. 'Twas a mercy you did her."

"Mother," Anna grumbled. "What an unexpected surprise."

Chapter 2

Abigail Jacobs cradled a glass of whiskey in her palm and gazed at her daughter from across the tavern table. "Now, tell me about this revenant."

They sat in a corner lit by a single candle in the back of the bustling Nobody Inn. Perched on the shore of Lake Champlain, the dockside tavern was the sort of public house where darkened corners were as popular as the dark deeds they concealed. It was a Saturday night, and for the motley assortment of fisherman, steamboat deckhands, lumberjacks, and warehouse workers who frequented the Nobody during their waking hours between shifts, the drinking and gambling would continue well into the early hours of the morning. Those with an extra coin or two in their pockets might even buy a few hours in the company of one of the many women of easy virtue who called the tavern a second home. Clouds of blue pipe-smoke swirled lazily in the dim candlelight as the sharp crack of dice rolling across the tables shot through the clamor of the cavernous room.

It was the last place women like Abigail and Anna would

be expected to be found—and exactly where they felt at home.

A little over an hour had passed since they had stolen away from the bloody scene at the governor's mansion. Anna had taken a moment to dispose of her bloody ball gown in favor of a simple dress and overcoat she had stashed near the edge of the estate's grounds. Days before the ball, she had arranged for a pair of mercenary resurrectionists to disguise themselves as servants to remove the headless corpse of the thing that was the Southerner. When confronted with the unexpected task of making the maid's body disappear as well, they had been skittish for fear of being charged as accomplices to murder.

But for men who made a living selling the bodies of the recently dead to be dissected as specimens in medical schools, there was little that money couldn't buy. By morning, the cart carrying the two corpses would be leaving the green mountains of Vermont behind on its way to New Hampshire and Dartmouth College. All that would remain was the strange mystery of a shattered window in the mansion's nursery, a smashed decanter in the governor's library, and a missing rug. All would be attributed to some drunken dinner guest.

Anna's expression remained grim as she stared into her own tankard of strong, dark ale. "I came across him in Cambridge several months ago."

"You never told me about him."

"I didn't see the need." Anna had an edge in her voice. "His real name was Stanton Vess. He was shot dead in a pistol duel in Savannah nearly ten years ago. I had mistaken him for a nosferatu."

"And what is the difference?"

Anna's response was that of a pupil reciting the answer to an examination question. "Nosferatu are an ancient breed of creatures that feast on blood to survive. A revenant is a human corpse reanimated by an evil spirit craving the warmth of human blood for pleasure."

"Very good. What of the evil spirit that reanimated Vess' corpse?"

"Vess' own grandfather, Harlon. By the time I pieced it together, he had already fled Cambridge and moved further northward."

"So you ran off here in pursuit."

"Suffer no evil to live… isn't that how you raised me, Mother?" Anna snapped and gulped her ale. "I had every intention of returning to Boston."

"Hmmm… I wonder." Abigail took a long sip of her whiskey and let the heat of it warm her from throat to chest. "I was about your age when I left my stepfather's home in Salem." She looked her daughter in the eye. "I had thought you might at least say farewell before you left."

"There *is* no leaving this life of ours, is there?" Anna replied bitterly. "Ours is a cursed bloodline. My great-great-grandmother was hanged for witchcraft in Salem. My great-grandmother drowned herself in a fit of madness. My grandmother sacrificed herself to save you from a vengeful spirit, and I can very well expect the both of us to die bloody deaths as well. Whether I like it or not, this is the life you've raised me into and there's no escaping it."

"No, I suppose there isn't. But truth be told, 'tisn't a terribly bad life." Abigail's blue eyes twinkled in the candlelight. "Remember the Gloucester haunting?"

Anna scowled and stared down into the dark galaxy of foam swirling in her ale.

"Tis not your fault the girl is dead." Abigail said after a moment. "Her fate was sealed the moment she happened across that abomination."

"But I—"

"Did what was required to save others from a bloodthirsty monster, no more and no less than we have always done." Abigail stretched a hand across the table and took her daughter's palm in her own. "You saved many lives tonight, but sometimes we must accept that we can't save them all."

The unexpected tenderness in her mother's touch felt strange to Anna. She pressed her full lips into a hard line and released her hand. This subject was over and not to be broached again. "How did you find me?"

"Truthfully, there's no need to find what has never been lost," Abigail replied. "I've had a Familiar bound to you since you were in swaddles."

Anna's ale froze halfway to her mouth as she stared at her mother in disbelief. "You've had a spirit following me my whole life?"

"Anna, after all we've been through, I would have thought there to be nothing left I could do to shock you."

Anna's eyes simmered with speechless fury. "How could you—"

"Oh, come now. Are you so surprised? How else was I to ensure your safety while I spent nights hunting monsters and banishing spirits? Was I expected to leave you alone in your crib unattended?"

"So you bound an undead spirit to be my *nanny*?" The muscles in Anna's jaw flexed as she clenched her teeth. "What is his name?"

"Anna, you know we don't speak their names aloud."

Anna looked away, gripping her tankard hard enough to turn her knuckles white.

Abigail read her daughter's anger and said nothing. Instead, her eyes caught those of a young man gazing at her from across the room. He stood out from the others, with a dignified refinement that suggested he was a student at the university up the hill and not one of the coarse fishermen and laborers. He was tall and slight with sandy blonde hair, deep eyes, and an angular jaw that came together at a dimple in his chin.

With Anna still brooding in silent fury, Abigail rose from the table. "I came here to see that my daughter was safe," she said with a new chill in her tone. "But I've come to realize that my concern was neither warranted nor welcome. I've booked two tickets on tomorrow's steamboat back to Whitehall. You're welcome to one if you like. If I don't see you at the wharf, I'll know your decision." Her attention strayed back to the young man across the room. "In the meantime, I believe I would prefer to spend the night in more pleasant company."

Anna's gaze flicked sideways and burned into her mother's back as Abigail turned and walked away. Through the smoky haze, she watched as Abigail sidled up to the handsome student.

And then Anna noticed something very strange.

A young girl sat on a stool at the end of the long bar. She

couldn't have been more than five years-old. Her strawberry blonde hair looked like it hadn't been washed in a while. Her mousy face was drawn and tired at this late hour and her eyes were heavy and glassy as she stared down at a cup of water sitting on the bar in front of her.

Something about the girl reminded Anna of herself and her own childhood. She had grown up in places like this in the company of her mother and Abigail's connections to the Boston underworld. It was in seedy harbor-front taverns like this one that Anna had been trained to fight by some of the city's toughest wenches and street-fighters. She had received her first fat lip from a barmaid at the age of twelve. Anna wore it like a badge of honor; a sign that she was getting stronger. A year later, she returned the favor and blackened the barmaid's eye. She had bloodied the noses of two men and knocked a tooth from a third by the time she was fourteen.

Anna's upbringing had been anything but common, and so it was still strange to see that little girl perched on her stool in a place like this so late at night. Anna glanced around. Where were the child's parents? Getting good and drunk at one of the tables? That was one thing Anna couldn't fault her mother for: Abigail enjoyed her whiskey, but she never allowed herself the shameful loss of control of drunkenness.

"Your sister won't have any luck with him tonight." The appearance of the barmaid at Anna's side pulled her attention away from the young girl at the bar. "Lad's lost his last coin on a game of Hazard and in debt up to his baubles."

The barmaid was a young and pretty Irishwoman with a mane of flaming red hair, delicate features, a pert nose, and luminous green eyes that gleamed despite the sleepless circles surrounding them. She was watching Abigail with amusement as she slipped out the front door with her new companion.

Anna gave a wry smile. Though she had never met her father, her luxuriant black hair was his legacy and the only outward difference between her and her mother. In every other respect, they did bear a striking resemblance, from their clear blue eyes to the slight downturn of their small noses. "She's no whore," Anna said. "And she's my mother, not my sister."

"Your ma?" the barmaid exclaimed. "Almighty Jesus, I hope to look half as good in motherhood. What's her game then? Pickpocket?"

"Simply a woman in need of an escort to see her home safely."

The barmaid gave a knowing grin and introduced herself. "Kitty Hayes."

"Emily Cuthbert." Anna rarely gave her real name.

"If you don't mind me saying so, Miss Cuthbert, you two look a might fancy to be hanging about a place like this."

Anna used the moment to satisfy her curiosity and nodded toward the young girl at the end of the bar. "If anyone looks out of place here, it would be *her*, wouldn't you agree?"

Kitty glanced back over her shoulder. "Cassie? Her da's Jericho Byrne." She spat the man's name as if it were so notorious that it should be instantly recognized. "Dosser's fresh from the lumber camps and crawling into a bottle or two tonight. Best Cassie not be around when he gets like that, so I'm looking after her until he passes out or dies and the devil take him."

"And the girl's mother?"

A quick shadow of grief flickered across Kitty's face. "She's one o' the missing."

Anna frowned and gave a slight nod. Everyone knew about the women who had disappeared over the past couple of months. They were what had drawn Anna to Burlington in pursuit of the revenant. Now that the creature was dead, it would claim no more victims.

"You knew her?" Anna asked.

"Sure I did. Mary works—*worked*—here at the Nobody." Kitty gave a sad sigh. "Hasn't been the same here without her this past month."

"I'm sorry about your friend." Anna knew it was the right thing to say, even if she lacked the emotional capacity to sympathize. She had never been close enough to anyone to call them a friend.

"Frightful thing," Kitty mused. "There's whispers of a killer on the loose, don't you know. 'Spose it was just a matter of time, what with the village growing so fast and all. Still, three women in as many months…"

A sudden bolt shot through Anna and seized her attention. "Three women?"

Kitty gave a grim nod.

"I had heard there were two."

"That's on account o' nobody gives a shite about a dead Indian girl. Most around here think she ran back to her people across the lake. But give up a paying job as a maid in the dean's house for the squalor of a reservation? It just dunna' make sense. No, if you ask me, Tabitha Brant was the first to go missing."

A clamor and outburst of impatient voices from a distant table snagged Kitty's attention. "Right, must crack on. Get you another pint o' the black stuff, Ms. Cuthbert?"

Anna nodded and Kitty scuttled off to fetch more ale and wine for her unruly patrons. Left alone, Anna's mind reeled as she twirled her near-empty tankard around on the table distractedly and considered the implications of this new revelation.

Three women in as many months…

Whoever this Indian girl was, she must have gone missing in July. The revenant Anna had killed had only arrived in Burlington in August.

It could only mean one thing.

Something else was preying on the women.

Chapter 3

Abigail lay propped in her bed with her bare back to the headboard and watched as the handsome student dressed himself across the room. His name was Nathaniel and their encounter had been brief. The young man had been eager to please but plainly too inexperienced to satisfy her. He faltered as most men did when he came across the crisscrossing scars that covered much of Abigail's arms from her wrists to her elbows. But the old lacerations were forgotten in the throes of lust.

And yet, whatever pleasure Abigail had hoped to glean from the encounter was spoiled by thoughts of Anna. She was too distracted by visions of their argument to enjoy herself. She had felt more than a bit of relief when the young man had brought their tryst to a shuddering and merciful end.

Now fully dressed, Nathaniel pulled on his tailcoat and was about to say something when Abigail raised a hand.

"Please don't speak," she said, sparing him the embarrassment of lying about why he had to take his leave of her so suddenly. She had heard all the excuses before. *My ship sails before sunrise... I've just now remembered that I've a lecture early in the morning... My ailing mother needs help with her firewood...*

Abigail had long ago found it easier to say as little as possible.

Her curtness caught the young man by surprise. He looked at her curiously as he lingered awkwardly at the door, as if sniffing out a trap. When Abigail's placid gaze finally convinced him there was no catch, he gave her a grateful smile, took his hat in his hands, and slipped out the door.

Abigail lay in bed a while longer while Nathaniel's footsteps receded down the corridor of the inn. Her thoughts were far away as she stared at the dancing shadows cast by the fire burning on the grate. Abigail's taste in lodgings was substantially more refined than her preferences for taverns.

The Steamboat Inn stood on Pearl Street, north of the harbor, on the edge of Burlington's common and old battery grounds. Abigail's accommodations comprised one square room divided in two by a comfortable four-poster bed. An unlit oil lamp stood on a nightstand to one side of the bed. A porcelain washbasin sat on a matching table on the other. Abigail had arranged her two travelling trunks beneath the plush damask curtains of the room's only window. The crackling fireplace suffused the space with the heartening scent of wood smoke.

The lavish room came at a cost, but money was no longer a concern for Abigail. By day she was a schoolteacher at a posh Boston private school, but come nightfall there was no one else who could do what she did. When someone encountered a problem with the paranatural, their path would inevitably cross Abigail's. Not all of her clients were wealthy. She often traded her services for something as fanciful as a book of poetry or a painting she found particularly pleasing. But Abigail's skills in the occult had still paid off handsomely over the years.

Abigail realized just how tense she had become as she lay alone with the soft blanket pulled up to her breasts and one lithe leg exposed. She was still damp between her legs and she entertained the thought of slipping a finger under the blanket and finishing what the young man had started. But she sensed it would be a futile effort. It was a strange sensation; it wasn't like her to be so easily flustered. What was it, then? Was she simply exhausted and impatient from the long journey she had just made from Boston? Or had her quarrel with Anna affected her more than she cared to admit?

This jaunt to Burlington wasn't the first time Anna had run off. Back in Boston, she sometimes vanished for three or four days on end. Abigail never asked where she had been and Anna didn't care to share. But this time had felt different—this time had felt *final*.

Two full weeks had gone by without a word from Anna. Abigail feared the worst. It was a terrible feeling, a debilitating dread such as she had never known. For the first time, fear had driven Abigail to summon the Familiar she had bound to her daughter the night of Anna's birth. Part of Abigail had been relieved when the spirit revealed that Anna had left Boston in pursuit of the revenant. But another part scratched at her thoughts, whispering a truth she was too scared to admit: *You are losing your daughter.*

As the fire burned low, Abigail grew more restless with each passing moment. Sleep would be impossible now, regardless of how exhausted she was. She slipped naked from the bed and went to the hearth to rouse the flames before crossing the room to the larger of her two trunks. There, she produced a warm nightgown and a bottle of deliciously peaty Scotch whiskey delivered to her personally from the Isle of Islay.

She tossed the nightgown on the bed and pulled the cork from the bottle with her teeth as she went to the window and swung it open to the cool night air. The view from her room looked west, across the rolling expanse of the lake, and there was no risk of her being seen as she stood and let the silver moonlight fall across her bare skin.

Abigail stared out at the shimmering water and tried to clear her mind as the whiskey bloomed its heat through her chest. Somehow, her thoughts always found their way back to Anna. There was a reason she had kept the Familiar a secret from her daughter for so long. Anna would be furious. It certainly wasn't the first time they had fought, but Abigail now had the troubling sense that it might have been the last.

And what if it *was* the last time they ever spoke? What if Anna didn't meet her at the wharf in the morning to begin the long trip back to Boston? What if she chose to vanish from Abigail's life? A sickening feeling twisted Abigail's insides when she considered her last words to Anna were that she would rather spend her time straddling a stranger half her age than spend another moment in her daughter's company.

A cool breeze swept off the lake and wafted through the open window. Gooseflesh prickled Abigail's skin and her nipples hardened as she pulled the window shut and turned away. She would need a better distraction.

Abigail shrugged into the warmth of her nightgown and turned her attention to the second of her two trunks. This one was much older and much more remarkable than the other. Imported from the Orient over a century ago, it was black as night, its exotic wood carved to depict a timeless battle among pagan deities. Two intricate wrought-iron straps bound it at each end.

Despite its apparent sturdiness, the coffer's antique paneling had grown dry and brittle with age. Abigail knew she should already have had someone construct a replacement for her. She had only held on to it this long because of one very distinctive feature: it displayed no visible lock. Instead, inlaid into its flat lid was a square iron plate comprising over a dozen smaller, overlapping square panels—a Chinese puzzle lock.

Abigail went to work at the puzzle with her fingers, sliding each panel up and down and side to side in a carefully memorized sequence. Less than a minute later, she solved the problem and the final panel slid aside to reveal a five-dial combination lock. Instead of numbers, each tiny dial was engraved with strange characters that very few could identify as symbols from ancient Chinese cosmology. Abigail aligned the characters into the proper order, sprung the lock, and swung open the lid.

Inside the trunk was an eclectic assortment of arcane objects, vials, and books. The volumes varied in size and age, but one stood out from the rest. It was old—*very* old. Its deep crimson binding gleamed like blood in the firelight as Abigail admired the exquisite filigree tooled into the leather cover. She held a hand suspended over the five-pointed pentagram embossed at the center of the thick tome, as if it were radiating some kind of strange heat. Of all the strange and wonderful items in her collection, Abigail's Book of Shadows was her most treasured possession.

Abigail brought the volume to the bed and lit the oil lamp. Under its warm glow, she turned the cover and perused the pages. Contained within was an extensive compendium of the occult, witchcraft, and the paranatural. Among its pages were powerful banishing spells, necromancy binding incantations, and fearsome hexes that could maim and kill. An exhaustive catalogue of spirits and monsters could also be found, as well as a vast accumulation of benevolent herb-lore, including the recipe for the foul-smelling tea that kept Abigail looking ever youthful.

And yet for the all the wondrous secrets Abigail's Book of Shadows contained, she had always felt it was incomplete. In the lonesome childhood years that followed the death of her parents almost forty years ago, she had often fantasized about discovering some way to bring them back. It was this very idea that had led her to witchcraft and sent her on her perilous journey to find the spell-book of Sarah Bridges, the infamous witch who had helped Abigail's mother that fateful All Hallows' Eve.

As a teenager, Abigail had braved unspeakable horrors in pursuit of the powerful grimoire. But when she finally claimed it as her own, she discovered her efforts had been in vain. There was no spell to return the dead to the living; such a thing simply did not exist. Once a spirit crossed over the Veil, there was no coming back—at least not without dire consequences. The Book of Shadows granted Abigail untold power, but it couldn't give her the one thing she truly desired.

Her parents were lost forever.

The ancient parchment now rustled and cracked as Abigail poured over the collected wisdom of generations of witches who had possessed the grimoire before her. Conscious thought left her as she cleared her mind and focused on the words before her with intense concentration. Enrapt, she lost all awareness of time. It was as if the book itself held her spellbound. The bottle of whiskey on the nightstand went untouched and hours passed like minutes until an unwanted thought clawed its way back into Abigail's consciousness: This Book of Shadows was Anna's birthright. Abigail intended to pass it on to her daughter when the time was right. But that wasn't likely to happen now, was it?

Abigail made a living vanquishing the things of nightmares, but she had never been as frightened as the night she had given birth to Anna. She had done it alone, the way she had done most things. There was no one there with her on the fearful night early in her pregnancy when she had felt lightheaded and fainted, only to wake with spots of blood between her legs and an icy dread that she was losing her baby. She was alone throughout the periods of nausea and the sleepless hours when her belly had grown so large she had no choice but to spend her nights on her back in the darkness.

And when the time came for her baby to leave her womb, no one was there to hold her hand as she pushed through the agony and screamed so loud it shook the candles on the nightstand. Still weak and trembling and slippery with blood, she had cut her daughter's umbilical cord herself. And as her precious newborn suckled at her breast for the first time, tears had streamed from Abigail's eyes as she wondered what kind of mother she would be. What the hell had she done, bringing a child into *her* world? What did she know about being a parent? How could she be a loving mother when her own had died when she was so very young?

Since that night, Abigail had done all she could for her daughter. She had weathered the scandal and derision of being an unwed mother and had ensured Anna benefitted from the same education that Abigail provided to the boys in her school. But in her heart, Abigail feared she had been a dreadful mother. Most parents would assure their children there was no such thing as a monster living under the bed.

Abigail had taught Anna how to kill it.

With her concentration broken, Abigail cast her Book of Shadows aside and allowed herself to admit what was truly disturbing her: she was afraid. Anna had been her only companion for seventeen years, her only source of love and comfort. Sure, there was the occasional reunion with her stepsister's family in Salem, but it was Anna who filled the void left by the deaths of Abigail's parents at such a tender age. The awful awareness that it was now ending filled Abigail with dread.

As she stared at the wall, Abigail looked past the dancing shadows and perceived a future that very much resembled what her life had been like before Anna came into it. What she saw was a hollow chasm of loneliness.

Before Anna, she couldn't have imagined her life with a child. Now, she was terrified of a life without one.

Chapter 4

Cassie Byrne had never been in the woods after dark. Her eyes felt heavy and her lids refused to stay open as she held Kitty's hand and trundled along the leaf-strewn path weaving through the trees. If it wasn't for the lone mosquito flitting around Cassie's head and whirring in her ears, she might have fallen asleep on her feet.

Kitty had been quiet since leaving the tavern. She kept her lantern held high to illuminate the path and a wary eye on her surroundings. More than once, she stopped and turned to peer into the darkness behind them, as if she were afraid of being followed. The idea gave Cassie a chill. Kitty was the bravest woman she knew; it wasn't like her to be scared of anything.

"Come along," Kitty prodded whenever Cassie's already sluggish pace nearly dragged to a halt. "We need to get you a few hours o' sleep before I take you home in the morning."

"*Must* I go?" Cassie yawned.

"Aye, Cassie. It's still your home."

Cassie lowered her head and went quiet. The damp cottage

hadn't felt like a home since Mama left. Whatever warmth and love it held had gone with her.

The mosquito fluttered Cassie's ear and she swatted at it with her free hand. Kitty said this meandering path through the woods was a shortcut from the harbor to her small cottage on the north edge of town. Exhausted as she was, Cassie saw nothing short about it. A cold prickle danced across her skin as her gaze wandered around the dark and foreboding forest. Century-old trees stood like iron-willed sentinels in the darkness. Many had already shed their foliage. Their bent and twisted limbs stretched toward the night sky like enormous talons scratching up from beneath the dirt. Silver shafts of moonlight knifed between their jagged fingers. The temperature was falling and a ghostly mist was rising. It crawled over the underbrush and grasped at the tree trunks. Other than the lonesome sigh of dead leaves shivering in the breeze, the woods lay silent and sprawling around them.

"Why can't I just keep staying with *you* until Mama comes home?" Cassie asked, as much to break the unnerving quiet as to get an answer.

"Because he's your da and he's a right to be with his daughter if he wants."

"I hate him," Cassie murmured before she could stop herself. "I wish he was gone instead of Mama."

Kitty drew to a halt and stood peering down at her in the lamplight. Cassie knew she was about to be scolded for saying such a wicked thing. She wished she could pluck her words out of the air and pop them back into her mouth.

Strangely, there was no anger on Kitty's face. Just that mingling of sadness and pity that Mama used to have whenever Cassie fell and skinned a knee.

"I know you miss your ma," Kitty whispered. "I miss her too, my little *a stór*."

Kitty used funny words sometimes and Cassie didn't know what the Gaelic expression meant, but the way Kitty said it made her feel good. Kitty gave her hand an affectionate squeeze and turned to continue on.

A sound from the forest froze them in place.

The low but unmistakable crackle of a twig snapping under foot.

Kitty held her lantern aloft and peered into the murk. "Who's out there?" she shouted into the phantasm-white mist. Her voice bounced between the trees until the darkness swallowed it up.

No one answered.

But they *had* heard it. In the suffocating silence of the forest, the noise had been as clear as a rifle shot.

Someone was out there, shrouded in the shadowy mist.

Kitty scanned the trees a moment longer. "Abe? Dirk?" she yelled. "Sure I catch you following me home and with the Almighty as my witness, I'll piss in your ale each and every night!"

Still nothing. The mist floated and spirited through the inky darkness of the woods, enrobing everything in its vaporous reach.

"Fucking *gobshites*," Kitty muttered under her breath. She waded into the underbrush, playing the lantern's light around to get a better look and peering into the darkened spaces between the trees.

The mist seemed to stare back at them and a slow feeling of

dread crawled into Cassie's gut. It was a queer feeling, like worms wriggling around in her belly. She didn't like this, and she certainly didn't want to know who—or *what*—was lurking out there in the woods.

"Kitty, can't we just—"

"Stay there, Cassie…" Kitty waved her back as she ventured further away from the path and searched the gloom.

Cassie heard a tremor in Kitty's voice and realized she was afraid. The revelation sent a cold wave through her as if someone had dumped ice water down her throat. Kitty was an adult. She wasn't supposed to be afraid. Whatever was out there had spooked her. What could be so dreadful? The question led to another and another, each more distressing. What if whatever was out there took Mama? What if it had come to take Kitty away too?

Cassie had heard the other children at the schoolhouse whispering when they thought she wasn't listening; she knew her mother wasn't the only woman who had disappeared. Something monstrous was stalking the town. Was it out there now? Watching them from the darkness? Waiting?

Cassie's pulse beat faster and harder with each step that Kitty took deeper into the woods. She was about thirty feet away now, so far away the glow of the lantern no longer fell upon Cassie as she stood waiting on the path. The black distance between them stretched like a bottomless void.

"Kitty, I'm scared," Cassie whispered after her. "Please come back. Can't we just—"

All at once, Kitty let out a stifled cry and the lantern was snuffed.

Darkness swooped over Cassie and she went rigid with

fright. There had been another sound just before Kitty's startled exclamation, one that froze Cassie's blood so deeply her skin tingled.

A low and bestial snarl.

Cassie stayed riveted where she stood. Was it a bear? Did bears wander this close to town? Or was it something even worse? Every part of her wanted to cry out for Kitty, but she was too terrified that whatever was out there would come for her next. Maybe if she stayed very still and very quiet, it might not know she was there. Maybe it might just move along and let her be…

A rustling broke the eerie silence of the mist.

The sound of something moving in the forest.

Getting closer.

Cassie's little heart pounded at her ribs and rattled her spine, but she still couldn't bring herself to move. It was as if her feet had sprouted roots that pierced through the worn-out soles of her shoes and screwed deep into the ground beneath her. Her chest shuddered and her breath bloomed in rapid puffs as the noise grew louder, closer. The sharp *crack!* of a stick shot through the darkness. Cassie imagined with awful certainty that it had been crushed under a heavy claw. A smell filled her nostrils: the musky stink of animal fur mixed with a coppery reek Cassie had only smelled once before when Papa had cut himself badly with the hacksaw.

A shape emerged from the mist—big and shadowy and so nightmarish it broke the fearful spell that held Cassie in thrall. She shrieked and spun on her heels, sprinting away as fast as she could. The looming hulks of the trees sped by in a dusky blur as she fled along the path, pumping her little legs so hard they burned and screamed at her to stop. Her form seemed to flicker in and out of existence as she raced through the silver shafts of moonlight.

Cassie had the crazy impression that someone was calling her name—perhaps it was Kitty—but she was too overcome by terror and her blood was pounding too hard in her ears to make sense of it. She could feel the monster lurking behind her, closing the distance between them with ease as if it were toying with her. No matter how hard she tried, she could never outrun it. It was too big, too powerful—and she was so very, very small. Soon it would be close enough to nip at her heels. She could almost feel its breath on her back, warm and fetid and heavy with moisture. Her only hope was to hide and pray.

Cassie darted from the path and dashed into the underbrush, heading straight for the hulking form of a fallen tree. The pungent reek of earth and rot filled her nose as she dove beneath the immense trunk and pressed herself flat onto the forest floor. Wisps of mist tickled her skin as it descended upon her and enshrouded her in white. She knew the monster had seen her veer from the path, but maybe it had lost sight of her in the mist and darkness of the forest. Maybe it didn't know she was down here on her belly in the dirt, helpless and terrified beneath this rotting tree.

Tears rolled down Cassie's cheeks. She struggled to stifle her sobs as she lay perfectly still and waited in the darkness. A stick jabbed painfully into her abdomen and something with tiny legs crawled across the nape of her neck, but she didn't dare move. The forest had gone dreadfully still around her except for the mournful whispering of the leaves. Sprawled in the soft dirt, Cassie's vision was limited to the brush and saplings of the bramble immediately ahead of her. She pricked her ears, listening keenly for any hint that the monster had somehow lost her.

A sudden sound stole the breath from her lungs and cut her hope to ribbons.

A rustling of leaves barely an arm's length away.

Cassie bit back on her scream and squeezed her eyes shut, her heart pumping so hard she struggled to breathe. Her breaths came too fast to squeeze through her tiny nose, and she was forced to open her mouth to let the air in and out. Her body quivered and her muscles ached with tension. She tried to remember a prayer, but her thoughts were too paralyzed with fright to conjure the words. All that came to mind was a garbled plea.

Please God, make it go away... Oh, please, please, please, make it go away...

Another stirring in the mist.

Cassie forced her eyes open in time to catch a hulking silhouette block out the moonlight as it stalked across her field of vision. Her stomach clenched and coiled, and an uncontrollable spurt of urine squirted into her undergarments. The monster was moving. Was it going away or circling around? Did it know she was under the giant log? Could it smell her there?

Please God, make it go away... Make it go away...

Cassie's pounding heart counted the seconds as she hid and cowered. What should she do next? Could she stay here until morning? Would she be safe once the sun rose?

Something seized her ankles with crushing force.

Cassie let out a piercing cry as she was ripped from her hiding place. Her fingertips gouged shallow trenches through the earth as something dragged her backward and lifted from her feet. She struggled to get away, but her legs spun uselessly in the air. Another scream rose in her throat, but it was choked back by the strangest sensation of being smothered in a furry blanket. She gasped for air, but the overpowering scent of animal hide suffocated her lungs. She kicked and thrashed until the fight went out of her and her eyes slid closed.

Silence returned to the forest as Cassie's nightmare came to an end.

Chapter 5

The reek of burning coffee greeted Anna as she approached the ramshackle cottage. After a sleepless night haunted by visions of the governor's maid staring at her with dead and accusing eyes, she had risen shortly after dawn to get an early start at finding answers to the lingering question of what exactly had happened to Burlington's missing women. Was the revenant responsible for only some of their deaths? If so, what happened to the others? Had they run off as some said? That a woman had gone missing in each of three straight months seemed like too much of a pattern for Anna to ignore. Was this the work of some sort of ritualistic murderer as many feared?

As she lay awake in the pre-dawn darkness of her dingy room, Anna had decided she needed to learn more about each of the women. Breakfast at the Nobody Inn had been meager, but it gave her the opportunity to convince the innkeeper to divulge the whereabouts of Jericho Byrne's house. He gave her a queer look, as if wondering why in hell she would be interested in visiting a man like Jericho, but he'd kept his questions to himself as he gave her directions and pocketed the coins she offered.

The walk from the inn took Anna south down Water Street. It was a Sunday morning and the harbor was quiet. The steamboat from St. Johns to Whitehall wasn't due for another few hours. The men who worked the docks were either sleeping off the revelry of the night before or rousing their families for church. The weather had turned overnight and the warm breezes had surrendered to a more seasonable chill, as if winter were already breathing down from the mountains. Choppy waves lapped against the shore as a stiff wind swept across the lake. The sky was a gray shroud pulled low to the horizon.

Anna was grateful for the fur-lined, skirt-length pelisse overcoat she had brought from Boston. Her thick black hair was tucked beneath a bonnet pulled in to frame her face, and she had a woolen shawl wrapped around her shoulders. The rich and heady scent of malted barley filled the air as Anna made her way past the brewery toward the village outskirts. She crossed a bridge spanning a gulley and the street became nothing more than a winding, leaf-strewn lane.

Now, Anna wrapped her shawl tighter around her shoulders as more of Jericho Byrne's cottage came into view. It squatted within a dense copse of maples atop a slight rise ahead. Here and there, Anna spotted sugaring pails hanging from spigots among the trees. The tin was rusted and pitted as if the pots hadn't been used in some time.

As Anna crested the low incline, more of the rundown property revealed itself. A column of white smoke—the telltale sign of wet firewood—streamed from a dented stovepipe snaking from the cottage's leaf-spattered roof. The roof itself sagged in the middle and its shingles were in need of repair. To Anna's right, the jagged end of a broken axe handle protruded from a heavy log near a woodpile. The abandoned axe head was still wedged deep within the timber. A pitiful animal pen stood to Anna's left. As far as she could tell, there were a couple of neglected chickens and a scrawny goat. The pitiful animal stared at her with its strange eyes as she swept past.

The planks of the rickety steps groaned beneath Anna's tread as she mounted the porch and knocked on the crooked door. When no reply came, she waited a moment before rapping again. After the shuffling of feet and a few muttered curses, the door was ripped open, and a bedraggled man appeared.

Jericho Byrne was in his late-twenties, lean and of average height, with sallow skin stretched taut across the lean muscles of his sinewy frame. He had a face that very much resembled that of the goat in the pen: a scruffy goatee sprouted from his pointed chin and his beady eyes were set slightly too far apart. But there was something dangerous lurking in those eyes as well, an unsettling sense of predatory intelligence.

No, not intelligence—*malice*.

Jericho said nothing as he gazed at Anna expectantly, preferring instead to slump against the doorframe while he sparked a grimy pipe.

"Jericho Byrne?" Anna pressed.

The bleary eyed man looked her up and down. "Uh, huh."

"Mr. Byrne, my name is Beatrice Colquitt with the Champlain Valley Historical Society." Anna had no idea if such a society existed, but she doubted Jericho did either. "We are in the process of tracing the genealogies of our local citizenry, and I had hoped you might help us confirm some branches of your family tree."

Jericho's greasy gaze slithered over Anna's slender figure once more. "Sure, I guess. Wanna come inside for some coffee?"

Another glint in Jericho's cruel eyes brought Anna's defenses springing to life. Nothing good could come from stepping foot inside this man's home. "Thank you, but our conversation should be brief and I've many families to visit before the morning is through."

Jericho's lip twisted with disappointment and he took a long drag of his pipe. "Suit yourself."

"Thank you, Mr. Byrne. Our records show you are of Irish descent. Is that correct?"

Anna wanted to warm the man up and get him talking. Her guess proved correct as Jericho nodded and said, "Parents came across from Galway."

"And their names?"

"Rory Byrne and Dolores Walsh."

"But you were born in America, yes?"

Jericho nodded again. "I'm a Native, sure."

"Thank you, Mr. Byrne. Now I wonder if I might I have a word with your wife?"

"Mary?" Byrne frowned and spit in the dirt. "Ain't seen her for near a month."

Anna feigned a look of surprise. "Your wife is out of town?"

Jericho shrugged. "She run off after I broke her lip. Burnt the goose that night." Byrne's grin revealed the crooked teeth clenched around the stem of his pipe. "She'll be back, though. Ain't the first time she run off, but I sure as hell can tell you it'll be the last. Soon as she gets back, I'm gonna hobble that bitch so's she don't run nowhere again."

Anna grit her teeth and willed herself not to give this cowardly brute the thrashing he deserved. She imagined the young girl she had seen last night at the tavern, Cassie Byrne, living here alone with this vile man. Anna didn't know what a father was supposed to be, but she was certain this man wasn't deserving of the title. An unpleasant conclusion came to her as she pondered what cruelties Jericho Byrne was capable of and why Kitty Hayes had thought it better for little Cassie to spend the evening at a seedy dockside tavern rather than in the company of her own father.

"Is your daughter home, Mr. Byrne?" Anna asked with growing apprehension.

Jericho spit again. "Nope. Kitty came by to collect her last night and I ain't seen her since."

"She never came home?"

Jericho shook his head and sent another cloud of blue smoke billowing into the air. "Say, I'm freezin' my balls off out here. Are you sure you wouldn't be more comfortable inside?"

"I think not," Anna replied. "It wouldn't be proper."

"Awww... nobody around here to give a shit." Jericho purred in what he undoubtedly thought to be a voice of seduction.

"All the same. You've been most generous with your time, Mr. Byrne. I wish you a pleasant day." Anna forced a smile and started away.

Jericho leered as he trailed after her across the porch and down the steps. "C'mon now... A lil' cunt's the best cure for a heavy head."

If Jericho Byrne hadn't grabbed Anna by the arm at that moment, he would have spent the rest of his morning nursing a routine hangover instead of broken bones.

It happened in a flash as Anna spun and broke free of Jericho's grip. In the same motion, she seized his wrist in her left hand, gloved his bent fist with her right, and twisted as she drove his knuckles backward into his inner elbow. There was a sickening *crack!* as his wrist fractured.

Jericho's scream was a mingling of surprise and agony as he dropped to his knees, cradling a hand that dangled at a grotesque angle like a doll's arm hanging by a stitch.

"You bitch!" he roared and sputtered. "*You damned bitch!*"

Anna might have relented if Jericho hadn't opened his mouth. Instead, she kicked him hard in the ribs and he flopped onto his back like a fish. She stood over him, her boots planted firmly on either side of his squirming body. His hair felt coarse and greasy in her grasp as she seized a handful and raised the fist of her other hand. She held it there for a fraction of a second, hovering in the air right in front of Jericho's face just long enough for him to see what was coming. His eyes flew wide with a dawning sense of panic, and Anna savored the instant before she rammed her knuckles squarely into his face.

The blood barely had time to spurt from his nose before her fist drew back and shot forward again. Jericho's head snapped back from the blow. He thrust a hand up to fend off Anna's assault, but she knocked it aside. Again and again she struck him, raining blows down on his face even as she felt him start to go limp in her grasp. She knew dimly that she should stop before she killed the man. But there was a familiar voice raging her head, urging her on.

Yes! it screamed. *Strike him down! Give him blood to drink!*

God, it felt good to hit him! To inflict pain and release the rage and aggression she seemed to carry with her at all times. A stinging heat lanced up from Anna's knuckles, but she was too lost in the catharsis of violence to care. Her blows split the skin of his cheeks, his chin, his lips. Jericho's face was a pulpy mess now, oozing gouts of blood from nearly a dozen gashes. Only when he lost consciousness in Anna's grip did she release her grasp on his head and let him drop like a sack of meat in the dirt.

Anna stood back, her chest heaving, the red fog of her fury dissipating as quickly as it had descended. She relaxed her clenched fists and shook the throbbing pain out of them. Blood seeped from her skinned knuckles and dripped to her fingertips. She took a moment to wipe them on Jericho's shirt before rolling him onto his stomach so he wouldn't choke on his own blood as he lay senseless. She glanced around as she stood over Jericho's crumpled form. He had been right about one thing: other than the scrawny goat still gazing at them from the rickety pen, there was no one around to witness what happened between them.

Chapter 6

It was mid-morning, and the harbor thrummed with activity when Abigail came to a numbing realization: Anna wasn't coming. Passengers and porters came and went around her as she stood on the pier with her back to the great machinery of the steamboat. She searched the faces in the crowd, hoping against hope that a familiar countenance would emerge from the throng, one whose features looked startlingly like her own.

But as the minutes crawled by, Abigail's hopes of seeing her daughter again dwindled. A cold and hollow hole opened in the pit of her stomach as she was forced to accept a grim reality.

Anna was gone from her life.

The unavoidable truth brought on a terrible ache that gripped Abigail's heart and left behind a pain no amount of whiskey could anesthetize. She tipped her head back and looked skyward, as if avoiding her daughter's absence from the dock might make the agony of the moment pass quicker.

The steamboat's massive engine belched black smoke

through its single stack as the crew got up steam and readied for departure. The twin paddle-wheels of the *Franklin* still sat motionless in the water, but Captain Sherman seemed eager to get everyone aboard and cast off ahead of schedule. Far across the lake to the west, a dark and angry army of storm clouds was marching over the hulking giants of the Adirondack mountains. The waters had already grown choppy and wind-blown whitecaps were forming on the crests of small waves. It would do the captain well to take his ship as far south as possible before the storm made sailing too dangerous.

The crowd on the pier known as the Pine Dock was dwindling now, the last of the passengers crossing the gangplank and either gathering by the ship rails or making their way directly to the warmth of their private cabins in the ship's stern. Abigail's own trunks were already waiting for her aboard. But she couldn't bring herself to turn around and put her back to the village. Once she did, the loss of her daughter would become an irrevocable reality.

The captain sounded the ship's horn, a single mighty blast that rattled Abigail's bones and boomed like a death knell as it reverberated up and down the valley. At last, she could put it off no longer. She let out a long breath and turned towards the gangplank. The ship's deck heaved and rocked in the rough waters beneath her and a deckhand stood ready to lend her a hand, but Abigail waved him off as she climbed aboard.

With another mighty blast of the horn, the crew cast off the lines, and the paddle-wheels chugged to life. Abigail stood by the rail as the ship pulled away from the pier and put a gulf of churning water between itself and the village of

Burlington. The newly built *Franklin* was a fast boat and they were soon well out into the lake and rounding Juniper Island. The island's new lighthouse tower came into view, but Abigail had her back to it. She stood huddled against the wind and watched the town of Burlington growing smaller in the distance, a collection of miniatures models perched on the windswept shore.

Abigail's thoughts soon returned to Anna. What had she expected of her daughter? Wasn't Anna exactly what Abigail had raised her to be? She was strong, cunning, and yes, even ruthless when necessary. Hadn't this parting always been inevitable? Had Abigail started writing the ending of their story long ago when she had initiated her little girl into the ways of the occult?

Abigail felt a shiver when she thought about what had driven her to make that fateful decision. Though it pained her to this day, she'd had no other choice—she had to protect her daughter.

To the south, a brilliant blast of lightning forked across the darkened sky. Seconds later, a booming peel of thunder rolled up the valley and crashed against the mountains.

A bell rang out several times and the ship's paddle-wheels came to an abrupt halt.

Abigail and the few remaining passengers who still lingered on deck exchanged quizzical glances as the big ship was tossed around in the choppy water. A moment later, the wheels churned back to life. Instead of continuing south, the ship began a slow revolution.

A crewman emerged from the pilot house. "Rough waters ahead! Too dangerous to navigate the Narrows! Captain's returning to Burlington to wait out the storm! Apologies for the inconvenience!"

Before long, the ship was pulling back alongside the Pine Dock in the harbor. The crew hustled to tie the lines and put out the gangplank as the disgruntled passengers reappeared on the windswept deck. Abigail was one of the first to cross from the ship to the pier. An unexpected sight gave her heart a jolt.

Anna was there.

ABigail's spirits leapt at the sight of her. But a voice in her head struck her like a slap to the face. *She didn't come to join you. She came here to watch you leave.*

Abigail pressed her full lips into a rigid line as she approached her daughter. She would never allow herself to reveal just how wounded she had been.

But Abigail's stony bitterness was quickly overcome by the troubled look on Anna's face.

Something was wrong.

"We must talk," said Anna.

A little less than twenty minutes later, they stood on a cliff overlooking the lake by the edge of the old battery grounds. During the walk north from the harbor, Anna had related the morning's events.

"You're certain she never returned home?" asked Abigail.

Anna shook her head. "I passed by Hayes' house myself. There was no one there. The chimney was quiet and the last time her neighbors saw her was last evening when she left for the tavern."

"Might she have kidnapped the girl and fled the village?"

Anna conceded a doubtful shrug. She had wondered the

same thing when she had learned that neither Kitty Hayes nor Cassie Byrne had made it home last night. It was a possibility, but a nagging tickle in Anna's gut told her it was an unlikely one.

"Tell me more about the other women," Abigail said.

"If Hayes is correct, the first to go missing was Tabitha Brant. She was a young Indian woman who worked as a handmaid in Virgil Stroud's house."

"The dean of the university?"

Anna nodded. "The second woman was a local spinster, Catherine Abell. Her father owns a prosperous sheep farm and her brother is a student of law."

"What about the third woman, Mary Byrne?" Abigail inquired. "Might she have tired of her husband's abuse and actually have run off?"

"And leave her only daughter behind with that bastard of a father?"

"Could he have killed her?"

Anna frowned. "Possibly. That doesn't explain the first two women."

"Have you been able to examine any of the bodies?"

"There are no bodies. The local constable hasn't been able to find any trace of the missing women. It is as if they simply vanished."

Abigail nibbled at her bottom lip as she thought it over. "Four women in as many months. There must be something that links them."

"There is," said Anna. "The moon."

Abigail gave her a questioning look.

"Each of the women went missing on the night of a full

moon," Anna explained.

"All except for Kitty Hayes," Abigail remarked. "Last night's moon wasn't full."

"But it will be *tonight*. Regardless, the full moon is still what links the first three missing women. It cannot merely be a coincidence."

"You believe we may be dealing with a lycanthrope?" Abigail seemed unconvinced.

Anna shrugged. "I don't know what I believe. It's possible."

Abigail gave a grudging nod and went quiet. Anna was right. In a village of this size, the disappearance of one woman could easily be explained away, perhaps even two. But four? And now a child? No; something else was going on, something sinister. But what?

A moment passed in silence as they stood together, each lost in her own thoughts.

"You had no intention of returning to Boston." Abigail said at last. It was a statement of fact, not a question.

Anna's gaze fell to the dirt between her boots. She didn't need to speak for Abigail to have her answer.

"What was your plan?" Abigail pressed.

"Take a steamboat north to St. Johns. From there, catch a stagecoach to Montreal."

"Where you would disappear and slip into a new life," Abigail finished for her.

Anna again couldn't bring herself to say anything more. She looked away as if the truth written on her face would betray her.

As the silence lengthened, Abigail turned her attention across the lake, where the hulking ramparts of the

Adirondacks stood. They were shadowy and indistinct now, partially obscured by the dark fury of the approaching storm. Snow was already visible on the rocky summit of the largest of the range, the peak known as Cloudsplitter.

"I met your father in those mountains," Abigail said.

Anna cast a quick glance at her mother from the corner of her eye. Here was something unexpected. Abigail never spoke of Anna's father. In seventeen years, the only scrap of information Anna had ever coaxed from her mother was her father's name: Glen Colvin. On every other occasion, Abigail had made it painfully clear he was not to be mentioned. It was, therefore, with no little surprise to Anna that Abigail continued.

"He was a good man, shot in the back by a vile one. I often wonder if he would still be alive had he never crossed paths with me." Abigail paused before turning to look her daughter in the face. "You've never known loss, Anna. Your father died before you were born. You never knew him and you haven't the slightest idea how it feels to be scraped hollow by grief. I've done all I can to shelter you from that sorrow. Perhaps if I hadn't, you would better understand why it falls to us to spare others from such a fate."

Anna's lips pressed into a mirthless smile. "Ah, but we both know that's not entirely true, is it, Mother? You say we must do what we do to save others, but what truly drives you—what has always driven you—is wrath. You do it to punish the evil that took your parents from you. But they are dead, and no matter how many spirits we banish or monsters we slay, nothing will ever bring them back."

Something wintry flashed in Abigail's clear blue eyes, and

Anna wondered if she had gone too far. But she couldn't help herself; the words had come out before she could stop them. She had quietly slipped away from Boston to avoid this exact confrontation, to spare her mother the hurt it would inevitably cause. Now that Abigail had tracked her down, the feelings Anna had pushed deep down for so long refused to stay locked away in their pit.

Abigail spoke with a cool and dry tone that made it clear she was choosing her words. "When you were born, I didn't know what to do. My whole life, I have pushed everyone away for fear that they would get hurt for being near me. And yet, here I was raising a beautiful and fragile and vulnerable little girl. At first, I thought to do the only thing I could think of to keep you safe: I thought to teach you to defend yourself. But even then, I resisted. I never wanted this life for you, Anna. You must believe me. I would have done anything to spare you from it. It wasn't until…"

Anna stared at her. "Until what, Mother?"

When Abigail looked at her again, there was a sorrow in her eyes Anna had never seen before. "There is a darkness about you, Anna. There always has been. A shadow that is not your own. I know not whence it comes, but I have my fears. You know of your great-great-grandmother, Rebecca Hale. You know she signed her name to the devil's black book on the eve of her hanging in Salem. You also know I was possessed by her spirit that terrible All Hallows' Eve when my mother sacrificed herself to save me. My fear is that some trace of Rebecca's malicious presence lingered within me long after that night, an insidious whisper that bided its time until it somehow found a voice in you while in my womb." Abigail drew a long breath and let it out. "I saw it in you at a young age, Anna. I had thought that initiating you into the ways of witchcraft and training you to kill monsters might give you a way to satisfy your darker impulses, to channel your violent tendencies into the cause of saving people before—"

"Before I hurt someone," Anna finished for her. She was struck by a clear moment of understanding. "You're afraid, aren't you, Mother? That's why you followed me here, why you refuse to let me go. You believe I'm dangerous. You're afraid, not for yourself, but of what I might do to others without you by my side."

Abigail's lips compressed and she said nothing—she didn't need to. Anna remained silent, too stunned by these revelations to put her troubled thoughts into words. She pictured Jericho Byrne, beaten within an inch of his life at her hands. What Anna couldn't admit was part of her was glad he had given her a reason to lash out. And while she knew there was no saving the servant girl last night, Anna also knew she hadn't hesitated to bury her knife in the girl's chest. She had been little more than an obstacle standing between Anna and her prey, an obstacle that needed to be eliminated so that she might satisfy her own lust for violence.

"No," Anna said at last, her tone low and icy. "I am not the puppet of a long-dead witch. *You* did this to me."

Abigail's eyes narrowed. "What do you mean by that?"

"Don't you see? There is no evil presence within me guiding my actions. These creatures that we hunt and kill, I don't do it to save others. I do it because I *enjoy* killing, because you *bred* me to be a killer. A person shouldn't enjoy such things, Mother. But you've spent your entire life so obsessed with revenge that you've passed your rage on to me as well. It was in the very milk you nursed me with. And now, I can't stop killing. It is for the same reason I can no longer have any part of witchcraft. I am too drawn to its power. I crave it in every moment, an uncontrollable desire simmering in my very blood. If I yield to it, I am certain that I will not stop. If I allow myself to walk that path, I will pursue it to its furthest ends, even as it leads me to the darkest arts and blackest of magics. I will be a slave to that thirst for power until it burns away my very soul." Anna looked away. "No, I must leave this life behind before it's too late, before I become like… like—"

"Like me."

Anna's stony silence spoke a truth she could not bring herself to utter. In that moment, she knew she had hurt her mother in a way no beast or spirit ever had. The two stood in silence, gazing at the shadowy mountains in the distance, each consumed by her own thoughts and wounds.

At last, Abigail drew herself up. Her voice was as brisk and cold as the wind sweeping across the lake. "Four women have now disappeared. A young girl is missing, a child younger than I when I lost my parents. Time is running short and it will take both of us if she is to be found alive. Help me this one time more and I will ask nothing of you again."

Anna squeezed her lip between her teeth as she thought it over. "What is its name? The Familiar you bound to me?"

Abigail hesitated a moment. Speaking the names of Familiars aloud was dangerous; it could give them power. But Anna didn't look like she would accept that answer again. "Gideon," she replied.

"If I help you, you will unbind him from me." Anna's tone

made it clear this was a demand, not a request.

Abigail nodded. "When there is time. Should you wish to never see me again, I will not follow."

Anna went quiet. Abigail thought she saw tears in her daughter's glacial eyes, but she couldn't tell if they were brought on by the stinging wind.

"What do you need of me?" Anna asked at last.

"Continue your inquiries into the other missing women. Speak to Dean Stroud about the circumstances of his servant's disappearance. She was the first of the women to go missing, correct?"

Anna nodded. "And you?"

"I intend to discover if the women we are looking for are already dead."

Chapter 7

Jericho Byrne needed a drink to numb his pain. Given the agony he was in; it would take several to do the job. All the bottles in his cottage had been drained the night prior, so he turned to the one place he knew he could find alcohol on a Sunday afternoon: The Nobody Inn. So great was Jericho's thirst that he was willing to risk the embarrassment of explaining his injuries to the rogues and roughnecks who would be the tavern's only patrons at this time of day.

As he drudged across town, supporting his broken wrist against his chest while hot bolts of pain went off in his cracked ribs, Jericho decided he would tell them he'd been high in a tree trimming branches over his cottage when the bough he was standing on broke beneath him. He had fallen at least twenty feet—a height that would surely increase with each telling—and cracked his face on another bough before breaking his ribs and wrist on impact with the ground.

It was a flimsy story that would earn him some snickers and derision—Jericho being a lumberjack and all. But there was no goddamn way he was telling anyone the truth that a girl had handed his ass to him and turned him into such a bloody mess.

Now Jericho hunched on his stool at the tavern's bar, cradling his rotgut with his good hand and waiting for the burning bliss of the alcohol to ease the dull throb in the back of his skull. He took another sip and made the mistake of glimpsing himself in the sooty mirror behind the bar. *Jesus!* The cowardly bitch had really done a number on him. What had she beaten him with while he lay unconscious? A hammer? His swollen face looked like a misshapen mass of lumpy mushroom heads. Both eyes were puffy, his eyelids fattened to narrow slits in the center of ugly purple rings. The flesh of his cheeks had been cut across the cheekbones and his lips were split all over. Dried blood still clung to the wiry hair of his scraggly goatee. Jericho had braved the agony of resetting his broken nose, but it was still bent in a strange direction.

As he gazed at the ruin of his face, Jericho now understood why women had turned away and children scurried to hide as he hustled toward the inn.

He looked goddamned monstrous.

Unable to stand the sight of himself any longer, Jericho averted his eyes from his own reflection. Maybe it was the impending storm, but it was a quiet afternoon at the Nobody. The dreary afternoon light filtered through the dingy leaded windows in gray sheets. The innkeeper, Quint Acker, didn't waste money on candles until sundown and the cavernous room was heavy with shadows. Other than a small gang of shady men huddled around a table in the gloom at the far end of the tavern, Jericho found himself drinking alone—

which was fine with him. He'd just returned from the logging camp and was flush with cash. There were many more drinks to come after this one. And since Mary had run off, there was one less mouth to feed. Hell, if Kitty Hayes wanted to keep his whelp of a girl, Jericho would have enough money to drink himself silly just about any damn time he wanted.

But what about when the winter logging season opened in a few weeks? What if his wrist or ribs weren't healed by then? Lumberjacking was no work for an invalid, and the north country was crawling with strapping young men eager to take Jericho's place. *Damn…* How long did it take ribs to heal? What was he going to do if he couldn't work? How would he survive the winter?

Quint sauntered over and wiped the wooden bar top with a grubby rag that smeared more grime than it removed. "Hope ya had your fall *after* that girl came calling on ya this morning," he said with a smirk.

Jericho cocked an eyebrow—or at least he thought he did; his eye was so swollen it was hard to tell. How did Quint know about the girl? The innkeeper was a burley man of shorter stature who sported a shaved head, cauliflower ears, and a crooked nose broken too many times in bar fights. He was no stranger to broken bones, and it was Quint who had helped tie the splint around Jericho's broken wrist. There was nothing to be done for Jericho's ribs, though.

"What girl?" Jericho grumbled innocently.

"Pretty thing. Black hair. Blue eyes. She was asking about ya early this morning. Figured it was no business of mine to ask why. Said her name was Emily something."

Jericho shook his head as if he hadn't seen her and let the

name roll around in his head. *Emily?* Jericho couldn't be certain, but he was pretty sure that wasn't the name she had given him. Which meant she had been lying.

"Cuthbert," Quint blurted. "Emily Cuthbert was her name."

Jericho attempted an indifferent shrug, his thoughts now bent to trying to remember the details of his exchange with the girl. She had come from some historical society and her name was… was… Beatrice Colquit! Yes, that was it! Certainly not Emily Cuthbert. But if she'd been lying about her name, who the hell was she?

"Hey Quint," Jericho croaked hoarsely. "This Cuthbert girl say where I can find her? Might be she knows something about Mary."

"Sure. She's staying upstairs. Paid up for another night but ain't seen her all day."

That sealed it. Byrne was now sure the girl's entire story was horseshit. What kind of historical society bookworm lied about her name and spent her nights in a place like the Nobody? And what kind of girl fought the way she did? No; whatever her real name was, this girl had come looking for him for a reason—and it sure as hell wasn't to ask him about his family history.

Maybe it was just to kick yer balls in, a taunting voice whispered in Jericho's head. It belonged to a ghost he hadn't heard in many years: his mother. Oh God, how Jericho Byrne hated his mother.

Dolores Byrne hadn't always been the cruel shrew Jericho had come to loathe. She had been young and happy in Galway where her husband Rory worked the docks. But when

Rory was accused of being a member of the United Irishmen intent on armed rebellion against the Protestants, he was branded a traitor and their Protestant landlord threw the Byrnes into the street.

Penniless and with nowhere else to go, they were huddled around a cheerless fire in a rat-infested alley near the harbor when Rory convinced Dolores a better life awaited them across the sea in America. *The only religion that matters there is money*, he had argued with a gleam in his eye. A few more nights of homeless starvation chased away any objections Dolores had. At the first opportunity, they stowed away on a ship bound for America and the promise of a new life.

On the sixth day of the crossing, a deckhand discovered Dolores and Rory below decks. Faced with the threat of being thrown overboard and drowned somewhere in the frigid North Atlantic, Dolores did the only thing she could: She sold her body to the crew in exchange for their silence. The next nineteen days and nights were a living hell for which Dolores never forgave her husband. It wasn't just that he merely stood by while the men took their turns with her; it was that he never even *objected* to her shameful offer. It wasn't fair, she thought. It was Rory's fault they had to leave Ireland. Stowing away to America was his idea. *He* should have been the one who suffered, not her.

Dolores's animosity for her husband only deepened when they finally reached New York, only to discover the streets weren't the rivers of gold Rory had promised her. In fact, Dolores was quick to remind him that *none* of his promises to her ever came true. The hard reality was that Catholic Irish were as welcome in America as the plague and work was hard to come by.

Illiterate and with no real skills to speak of, the Byrnes had migrated away from the city, moving ever further toward the lonely logging camps of the great northern wilderness. Perhaps they would find themselves more welcome among the Catholic French loggers of Lower Canada, Rory reasoned. Somewhere along the way, Dolores discovered she was pregnant. Whether the baby was Rory's or that of one of the many deckhands she had lain with during their crossing, no one would ever know.

Rory spent the winters at the logging camps, leaving Dolores to endure the hardship of raising little Jericho alone in the sad cottage Rory had cobbled together in the forbidding woods. Isolated and wretched, with barely enough firewood and food to make it through the winters, Dolores's mind began to unravel. When Rory finally returned in the spring, she would vent her frustrations on him mercilessly.

With little money, a bastard infant to feed, and a raging harpy for a wife, Rory fell into drinking for escape—a vice that only infuriated Dolores even more. Some of young Jericho's earliest memories were of his mother berating and beating her husband with anything she could get her hands on. The fireplace bellows, pieces of crockery, a splintered piece of timber, her bare fists; any weapon was good enough for Dolores so long as it sent her husband scurrying before her.

So it went until one Sunday afternoon when Rory's head slumped back in a drunken stupor in his favorite chair and Dolores slit his throat with his straight-razor.

Jericho was eight when he came home from trapping that night's dinner to find his father's chest awash in blood. The crimson slash across Rory's throat stared back at him like some sort of ghastly grin. Rory Byrne had never been much of a father, but having grown up in near solitude, he was the only man Jericho had ever known. Something about the stricken look on her son's childish face as he gaped at his father's severed windpipe must have roused Dolores to the atrocity she had committed. It was too much to bear, and it snapped the last frayed threads of her sanity. She still held the dripping razor, and while Jericho looked on in horror, she calmly and neatly sliced both wrists from hand to elbow in front of him. She missed an artery in one arm and it took her almost ten minutes to bleed out.

Jericho didn't cry or scream for help as his mother slowly went a ghostly white—not that there was anyone within earshot to hear him. He remained by Dolores's side the whole time until she stopped breathing, but not because he cared for her. He wanted to make sure she stayed dead so she could no longer torment him and his father.

It must have been the hateful girl's questions about Jericho's family that morning that had dredged up his painful memories of childhood and awakened Dolores's ghost. And now that she had found a comfortable place in Jericho's head, she wouldn't stop haunting him.

Just like yer da, she taunted. *Too much of a mewling fairy to defend yerself. And from a wee girl, no less!*

Despite the spike of pain it drove into his battered skull, Jericho ground his teeth together in impotent rage and gulped his whiskey. He hated the girl who'd done this to him as much as his mother—maybe even more. *She hadn't fought fair*, he thought. She'd suckered him. All he'd wanted to do was talk to her, and she'd hit him with a cheap shot. What a gutless bitch she was. Things would be different if he saw her again. He'd be the one to knock *her* cold and leave her for dead. Maybe he'd even have a little fun with her first.

Oh, you keep telling yerself that, fairy, Dolores sneered. *But we both know yer balls ain't grown none since I used to flick 'em for fun, don't we? Balls 'bout the size o' pumpkin seeds, just like yer da's, ain't that right boy-o?*

Jericho winced at the old, familiar taunts, the ones Dolores used to torture her husband with until there was nothing left of him but the pitiful excuse of a man Jericho had called his *Da*. Jericho had long ago sworn he would never be like his old man. Sure, he had followed his father into the bottle, but that was different. He would never allow himself to be treated so shamefully by a woman, to be so ridiculed and browbeaten. In fact, he would make damn sure any woman he came across knew enough not to test his patience, not even a little.

Ha! his mother cackled. *Have another look in that mirror then, won't ya, faggot?*

Jericho's good hand ground into a tight fist. He'd strangle his mother if she weren't already dead. He'd kill her a thousand times over. But somehow he knew she wouldn't stay dead. He had known it even as he sat by her side as a boy and watched her blood drip through the cracks in the floorboards to the root cellar below. Someone would always be there to summon her ghost—someone like his treacherous wife or the lying bitch who'd beaten and humiliated him that morning. Jericho had never wanted to kill someone as much as he wanted to kill the black-haired girl who had invited his mother's unwelcome spirit into his head.

Jericho realized his glass was trembling in his fist and he released his grip. His gaze wandered to the small gang of men shrouded in pipe smoke in the shadows in the tavern's rear. They were getting louder the more they drank, their braying laughter more boisterous. Rising above the table like a mountain in their midst was Dirch Gray.

Jericho knew the man from the logging camps. Dirch was easily the biggest and meanest son of a bitch he had ever come across. Jericho had once witnessed him beat another man to death over a stolen tin of beans. The man was a known thief, and no one reported his death or mourned his loss. But the thing was, Dirch had *giggled* while he bludgeoned the man with his meaty fists.

There were rumors he wasn't the first man Dirch had killed. Jericho had always suspected the huge man had enjoyed the murderous eruption of violence, that he had actually sought it out. There was a perpetual look in Dirch's stony black eyes that chilled Jericho to the bone. It was as if the giant was drawing himself a silent mental image of the many ways he could kill you with his bare hands. What kind of man entertained such thoughts? One with a very tenuous grip on sanity—one of the very few Jericho Byrne actually feared. And then there were the stories of what Dirch did to women, things so sick and deranged they made even Jericho cringe. Lots of loggers were mean; Dirch Gray was outright maniacal.

An idea slipped into Jericho's head, one that might have made him smile if it wasn't for the hurt it would bring him. For the first time since that hateful girl had shown up at his doorstep, he felt his spirits rise. Maybe it was time to have another drink.

There ya go! Dolores jeered in his head. *Go get a real man to fight yer battles for ya! Bet that one's got a* real *set o' ball on 'em!*

Jericho ignored her as he slipped off his stool and sauntered across the room to Dirch's table. The giant's soulless eyes leveled on him through the smoky haze. Dirch's three companions swiveled in their chairs to see what he was looking at. One man was missing an eye. He didn't wear an eye-patch to conceal the empty cavity; he just let the world shudder at the gruesome wound, as if he took pleasure in the discomfort it provoked.

Jericho's stomach did a somersault as he drew near, but now that his plan had taken shape in his mind, there was no letting it go. After what she had done to him, the gutless bitch deserved everything she had coming to her.

"Hey Dirch." Jericho managed the words through his cracked and swollen lips. "How'd you feel about a little fun tonight?"

Chapter 8

Virgil Stroud collected insects. Hundreds of specimens were pinned to boards and displayed behind protective glass in the private study of the dean's sizable house on the eastern end of Pearl Street. Anna stood by and watched as Stroud hunched over his desk and squinted through a large magnifying glass. His thick eyebrows knit together as he carefully inserted a pin between the wings of a large red dragonfly.

"*Sympetrum fonscolombii*," Stroud explained without looking up or breaking his concentration. His voice was a rich baritone that seemed to come from some bottomless catacomb deep within him. "Otherwise known as a red-veined darter or nomad of the *libellulidae* family. 'Tis not a terribly rare species, but a fine specimen nonetheless. The Japanese consider them sacred as symbols of strength and courage, while our own Indians believe they bring renewal after times of hardship."

As she watched him work, Anna thought Stroud himself was somewhat insect-like. He was unusually tall and lanky—well over six feet—with long limbs and bent knees that brought to mind images of a praying mantis. Anna surmised he was in his mid-sixties, but still robust for his age. He had a hooked nose and a long face that ended in a thick but well-groomed goatee. His hair was completely white and swept back like a snowdrift above the sharp widow's peak of his forehead. Incongruously, his eyebrows remained dark and bushy and his eyes were tenebrous and piercing. The pallid light streaming through the study's only window struck one side of his face and cast the other half in shadow as he focused on the delicate task at hand.

With the dragonfly secured to its board, Stroud used a pair of tweezers to position the specimen so that it rested perfectly straight about an inch below the head of the three-inch pin. He then spread the iridescent wings and gently pinned them open as well.

"Ah..." Stroud exhaled with satisfaction and a certain measure of relief as he leaned back in his chair. He looked at Anna for the first time since her arrival. "I apologize for keeping you waiting, Miss Bell, but once a specimen has been captured, there is but a brief window of time for its preservation."

"Not at all, Dean Stroud," Anna replied. "It is I who must beg your pardon for this unexpected intrusion and thank you for the indulgence of your time."

Stroud rested his elbows on the desk before him, tented his fingers, and leaned into the light as he fixed his piercing gaze on Anna. Even seated, his head was almost level with her own. "How exactly may I help you, Miss Bell?"

"As I mentioned to your wife, I am a graduate of the Ursuline School of Boston and I am searching for a former classmate, Tabitha Brant."

Stroud arched a bristling eyebrow. "Ursuline? You're a nun?"

"No, I have taken no such vows. I am simply a woman who was fortunate enough to benefit from the benevolence of the Order when I was but a young orphan."

"You've traveled all the way from Boston to find a childhood friend?"

"Tabitha and I became quite close in our time together at the Ursuline. It broke my heart the morning we discovered she had run away. In the years since, I have married a man of comfortable wealth. He has encouraged me to seek out and see to the financial security of the one girl who held my hand as I lay crying in the darkness of the orphanage." Anna paused, acutely aware that the effectiveness of any lie hinged on the seemingly inconsequential details it afforded. "My search has led me here to Burlington, where if I'm not mistaken, Tabitha has been a servant in your employ. Am I correct?"

"*Was* a servant in my employ."

Anna feigned a look of surprise. "I beg your pardon?"

"It would seem that Tabitha has not outgrown her habit of running off. She disappeared from here without a word nearly four months ago."

"Disappeared? Have you any idea where she might have gone?"

Stroud shrugged his broad shoulders. "She sometimes spoke of returning to her people on the islands at the northern tip of the lake. The Abenaki, if I am not mistaken. I assumed she grew homesick and struck out to be reunited with them. I had no idea she grew up as an orphan in Boston."

"She was abducted from her village by traders at a young age." Abigail lied easily. "Have you any reason to suspect Tabitha might have been unhappy here?"

"Not in the slightest. My wife hired her upon our taking residence here nearly a year ago, shortly after I accepted my position as dean of the university. Since then, she performed her duties with diligence and we treated her with kindness. We even brought her to see the local physician when she complained of a toothache. It saddened us to learn of her sudden departure. Good help is terribly rare in this graceless town and we have yet to find a suitable replacement. Otherwise, I assure you, it would not have fallen to my wife to have undertaken the household duties."

Anna nodded. It had surprised her when Stroud's wife had greeted her personally at the door when she had come knocking unexpectedly. Lucretia Stroud was likely ten years younger than her husband, somewhere in her mid-fifties. She was an unassuming but handsome woman with pale green eyes. Her long hair must have once been dark, but was now streaked with various shades of silvery gray. Anna had noted the trim taper of Lucretia's waist and wondered if she had taken up the new fashion of wearing a tightly laced corset beneath her garnet muslin bodice. As she led Anna to her husband's study to be introduced, Lucretia had spoken with dignified politeness and paid close attention to her manners.

"Wherever Tabitha went, I pray she made it there safely," Stroud went on. "The journey north of here is long and not without peril."

Anna let her shoulders sag in mock disappointment. She allowed her eyes to roam over the dean's impressive collection of insects. Winged butterflies, moths, and dragonflies seemed to dominate, but there were also colorful beetles and scarabs, as well as a few display cases dedicated to spiders of all sizes. "Am I correct in assuming you are a professor of entomology, Dean Stroud?" she asked.

"Actually, no," Stroud replied with a wry twist in his lip. "In this endeavor, I am an amateur. This collection is merely a pastime through which I find calm, much the same way a builder of miniatures finds peace in concentration and focus, I suspect. My particular area of study at the university is botany and the pharmacological use of plants."

"How plants may be used for medicine."

"Indeed. Since ancient times, plants have been the basis for all manner of cures. I have personally cultivated nearly two hundred species, some from as far away as the Orient." Stroud rose and rounded the desk to Anna. Despite the bend in his knees, his legs seemed as long as broomsticks. "Would you like to see them?"

"Oh no, I couldn't take up more of your time."

"Nonsense. With the weather growing colder, we will so rarely have visitors and it would be my pleasure."

Anna considered the offer. Stroud seemed kindly enough, simply eager to impress, but she didn't have time to waste admiring the aging academic's garden. Still, there were more questions she wanted to have answered. Did Tabitha have friends in the village? Someone with whom she may have confided her intentions? A man she may have eloped with? Anna sensed that if she insisted on peppering Stroud with more questions now, it might only make him suspicious of her.

"Very well," Anna replied. "I would be delighted to join you if it is not too much trouble."

"Splendid. I'll have Lucretia bring us some tea." Stroud grinned and gestured for the door.

Anna followed him from the room and through the stately house. As they went, Stroud elaborated on the wondrous history of plant-based medicines. Anna listened with exaggerated interest and imagined what the dean would give to access the miraculous secrets contained within her mother's Book of Shadows. Anna herself had little interest in herb-lore; she was more drawn to the power of the dark arts of necromancy.

They passed through the kitchen and the butler's pantry before arriving at the back door. Stroud cast it open and led the way into a grand conservatory surrounded on all sides by enormous glass windows.

Anna sucked a sharp breath into her throat as she entered, struck by the lush beauty of the dean's indoor garden. Except for Harvard's famed arboretum, she had never seen such cultivated splendor. Despite the October chill creeping across the land outside, the air in here was almost steamy and Anna wondered how Stroud kept it so humid and saturated with the moisture of a tropical forest. Two parallel flagstone walkways stretched toward the windows at the rear of the conservatory, which had to be at least a hundred feet away. The rows in between and on either side of the paths were bursting with a resplendent assortment of exotic and luxuriant plants. Such a garden must have taken years to cultivate and yet, hadn't Stroud said he and his wife had only taken residence here a year ago?

As if reading Anna's thoughts, Stroud said, "I brought much of what you see here from New Haven, where I was a professor at Yale for many years. Their transport came at considerable expense, but it was one of my few conditions for accepting the position as dean here at the University of Vermont. Sadly, not all the specimens survived the journey. Even so, I remain pleased with their progress."

"It's wonderful," Anna said, unable to conceal her admiration. She moved to examine a curious red cone blooming from an abundance of green foliage. It must have been nearly eight inches tall and had elliptical leaves that spiraled up and around its slender stem.

"That species is known as a spiral ginger," Stroud explained. "'Tis common enough in the warmer climate of the southern Americas."

Lucretia arrived bearing a pewter tray, which she set on a nearby bench. Her long hair was now tucked in a bonnet and she wore a white apron over her bodice. If the lady of the house was put off by the indignity of playing the role of servant, she didn't show it.

"You've not had lunch, Virgil," she said. "I thought you and Miss Bell might enjoy something to eat with your tea." She indicated a plate of biscuits sitting on the tray next to the teapot.

Stroud gave a thin smile and nodded. Lucretia stood by for a moment, as if waiting to be invited to join the conversation, until Stroud gave her a curt glance and said, "Is there anything more, Lucretia?"

"No, I… I will leave you to your business." With a polite nod to Anna, Lucretia turned and left the conservatory.

"You must smell the plumeria there." Stroud pointed with one long finger while he poured their tea with his other hand. "Their scent is that of Elysium itself."

Anna followed his direction a few paces down the path to a small shrub bursting with flowers. They were bright yellow at the center, with a dusting of light pink at the rounded tips of their overlapping petals. Anna bent her nose to the blooms and breathed deep of their sweet fragrance. They instantly reminded her of fresh peach and warm honeysuckle.

Stroud joined her and handed her a teacup. The tea was an uncommon variety, with a slightly bitter tang that Anna didn't find unpleasant. There came a soft tapping from above now. She glanced up to see the first fat drops of rain splashing on the glass roof.

"Come." Stroud motioned for her to follow him further down the aisle. "Let me show you something truly unique." He led the way past an assortment of lush ferns and dazzling orchids to a curious patch of large grayish-green seed pods perched atop thick stalks.

"*Papaver somniferum*," Stroud announced proudly. "Commonly known as the opium poppy."

"Opium?" Anna asked between sips of her tea, pretending she wasn't already familiar with the drug or its use in treating pain, particularly sick and wounded soldiers. Her own mother had made use of it to numb the pain of a broken rib she had incurred while putting an end to an especially nasty haunting.

"Indeed. This variety was imported from India itself and is

among the rarest in my collection. It is the center around which all of my current research revolves."

"How so?"

"I seek a new treatment for female hysteria," Stroud explained. "For centuries, we have considered the disease from a multitude of perspectives, both scientific and demonological. Women are particularly susceptible to the disorder—through no fault of your own, to be sure. It is simply a consequence of the weaker nature of your sex."

Anna sipped her tea and bit her tongue. She wondered with some amusement if Jericho Byrne might have something to say about the weaker nature of women.

"Outlandish remedies ranging from abstinence to hysterical paroxysm and even purification of evil through exorcism have all been attempted, unsurprisingly without success." Stroud's tone and cadence had now slipped into that of the professor. "But I believe we may develop a more effective treatment from the medicinal properties of the plants you see before you."

"How do you…" The rest of Anna's question came out strangely slurred. She blinked in confusion. The sound of her own voice had seemed to come to her from a great distance, as if she were hearing its echo resounding from within a deep cavern. The pattering of the rain on the glass above was somehow amplified now, each drop a booming reverberation in Anna's head. And they were becoming louder, more resonant by the moment. Anna was gripped by a swift moment of panic. Something was terribly wrong.

And yet, she quickly discovered she didn't quite care anymore. An odd but blissful sensation was spreading through her. She felt as if she were being wrapped in a warm blanket—no, not a blanket, but the heavy fur of some magnificent beast. Its comfort made her feel inviolable and carefree. It was a euphoric rapture the likes of which she had only known when lost in the ecstasy of witchcraft. She felt weightless and wanted nothing more than to close her eyes and let the floating current of elation carry her away.

Anna staggered on wobbly legs. Her teacup crashed to the hard flagstone as her hand shot out to steady herself. She blinked and her drowsy eyelids stayed closed for longer than she intended. Through the deepening fog of her mind, a dim thought occurred to her: Stroud wasn't making any effort to assist her. Strangely, he didn't seem the slightest bit surprised or alarmed by her sudden disorientation. Instead, he stood by and studied her as she swooned, his gaze radiant and intense and imbued with something Anna couldn't quite name. Fascination? Anticipation? Exultation?

A sickening dread wormed its way into Anna's gut and cut a shadow through her paralyzing sense of bliss. She now recognized the bitter tang she had tasted in her tea: laudanum. She remembered the moments when her back had been turned to Stroud as she smelled the plumeria flowers at his insistence. The instant had been fleeting—barely a few seconds—but long enough for Stroud to dose her tea secretly with the powerful tincture of opium and alcohol.

Anna cursed herself for being so careless, so trusting. As her thoughts dissolved further into a swirling pink haze, she struggled to remember what her mother had taught her about the opiate. How much laudanum had Stroud given her? Enough to kill?

"What did you—" Anna's voice was that of a woman speaking in her sleep. Her garbled question trailed off as the floor seemed to tilt like a listing ship. She stumbled and pitched forward toward Stroud. He retreated a step out of reach, and she lost her balance. This time there was nothing with which to catch herself. She fell, and for an instant it felt like she was flying until she crashed to the ground like a boxer taking a haymaker to the jaw. Despite the force of the impact, there was no pain, no distress. There was only a bizarre sense of detachment and a feeling that nothing mattered more than closing her eyes and letting herself be lifted away. Abigail, Cassie Byrne, the missing women, Stroud—all of them were washed far out to sea and pulled under by a tide of indifference.

From her skewed point-of-view, Anna was conscious of Stroud's large slippers treading across the flagstones toward her. She struggled to rise, but the warm and comfortable fur blanket that had enveloped her weighed her down and made her limbs too heavy to lift.

Stroud knelt over her, and his long face came into view. Prone and listless, she stared up at him, his gaze searing into her own until her glazed blue eyes rolled back in her head and slid shut. As she gave herself over to oblivion, Anna felt her spirit carried aloft from its corporeal cage.

But far below her, there lay nothing but darkness.

Chapter 9

The night before the governor's ball, Jezekiah Whipple had died of a heart attack in his bed at the ripe age of seventy-six. But he hadn't died alone. The teenage prostitute who had precipitated the heart attack was there with him. The old man's hands had fallen away from her small breasts and she thought he had fallen asleep beneath her. When she slid down between his knobby knees and failed to rouse him with her mouth, the awful reality of what had happened slammed into her and sent her scurrying for her clothes.

Whipple's maid came across his naked body the next morning and wisely stuffed him into his long nightshirt for fear of scandal. The half-dozen servants he kept on staff knew of the young women who came to the house late at night and left by the back door in the small hours of the morning. Of course, the servants turned a blind eye and said nothing. Now that their employer was dead, however, there was no telling what vicious rumors they might turn loose on the small town.

A wealthy timber baron, Whipple had no family left to mourn him. His only son was killed fifteen years earlier in the

Battle of Lake Champlain during the War of 1812, and Whipple's wife had died of bronchitis shortly after. Since then, the aging widower had slid into a daily routine of drinking and shooting at things on the eighty acres of farm and orchards upon which his home was nestled.

Naturally, Whipple's sudden death—and the scandalous intrigue surrounding it—was a tantalizing topic among the wealthy gossips at the governor's ball. It was there that Abigail had overheard the salacious speculation circulating throughout the evening and it was why she now stood over the dead man's body where it lay on a mahogany table in his plush parlor.

The rain had eased somewhat, and it was now late afternoon. Whipple's groundskeeper, a stooped rake of a man named Hoag, had been outside the house, hewing the pine boards for Whipple's coffin, when Abigail arrived and announced she had come to lay out the old man's remains. Hoag seemed perturbed and squinted in confusion at her as she stood waiting expectantly in the rain.

"But… where's Ruth?" he asked. "Isn't she—"

"Ruth's not feeling well, poor thing," Abigail replied. "She sends her condolences and bade me to come from Shelburne in her stead."

Hoag now leaned against the door-jam to the parlor's wide double-doors and kept an eye on Abigail as she stood over Whipple's nightshirt-draped body. With a showy sign of the cross, she closed her eyes and murmured, "Mary stood at his feet behind him weeping, and began to wash his feet with tears, and did wipe them with the hairs on her head, and kissed his feet, and anointed them with ointment." Though she kept her voice low, Abigail still spoke the words of Scripture loud enough for the groundskeeper to hear and lend credence to her ruse. She opened her eyes again and asked, "Has the house a coffin door?"

"Aye." Hoag pointed across the room. There was a nondescript door set in the corner of a sidewall.

"Very good. Wouldn't do to remove Mr. Whipple's remains through the same door used by the living, would it?"

The groundskeeper nodded and gave a thin smile.

"This may take some time," Abigail said. "Please don't let me keep you from your work."

She turned away, but Hoag seemed hesitant to leave her alone. He lingered at the door and shifted from foot to foot.

"I assure you I have brought everything I need." Abigail patted a leather bag she had set on the table next to the dead man's wrinkled and bluish feet. "Please, Mr. Whipple expired nearly thirty-six hours ago. If I don't begin the shrouding process at once, his body will soon become... *unpleasant*." She produced a scalpel from the bag and motioned tactfully for the door.

The appearance of the razor-sharp blade in Abigail's hand —and the mental image of what she was about to do with it —was enough to convince the groundskeeper. "I'll be out where you found me if you need me." With a tip of his cap, he shuffled out the door and left her alone with the corpse.

Abigail went to work. Were she indeed a shrouder responsible for washing, dressing, and grooming the bodies of the deceased, she would now remove the internal organs, block the orifices, apply alcohol to the corpse's skin, and fill the cavities with charcoal to delay the onset of putrefaction.

Abigail had no intention of doing any of those things. She required one thing of Jezekiah Whipple and one thing only.

Abigail first turned Whipple's body on the table so that the feet faced East, the direction of the dead. She then placed the unused scalpel on the table next to her leather bag and produced another more curious instrument. It was made of silver and resembled a spoon combined with a fork. Three sharp tines were cut into the edge of its unusually round and deep bowl. The handle was inlaid with intricate arcane patterns and sigils.

From somewhere outside, Abigail could now hear the rhythmic sound of sawing as Hoag resumed work on Whipple's coffin. With her strange implement in hand, she rounded the table and stood over the corpse's head. Gravity pulled the slack jowls of the dead man's ashen cheeks downward toward the tabletop so that his wrinkled lips stretched back in a macabre grimace. His eyes were closed and Abigail took a deep and steadying breath before proceeding.

She reached for the dead man's left eye and parted the cold lids with her fingers. The sightless orb was fixed straight up toward the coffered ceiling in a ghastly stare. The iris was milky-gray, and the whites were a jaundiced shade of yellow. Abigail kept the eyelids apart with one hand while her other hand dug the tines of her instrument into the eye socket. Careful not to rupture the eyeball, she twisted the tool until the spoon cupped the eye from behind. With a deft snap of the wrist, she severed the tough optic nerve with the sharp tines and scooped the eyeball from its socket.

Experience had taught Abigail not to think about what came next. Without hesitation, she plucked the eyeball from the spoon, popped it into her mouth, and chewed.

The slippery orb burst between her teeth like a cherry tomato. A scorching rush of bile surged up her throat, and she fought back the reflexive urge to gag as she continued to chew. The meat inside the sclera was spongy and gelatinous and gave a faint impression of pork. There was also a slight crunch as Abigail ground the cornea beneath her teeth until it was soft enough to swallow. As the masticated eye slid down her throat, she closed her eyes and murmured a quiet chant in an ancient and serpentine language. An ecstatic tingle pulsed through Abigail's flesh as the dark energy of her spell flowed through her, satisfying her in ways no man ever could.

When she opened her eyes, it was as if night had fallen. The surrounding room was drained of its color. All that remained was a monochrome blue, as if her surroundings were now illuminated by the ghostly light of a full moon.

An electric thrill ran through Abigail. Her spell had worked; she was looking through the invisible Veil that separated the living from the dead. While she remained safely rooted in her own world—Whipple's corpse was still laid out on the table before her and the sound of Hoag's steady sawing still drifted from beyond the rain-spattered window—ingesting the dead man's eye temporarily revealed the hidden realm of spirits and monsters that roamed the earth unseen behind the Veil. Abigail had learned a hard lesson long ago that it was far safer to commune with the dead while they remained in their world instead of inviting them into her own.

Abigail's pulse quickened as she returned the silver instrument to her bag and retrieved the scalpel from the table.

She pulled the sleeve of her Spencer jacket up to her elbow, revealing the crisscrossing spider web of old lacerations. With her hand balled into a tight fist, she pierced the milk-white skin of her forearm with the blade. A spasm of pain crossed her face, but it was fleeting. The ritual to summon a Familiar had become a common one and Abigail flinched no more as blood welled from the wound. Instead, she closed her eyes again and murmured another sibilant incantation.

"Warm thyself of my blood offering and do my bidding," she finished, and opened her eyes. She crossed the room to an ornate mirror hanging on a wallpapered wall. There, she smeared her blood across its polished surface.

Within moments, there was a stirring in the mirror.

A ghostly mist materialized behind Abigail's reflected face. It swirled and writhed with a life of its own as it expanded and thickened inside the mirror. Soon, the mist completely obscured her reflection and the room she stood in. She was no longer looking at a mirror, but a window into a shadowy realm.

Now filling the gilded frame from corner to corner, tendrils of the spectral mist twisted into the ghostly impression of a man. The apparition smashed both fists into the mirror as if he were trying to free himself from a glass cage. He then pressed his vaporous mouth to the spot where Abigail had smeared her blood. The crimson streak faded and disappeared as the apparition sucked it through the surface of the mirror itself.

Abigail raised her arm and pressed it to the mirror, offering the bleeding wound to the spirit that was her Familiar. The ghostly mist surged against the invisible barrier and seized upon her with ravenous desire. There was a dizzying moment of lightheaded vertigo as the spirit sucked the warm blood from Abigail's flesh through the glass. A moment passed before she drew her arm away.

The mass of ghostly mist shot forward again, hungry for more. It crashed up against its side of the mirror and Abigail brandished an iron talisman she wore around her neck at all times. The spirit recoiled and shrank back as she held the rune-shaped charm aloft. If her Familiar found a way to cross through the mirror, the talisman was the only thing that prevented the hungry spirit from ripping her to shreds and emptying her veins.

A voice issued from the depths of the swirling mass, bottomless and hollow and chilling to the ear. *What would thou ask of me, my mistress?*

"I seek spirits of the recently dead," Abigail replied. She gave the Familiar the names of the missing women. "If any are there beyond the Veil, find them and bring them before me."

With a swirling gust, the mist vanished from the mirror as it sped on its way to follow Abigail's command.

As she gazed at her own reflection in the eerie midnight blue of the world beyond the Veil, Abigail didn't expect to be kept waiting long. If any of the women were dead, their spirits wouldn't be strong enough to travel far from their final resting places. It would take years for them to gather enough strength to move about behind the Veil. Ancient and powerful spirits such as those that Abigail bound to her service as Familiars could travel vast distances in the blink of an eye. And they were also infinitely more deadly.

Moments went by before Abigail became aware of something troubling.

Hoag's sawing had stopped.

In its place, Abigail could now discern the hushed rasp of the groundkeeper's voice. She hurried to the window and peered outside into the drizzle toward where Hoag had been hewing the lumber near a shed some distance away. He was now talking to a gray-haired matron—presumably Ruth, the real shrouded who had arrived to lay out Whipple's corpse.

Hoag looked perplexed. He gestured animatedly toward the house a couple of times before they both started across the expansive lawn in Abigail's direction. Ruth walked with a stick and a noticeable limp and Hoag was obviously torn between waiting for her and hustling to the house to confront Abigail, the intruder. Either way, they would come upon her soon enough.

Damn! Abigail thought. She needed more time!

The pair outside were nearing the house now. Soon they disappeared from sight, hidden by the front corner of the building. Abigail tried to remember how many yards remained until they reached the front steps. Twenty? Ten?

At last, the Familiar reappeared in the mirror in a burst of white smoke.

"What have you discovered?" Abigail demanded. "Tell me quickly!"

Those you seek are not to be found, Mistress, the hollow voice intoned.

Abigail took heart at the news. The missing women were still alive. But where had they gone?

Color was returning to the room as the potency of Abigail's

spell waned. The primary colors of blue, red, and yellow were the first to appear, as if an unseen artist were rendering the scene with painstakingly slow strokes. If Abigail wanted to renew the spell, she would have to ingest the dead man's other eye. But there was no need; she had gotten what she came for. She could already hear the slow tread of footsteps mounting the steps at the front of the house. They would discover her within moments.

With a word, Abigail dismissed the Familiar and snatched up her bag. The color had now fully returned to the room as she turned to escape through the coffin door.

The corpse's hand suddenly lashed out and seized her wrist.

Abigail whirled around and an icy prickle of fear shot through her at what she beheld. This wasn't possible! Something was clutching at her from beyond the Veil, something incredibly powerful. But what? Her spell opened a window into the Veil, not a door. Nothing could cross over.

Abigail's mind raced as she struggled to free herself from the corpse's freezing grip. How had her spell gone wrong? And how dire would the consequences be?

A grotesque erection protruded like a tent pole from beneath the dead man's long night-shirt as he swung his bony legs from the table and stood. The corpse's jaw dropped open, and it advanced. A voice crawled out of the gaping mouth. It was dull and raspy and hollow all at once.

Mistress…

That voice! Abigail recognized it at once! It was Gideon, the Familiar she had bound to Anna. What was he doing here, using the dead man's corpse to communicate? The binding spell was a powerful one; Gideon was to remain with Anna at all times like an invisible shadow. He was never to leave her unless summoned by Abigail or…

"What is it, Gideon?" Abigail demanded with a rising sense of anxiety. "Why have you come to me?"

Your daughter, Mistress…

A spark of alarm went off in Abigail. "What? What about my daughter? Speak!"

She is about to die…

Chapter 10

A splash of something cold on Anna's cheek roused her from oblivion. As a child, she had once awoken from a nightmare inspired by one of her mother's many lessons on the frightful beings that lurked beyond the Veil. As she lay trembling in her darkened bedroom, Anna had known it was foolish to be so frightened of a bad dream—a fact her mother often reminded of. And yet, little Anna couldn't help herself; she still craved soothing. She had slipped from beneath the blanket and crept across the small room to the door. When she pulled it open, the hallway beyond lay cloaked in inky darkness. At the far end, the door to Abigail's private study stood open. A single candle burned within. Anna felt drawn to it, that tiny beacon and its comforting glow flickering like a star in a vast, black void. It pulled her forward, almost against her will, through the darkness of the hallway toward the light where her mother sat reading.

Anna had the same sensation now as she regained consciousness. She felt herself being drawn up from a black and shapeless nothing toward a glowing pinhole that swelled in size until her eyes fluttered open.

The heart-stopping sensation of being smothered seized her immediately. She couldn't get air in or out of her mouth. In her daze, it took her a terrifying moment to realize she was gagged. Panic gripped her. Her heart thrashed against her ribs and she could feel the constricted air in her lungs screaming to get out. If she didn't slow her breathing, she would asphyxiate. She fought off another assault of panic and willed herself to remain calm, to breathe deeply through her nose and slow her galloping pulse. Another tiny splash landed on her cheek and she had a dim realization that it was a raindrop. Why was she in the rain? And why was she frozen to the bone?

Anna glanced around, trying to discern where she was. Fear and confusion gnawed at her belly. The surrounding darkness was impenetrable, the silence menacing. But as her breathing became more regular, more of Anna's wits returned.

She was lying sprawled on a smooth surface of cold, hard stone. Her body shivered from a chill that sank deep into her marrow. She struggled to sit up and found her arms felt strangely weighted. A terrible clanking filled her ears, and she realized with rising dread that her wrists were shackled with manacles. The chain that linked them together was unusually long and passed through a heavy iron ring anchored into the stone between her feet.

The cold metal biting into her skin burned away the laudanum-induced fog clouding Anna's thoughts. The memory of Virgil Stroud drugging her came crashing down on her with awful force. With it came a stark awareness of her surroundings.

She was imprisoned at the bottom of a tall tower that seemingly had no roof. It was night and jagged streaks of lightning blasted across the darkened sky nearly a hundred feet above her. The afternoon drizzle had intensified to a raging storm. But while booming peels of thunder reverberated down through the tower, the worst of the heavy rain didn't penetrate all the way to the bottom; only the occasional drops.

A spiral staircase supported by round pillars was carved into the tower's curving granite walls. Arched alcoves gave shadowy glimpses of a series of interspersed landings as the steps corkscrewed upward. The circular floor beneath Anna was maybe fifty feet in diameter and made of polished marble. Inlaid within it in darker marble was a seven-pointed star Anna recognized as a heptagram, a powerful occult symbol of warding and protection.

Anna was chained at the center of the star. She didn't bother testing the strength of the chain or the iron ring through which it passed. The exertion would only sap what little strength she had, and she suspected she would need all that should could muster for whatever was to come.

A freezing shiver ran over Anna's goose-pimpled skin, and it was only then that she noticed she had been stripped down to her thin cotton chemise. It wasn't soaked from the rain, but it was wet enough that her nipples were visible through the thin fabric clinging to her breasts. Her thick black hair was damp and plastered to her face and neck. Behind whatever cloth was bound around her mouth, her tongue felt thick and dry. Where the hell was she? How long had she been unconscious and what had Stroud done to her while she was so vulnerable?

An angry blast of thunder cracked high above. Anna staggered to her feet and glanced up again. This time, she noticed something she hadn't before. Looming over the edges of the open hole at the top of the tower were the skeletal fingers of tree branches silhouetted against the brilliant flashes of lightning. But that was impossible, wasn't it? How could any tree be so much taller than a tower such as this?

Unless this wasn't a tower.

It was a well.

But this enormous well spiraling deep into the earth was never intended to collect water. Discreet drains cut into the marble around the floor's perimeter drained away what little rain managed to filter down to the ground. Who had built this elaborate inverted tower? And for what purpose?

A sound broke the eerie silence and startled Anna out of her contemplation. From somewhere high above came a squeal of hinges and the grinding of a heavy door creaking open. The faint glow of torchlight appeared at the uppermost level of the winding stairs. It seemed to float through the air like a fiery apparition, growing brighter as whoever bore the torch descended, pausing to light more torches at each of the seven landings.

The garish radiance of the flames spilled down on Anna from above. She could now discern a procession of robed figures passing behind the pillars and through the alcoves as they descended the long staircase toward her. The first three wore black robes; the remaining four wore crimson. All of them were hooded, their faces obscured in heavy shadows. The torchbearer leading the procession was remarkably tall, and Anna immediately suspected Virgil Stroud to be the man beneath the black robes.

The robed figures silently encircled the perimeter of the well to surround Anna. A violent curse leapt into her throat, but the gag in her mouth kept it from escaping. Instead, she eyed the figures warily as each came to a stop at one of the seven points of the heptagram. The three in black stood facing her, with the tall figure she suspected to be Stroud directly in front of her. It wasn't lost on Anna that he stood just out of reach of the length of chain that bound her wrists to the ring in the floor.

The four crimson robes took up positions around her. Anna noticed they all bore the same symbol embroidered on the left breast of their robes: a five-pointed pentagram adorned with additional parallel lines, circles, and glyphs.

The tall figure before Anna fixed his torch in a sconce, faced her, and raised his arms high in the air. The long fingers of two spidery hands stretched from the cuffs of the black robe toward the night sky.

"Hear our prayer, mighty Astaroth!" Virgil Stroud's deep baritone boomed off the stone walls and reverberated up the well. "Guardian of Wisdom and ruler of forty legions! Exalted Duke, we humbly invoke you from the eternal Abyss to this mortal sphere! Accept our offering and appear before us in our Circle of Seven! Reveal yourself that we may glory in your presence! Hail Astaroth!"

The robed figures echoed his words in thundering unison. "Hail Astaroth!"

Astaroth. The name struck a chord in the recesses of Anna's memories. It was that of an ancient demon. Anna struggled to remember her mother's teachings. Abigail had become obsessed with demonology while pregnant with Anna. She had schooled her daughter on both Johann Weyer's *Pseudeomonachia Daemonum* and the *Lemegeton*, the notorious 17th century grimoire on demonology, also known as the *Lesser Key of Solomon*. By the time Anna was ten, she was as familiar with the names of demons as she was with the alphabet.

Astaroth was a great and terrible Duke of Hell. He appeared to mortals in the shape of a foul angel sitting astride an infernal dragon, carrying a viper in his right hand. To a conjuror powerful enough to summon and bind him, Astaroth was believed to unlock the riddles of mathematical sciences, make men invisible, lead them to hidden treasures, and make known all secrets asked of him.

Anna now recognized the symbol emblazoned on her captors' robes as Astaroth's sigil, a pictorial representation of the demon's name used for summoning.

"Acolytes," Stroud went on. He had lowered his arms and was addressing the crimson robes now. "We are come unto this sacred Tomb to observe the ancient Rite of Initiation. Before us stands our offering," Stroud motioned at Anna before sweeping his hand toward one of three doorways that led away into darkness from the bottom of the well. "She shall be freed unto the labyrinth. Let he who catches her spill his seed and visualize Astaroth clearly in their copulation. Thus shall he lend energy to our evocation of our master, in whose name we beseech the gift of esoteric truths of the ancient past."

Anna felt a chilling horror creep through her like frost on a window. She was to be hunted through whatever dark, underground domain it was that Stroud called the labyrinth, her fear serving as an enticement for the demon, Astaroth. And once they caught her, one of these men would have his way with her to amplify her terror.

Anna's stomach tightened into a pit of revulsion and dread. For the first time in many years, she knew what it meant to be afraid.

Lightning lit the sky and thunder crashed down upon them as Stroud continued. "Her blood will give glory to Astaroth. Let he who drinks of it be rewarded with ascension to the Second Order of the Crucible of Night."

"Hail Astaroth!" The crimson robes chanted in eerie unison.

Except for one.

"No," the man said a firm voice.

Anna's head whipped around to the crimson-robed acolyte who had spoken. Nothing of his face was visible, but he was broad-shouldered and slightly taller than the others.

Stroud's hooded head swiveled to the acolyte as well. "What say you, acolyte?"

"We cannot—" The acolyte started to protest but faltered. His voice lost some of its confidence, but remained resolute. "This is wrong."

"The ritual is sacrosanct," Stroud admonished. "The demon is drawn to fear and carnal desires. He must be satisfied by our offering before he may deign to appear before us."

"Even so, she's but an innocent woman. You never told us the ritual would require her rape. I'll have no part of it."

"Will you not?" Stroud's baritone sank to a soul-grating

growl. "Consider your actions wisely, acolyte. Will you truly forsake your initiation into the Second Order? Think of the mysteries yet to be unveiled to you, those revelations concealed from the average man. The wonders of alchemy; the power to recall the precise details of images and texts with but a single viewing; the instantaneous learning of mathematics and sciences; the answers to questions ancient and arcane that only Astaroth may reveal. These secrets may be yours as they are mine, if you but satisfy yourself of this paltry woman."

The acolyte shook his hooded head. "Of what good is knowledge without conscience?" He hesitated a moment longer, mentally committing himself to a course of action. Then he broke from the circle and strode toward the stairs.

For a brief moment, Anna allowed herself to take hope as she observed their dispute. Might this young man save her? Might his objections somehow sway others to intervene before it was too late?

But as she watched the man ascend into the shadows above, any spark of hope vanished with him. He had no intention of saving her; He was saving himself from the guilt of what they were going to do to her.

One of the other crimson-robed acolytes made a move to go after him, but a slender finger extended from Stroud's robe and kept him in his place. "There will be time enough to deal with him. Our evocation has already begun and our master, Astaroth, grows impatient. We must not keep him waiting lest he become displeased. *Tasa. Alora, Foren. Astaroth!*"

"*Tasa. Alora, Foren. Astaroth...*" The others echoed in concert. They chanted the phrase over and over. Anna recognized it as Astaroth's *enn*, a ritualistic chant of invitation and admiration for the demon.

"*Tasa. Alora, Foren. Astaroth...*"

While the others continued the chant, Stroud stepped to Anna and removed the gag from her mouth. His hooded face was inches from hers as she sucked in air and glared at him defiantly. She could feel the warmth of his breath flowing from within his hood, sense his eyes slithering from her full lips down to the pink nubs of her nipples poking through her damp chemise.

"What a pity that I may only be initiated once," Stroud whispered lasciviously into her ear. "I would warn you not to scream, Miss Bell, but that is precisely what we require of you. So please, do scream... loud and often."

"*Tasa. Alora, Foren. Astaroth...*"

Another black-robed man produced a ring of keys and released Anna from her manacles. Anna noticed age spots on his thin hands as he manipulated the locks. She resisted the urge to cave his nose into his face while he was still within striking distance. Attacking him now would accomplish nothing. She must still be patient and bide her time until a better opportunity presented itself.

The manacles fell to the floor with a clatter and Anna glowered at Stroud as she rubbed the circulation back into her sore wrists. "Is this what happened to Tabitha? Is this what you did to the other women? You will kill me now as you did them?"

Even veiled in shadows, Anna could tell Stroud's face had twisted into an amused sneer.

"Kill you?" He scoffed. "No, my dear. There is more than

one way to claim the blood of a virgin."

His words struck Anna speechless and stripped her of her vehemence. *Virgin?* How could Stroud possibly know that about her? That she had never lain with a man? Unless… unless he spoke the truth about the arcane powers he wielded.

"*Tasa. Alora, Foren. Astaroth…*"

"We will allow five minutes before we come after you," Stroud warned. He motioned toward one of the three portals to darkness. "The labyrinth does have another exit. I suggest you attempt to find it as quickly as you can."

"*Tasa. Alora, Foren. Astaroth…*"

Anna glanced around at the circle of hooded faces staring back at her. She could almost feel the depraved lust radiating off them as they chanted. The cool air of the well seemed to vibrate with their anticipation of the chase, of the gratification they would take in her unwilling fear and violation. Anna's eyes darted around the chamber. The men blocked the stairs. There was no escape except for the entrances to the dark labyrinth. She searched desperately for something she could use to her advantage. She found very little.

A numbing sense of despair took hold. The situation was hopeless. There was no way she could overcome all six men. Still, she had to try. She would rather die fighting than let herself be defiled at their hands. She had to find some way of getting the upper hand, of evening the odds no matter how slim they might be. But how?

Her gaze passed once more over the gathering of chanting men surrounding her. Anna knew she had only one card to play. These men wanted her to run for sport, to be afraid and cower before them. She decided to give them one out of the two.

Without warning, she charged.

Straight at Stroud.

Chapter 11

Anna dropped her shoulder and speared Stroud right in the middle of his long torso. The force of her tackle carried him backward off his feet and his heels swept up into the air from beneath him. Anna drove him down into the hard stone and felt his ribs snap with a sickening *crack* beneath her weight. He let out a wheezing gasp as the air went out of him. Anna hoped she was lucky enough to have punctured one of his lungs with a jagged shard of bone.

There was a stunned instant while the others stood in mute stupefaction before they recovered from their shock and leapt into action. The black-robed man who had freed Anna of her manacles grabbed her by her shoulders and ripped her away from the groaning Stroud.

Anna expected his move and let her momentum carry her into a backward roll toward the center of the heptagram. She landed within reach of the iron ring and snatched up the chain just as one of the crimson-robed acolytes lunged for her. Anna swung the chain with all her strength and brought a heavy manacle smashing into the side of the man's hooded head. Blood and teeth sprayed from within the hood's dark depths as the acolyte spun on his feet like a child's top before collapsing in a motionless heap.

Anna didn't have time to wonder if she killed the man. Another acolyte was already grabbing for her from behind. Anna ducked beneath his grasping hands and whipped the manacle through the air again. It collided with the front of the man's knee and crushed it backward. His foot shot forward the wrong way, his lower leg now jutting out below the knee at a forty-five-degree angle. The man let out a strangled cry and crumpled, writhing in agony and clutching at his ruined leg.

The chain was suddenly ripped out of Anna's grasp; the links sawing at her palms as it slid through her grip. She whirled and discovered one of the black robes had seized the manacle at the other end and had yanked the chain away. The manacle skidded across the floor and out of reach before it struck up against the iron ring with a clang.

With her makeshift flail now gone, Anna assumed a defensive stance and took stock of the situation. The remaining robed figures circled her warily. Stroud lay curled on his side, his stick-like legs crunched up to his chest as he gasped and struggled to suck air into his pulverized lungs. The first crimson robe still lay unconscious or dead where he fell. The second had degenerated into weeping sobs. He was likely only moments away from going into shock from the pain of his shattered knee. His hood had fallen back and Anna now saw the youthful face of a man about her own age under a mop of red hair.

She had incapacitated three of her six captors, but the odds still were not in her favor. Two black robes and a single acolyte remained. It was the latter that concerned her the most. If the color of their robes was any indication of their experience and status, the black robes were likely aging men like Stroud. But the acolytes were young and strapping… and hungry.

Anna's eyes darted to the stairs, but one of the black robes still stood in her way. She considered another charge, but without the element of surprise, the other two men would swarm and overwhelm her. She no longer had any choice. If she had any hope of escape, she would have to take her chances in the underground labyrinth.

Before anyone could stop her, Anna bolted for the nearest doorway. She heard shouts behind her as she plunged into the blackness. There was the pounding of heavy footfalls in pursuit, but Anna was faster, and she quickly outpaced them. She raced headlong through the twisting stone corridor, the darkness so thick it was smothering. She collided with a wall and ricocheted into another, her shoulder throbbing from the impact. Instead of pressing on blindly, she risked a moment to listen for her pursuers.

The corridor had gone silent.

Were they still lurking in the darkness behind her?

Anna's blood pounded in her ears as she considered her options. Stroud could have lied about there being another exit from the labyrinth. What better way to heighten her fear than to give her false hope as she fled through the darkness? Without hope, there was no reason to run, no chase to ratchet up her terror as a gift for Astaroth.

A taunting voice rolled through the corridor toward her.

"Come, come, little rabbit…"

The robust voice was that of a young man: the acolyte. He was still distant, but close enough to get Anna moving again. She pressed on with her hands out, feeling her way through the blackness. Despite swearing off witchcraft, she now tried to recall a spell that would allow her to see in the dark. But her thoughts were too rattled with adrenaline to summon the words.

The tunnels had been carved from the earth's bedrock and they were getting narrower now, the twists and turns more convoluted. The air down here was stale and reeked of mildew and wet stone. Anna had never feared tight spaces, but the thought of being so far below ground—the weight of thousands of tons of rock bearing down and standing between her and fresh oxygen—was enough to make her feel like she was already suffocating.

"*Tasa. Alora, Foren. Astaroth…*"

The acolyte's toneless chant rippled through the silent darkness. The sick bastard still meant to satiate his demonic master. Anna's bare toes crunched painfully on what she thought was a small pile of sticks, but soon understood to be the bones of some long-dead vermin.

Anna realized she could now make out the desiccated skeletal remains in the dark. She couldn't see much, just the barest contours of shapes, but there was now the faintest of light in the corridor. It was like that cast by a candle flickering through the keyhole of a darkened room. The revelation didn't bring Anna any comfort. It was the faint glow of a torch bleeding around the curves of the tunnel.

The acolyte was getting closer.

Anna knew she couldn't keep evading him. She was at too much of a disadvantage, fumbling along blindly while he stalked her unhindered. He was going to catch up to her soon. The further she ventured into this subterranean maze, the more likely she would become hopelessly lost. She already wondered if she could retrace her way back to the well if necessary. She had to change tactics, to turn the tables on her pursuer.

Fissures and niches honeycombed the stone walls of the tunnels. If she could only find one deep enough to slip inside and hide, she might ambush him.

"*Tasa. Alora, Foren. Astaroth…*"

The acolyte's voice was now so clear, it was almost a whisper in her ear. He was very close now. As much as she resisted the idea, Anna had to keep moving.

She reached out her arms and dragged her palms along the walls as she went, feeling for a crack wide enough to fit into. The tunnel grew narrower with each step. As she ventured further, hope started to abandon her. What if the tunnel continued to narrow into an impassible wedge? Already, she had the terrifying sense of being buried alive and entombed. She couldn't go on like this. If she didn't find a hiding place soon, she would have to turn and face her pursuer. If he was alone, she at least had a chance. But if the others were with him…

At last, the choice was made for her. The corridor widened unexpectedly into a natural cavern. Anna had no way of knowing how large it was, but a change in the reverberations of her footsteps off the stone indicated it was sizable. She explored the walls with her hands, but found herself walking in a wide circle. There was no other exit; the cavern was a dead end.

This was it. She would have to make her stand here.

An icy finger of fear traced a line up Anna's spine as she wondered how well the acolyte knew these tunnels. Would he know she had walked into a trap? Or was he as unfamiliar with the labyrinth as she was?

A flickering glow appeared within the tunnel. Anna pressed her back flat against the wall to the right of the entrance to the cavern. It wasn't the best spot for an ambush, but she didn't have time to further probe the darkness of the cavern for something better. She was playing the odds that the acolyte was right-handed and bearing his torch with his dominant hand. If that was the case, he would likely lead with that arm and turn immediately to his left if he grew suspicious of an ambush as he approached the cavern. For that split second, he would have his back to Anna.

Of course, there was a fifty-fifty chance he would turn the other way, right into her.

Anna held her breath as the glow of the torch grew brighter, closer…

Closer…

She could hear the man's footsteps approaching now, only yards away.

Closer…

Anna's pulse pounded so hard she was sure it would give her away.

Closer…

"*Tasa. Alora, Foren. Astaroth…*" The acolyte's malevolent chant swelled louder, louder.

Closer…

Just a few more feet…

There he was.

Light flooded the cavern as the acolyte emerged from the tunnel. His crimson hood was cast back now. As he swept by, Anna glimpsed his dark hair, his heavy, protruding brow, and a chin as solid as the square end of an anvil. He was larger than Anna had thought—much larger. Instead of being alert to an ambush, he seemed unaware of Anna lurking in the shadows behind him. In his smug arrogance, he likely assumed she was too scared to stop running and mount any sort of defense, despite the desperate fight she had put up back at the well. For a fraction of an instant, Anna had the idea that she might slip into the tunnel unseen behind his back and attempt to double-back to the well.

But it wasn't in her nature to run from a fight.

Anna rushed the man. She locked her fists together and leapt up, clubbing him hard at the base of his skull. He grunted mid-chant and went down on one knee. His torch tumbled from his hand and rolled across the stone floor. Anna planted a foot and cracked his head with a vicious kick that should have knocked him senseless. His eyes glazed over and he teetered but didn't go all the way down.

Instead, he spun around, cocked a fist, and smashed it into her temple.

Anna spiraled and fell sprawled on her stomach, her mind spinning from the man's staggering blow. The torch still burned on the ground a few feet away. In a daze, she moaned and stretched a hand for it, but the acolyte seized her by her ankles and dragged her back. She kicked at him, but her foot only bucked across his shoulder. He grunted and flipped her onto her back. Her head bounced off the hard stone and sent her mind reeling again. The acolyte pounced on her and bunched the hem of her cotton chemise up to her waist while fumbling with the crotch of his breeches to release himself.

Anna clenched her knees together and tried to roll to her side, but the big man balled a fist and rammed it into her stomach. The air exploded from her lungs with a burning whoosh and he used the opportunity to pin her wrists to the ground over her head with one hand. She struggled to catch her breath and thrashed beneath his weight while he fought to slip himself inside her. God, he was strong! Far too strong to resist.

Never had Anna felt so powerless. His voice was husky and laden with lust as he resumed his chant in praise of Astaroth, bringing it to a fervent crescendo. In the hellish light of the flickering torch, his face was twisted and savage, his sunken eyes those of a soulless predator. His breath was hot and panting on Anna's face like a dog's as she fought him off. She felt his erect hardness brush against her upper thigh and strained against him with more desperation. His free hand snarled a fistful of her black hair and slammed her head back into the stone. Her thoughts whirled around in a buoyant daze and stars burst in her vision as the world went misty.

Weakened by the repeated blows to her head, all of Anna's ability to defend herself deserted her. The man sensed her vulnerability and ground himself against her, fumbling between her legs, his fingers slithering for her unguarded crotch. Her eyes slid closed, and she had a dim but sickening awareness that she was about to be violated and victimized.

That's when the screams began.
Except they weren't Anna's.

Chapter 12

A blood-curdling wail cascaded through the corridor. It was distant, but so filled with terror and agony that it arrested the acolyte's attention and distracted him from the revolting horror he was about to unleash on Anna.

It was just the opening she needed.

She lashed out with both hands and raked his face with her fingernails. He yelped and clamped his big hands around her wrists, but she still wouldn't stop harrowing his flesh. She dug her nails in deeper, as if his face was some All Hallows' Eve mask she intended to rip right off his skull. Blood seeped into the jagged gashes and spilled across his face from his hairline to his chin. When he finally pried her nails away, she thrust a hand beneath his robe and seized his genitals. She squeezed and yanked downward with all her strength. She didn't succeed in tearing them away completely as she had hoped, but she still felt a satisfying pop in her hand.

The acolyte let out a yowling scream that was almost inhuman and slumped over on his side. Anna scrambled out from beneath him and threw herself on his back. She grabbed a fistful of his hair and bashed his face into the stone floor. Again and again and again she rammed him down, filling the cavern with wet, smacking sounds and pulverizing the acolyte's face into an unrecognizable pulp.

Yes! Yes! Open his skull and dash his brains! A voice shrieked in Anna's head and she no longer cared where it came from. All that mattered was obliterating this vile bastard from existence. Blood sluiced across the ground and still she did not stop, not until long after he lost consciousness.

Breathless and panting, Anna drew herself up and went for the torch.

The flame had guttered during their struggle but flared back to life in her grip. Its light spilled across the acolyte's ruined face as Anna stood over him. He was still alive—barely—his breathing ragged and croaking through his imploded nose and blood-choked throat.

Anna's expression was a stony mask as she lit him ablaze.

The acolyte's crimson robe went up in a whoosh of flames. The searing heat seemed to rouse him from his stupor. His swollen eyes blinked open and a panic-stricken moan escaped his bloody lips. But the trauma Anna had inflicted on his skull was too severe for him to do anything but convulse and whimper as the fire consumed him. Anna didn't look away, even as his skin blistered and his flesh blackened. She had never killed a man before, but she felt no different than if she had slain any other monster. The cavern filled with oily black smoke and the acrid stench of sizzling fat assaulted her nostrils. Only when her attacker's burning body went still and motionless did she finally turn her back on his charred carcass and leave the cavern behind.

Another strangled cry of agony echoed through the tunnel.

Anna paused as she retraced her steps through the narrow passage and held the torch aloft. How long had she been down here? It felt like hours, but was surely far less. Where were the unsettling screams coming from? Somewhere in the labyrinth? Back at the well? And who was wailing in such unrestrained torment?

Another question presented itself as Anna stood still and thought it over: Should she be headed toward the screams or away from them? The cavern behind her was a dead end, but there had been other intersections and forks in the passages along the way. Perhaps one of the other corridors might lead her to the second exit Stroud had promised? But that would mean taking the word of a man who had drugged her and nearly orchestrated her rape to satisfy the unholy hunger of an ancient demon. There could be miles of tunnels and caverns down here. She could spend weeks searching for another way out. No; Anna would rather take her chances with the one exit she was certain of: the well.

The screams swelled in volume as Anna pressed on. She was getting closer now.

Soon, another sound arrested her attention: footsteps ahead. Loud and pounding and full of purpose. Something was barreling through the darkened corridor toward her.

Anna gripped the torch and held it high, but could see nothing beyond the flickering glow of its radius. Still, the footsteps grew louder. Whatever was out there in the darkness was moving fast and drawing nearer, nearer…

A black figure burst from the gloom.

Anna had time to drop into a defensive crouch before one

of her black-robed captors collided with her and went hurtling through the air. He flipped and crashed onto his back in a tangle of robes. Anna spun and stomped a foot into his chest, brandishing her torch with one hand while the other balled into a fist. The startling look on the man's face kept her from bashing it in.

Never had she seen such unbridled terror in a man.

The man's aging face was alabaster white, his gray eyes wild and panic-stricken. They boggled and rolled around in their sockets while his slack jaw hinged open and shut over and over in a paroxysm of fright. Anna recognized him as the key-bearer who had freed her. Hoarse moans escaped his trembling lips as he stared up at her sightlessly. She realized he was trying to speak, but fear had stolen his voice. All that came out were mute gasps and what could have sounded like the word *run* repeated endlessly.

Anna recognized that the petrified man was no threat to her. She removed her foot from his chest and allowed him to roll to his knees. He remained there for only an instant to catch his breath before he lurched to his feet and sprinted away down the corridor without glancing back.

An icy dread stole into Anna's gut as she watched his fleeing shape vanish into the darkness. She turned and cast a wary eye at the way ahead of her. What was so dreadful to have scared the sanity from such a man? One who made pacts with demons and took part in the rape of women?

Just then, a low and bestial growl chilled Anna's flesh to the point of withering.

It came from behind her, in the direction the black-robed man had just fled. It was followed by a tortured shriek that billowed through the darkness toward her.

All the hairs on the back of Anna's neck raised as one. In that instant, she knew that she too must flee.

With her heart slamming against her breastbone, Anna spun and raced away. The screams ahead had abated, but she no longer had time to question her direction. She wasn't alone in these tunnels. She was sure of it. Something was in there with her, something far worse than any man. Anna could sense its evil presence stalking the darkness behind her. She twisted around a corner, then another and another, expecting to be overtaken at any moment by the unseen horror lurking in the shadows. It couldn't be far behind her. Yards? Feet?

Warm torchlight spilled into the corridor through a doorway about twenty yards ahead. She was nearing the entrance to the well now. Anna chanced a glance over her shoulder and saw nothing past the glow of her torch. She slowed and cast the flame aside as she crept toward the end of the tunnel. The stone was cold as she pressed herself flat against the wall near the opening and peeked into the well.

What she beheld there was a scene of unspeakable nightmares.

A monstrous beast held Virgil Stroud's body high in the air above its head. The creature was enormous, easily seven feet tall, and bore a chilling resemblance to an upright wolf. Its long and pointed ears stabbed upward from its huge and hairy head like spearheads aimed toward the night sky. Tight bunches of powerful muscle flexed and bulged beneath the silvery-gray fur that covered the beast from its huge head to the wicked claws of its feet. Its black lips were peeled back and its snout was long and slender, like a wolf's. And yet there was also something eerily human about its hideous face. Blood and slather dripped in viscous ropes from the rows of jagged fangs jutting from the creature's fearsome jaws.

Most dreadful of all were the beast's eyes. They blazed as if alight with the fires of Hell itself, radiating malevolence and an ancient, bloodthirsty promise of savage cruelty.

Anna had never seen a lycanthrope before—and she was sure that was what this beast was. Since childhood, she had witnessed and vanquished untold terrors as her mother trained her in the ways of the occult. But nothing had prepared her for the mind-shattering fear that gripped her now. Lightning exploded high overhead and filled the well with hellish flashes as she took cover in her spot at the edge of the entrance. She watched in dumbstruck horror as the werewolf pressed Stroud higher into the air. The professor's gaunt face was a mangled mess now, lacerated and torn in dozens of places, but Anna could see he was still alive. Illuminated in the blinding blasts of light, his bloody cheeks puffed in and out as he struggled for air.

For a fleeting moment, Anna had the awful impression that his tortured gaze had fastened onto her from across the round chamber. From behind a mask of blood and gore, his dark eyes bore into her as if silently imploring her for help. Then the giant beast brought him crashing down across its knee with all of its fearsome might. Stroud's spine snapped like kindling as the werewolf's power almost broke him in half at the waist. His stomach split open with a spray of gore. The creature threw back its head and let out a spine-chilling howl of exultant triumph before it buried its vicious teeth into the vital organs of Stroud's insides.

Anna was so shocked at the savagery playing out before her that she only now noticed the rest of the horrific scene at the bottom of the well. A second werewolf hunched over the mauled corpse of the red-robed acolyte whose knee Anna had shattered. The beast's fur was the color of rust and it seemed unaware of Anna's presence as it feasted hungrily on the acolyte's ropy innards. The burning light of the torches illuminated the beasts as they filled the round chamber with the revolting sounds of ripping flesh, grinding bones, and ravenous tongues lapping up blood.

A few yards away from where the second werewolf fed, the acolyte that Anna thought she may have killed had now been decapitated. A pool of blood was spreading steadily outward across the marble floor where his head should have been. Further back, the last remaining black-robed man lay sprawled across the base of the spiral staircase. His left leg was torn away mid-thigh as if he was caught fleeing. Blood spurted in gouts from the ragged stump. It ran in crimson rivers down the steps beneath him and streamed across the floor before falling away into the well's drains. The man's hood was cast back, revealing a balding pate and a wrinkled face that was now ghostly white from shock and blood-loss. He had screamed himself hoarse and now all that came out of his slack mouth was a high-pitched whistle like wind through a hollow tree.

Anna watched with sickening dread as the man squirmed onto his stomach and tried to drag himself up the steps. The movement caught the reddish werewolf's attention. It drew its blood-soaked maw away from its grisly feast and, in a single bound, sprang upon the helpless man. He let out a despairing wail as the creature hauled him away from the stairs. It slashed at him and cut his flesh to ribbons with the long black nails of its claws. When the white of his denuded bones appeared, the beast seized an arm and tore him limb from limb.

Anna ripped her attention away from the gut-churning carnage and gauged the distance between herself and the stairs on the opposite side of the well. It was perhaps about fifty feet. She would either need to dash straight across the blood-drenched floor, or stick to the curved wall and try to sneak unnoticed through the shadows around the perimeter. Neither option seemed to hold much chance of success or survival. For the moment, the pair of werewolves seemed lost in their ravenous bloodlust. But it would only take an instant for one of them to sniff out her presence and cut her down before she escaped.

A noise from behind sent an electric jolt racing up Anna's spine.

Goosebumps rose on her exposed flesh as she revolved around and peered into the gloom of the corridor.

Anna had the crazy impression that two fireflies had materialized from the darkness, their effervescent shapes glowing a pale yellow. Except there was something strange about them. Their movements were identical, the distance between them unwavering as they swayed slightly from side to side in the air. And they were growing larger as they drew closer, swelling from glowing pinpricks to the size of gold coins. A numbing wave of terror crashed over Anna as she realized they weren't fireflies at all.

They were eyes. Yellow eyes.

And they were getting closer.

Anna's heart shuddered. She was trapped between monsters in either direction.

The baleful eyes grew bigger as the creature approached. Anna had no doubt it was a third werewolf. She could smell the coppery reek of blood and viscera clinging to its fur as it stalked toward her. It let out a low and throaty growl and Anna felt the hot wind of its foul breath billow over her skin. Without thinking, she shrank away and backpedaled, retreating from the malevolent monster that was coming at her in the dark. Her bare feet sloshed through a warm and sticky pool of blood. She looked down and realized she had backed through the portal and into the open space of the well.

And the murderous eyes of the other werewolves were now upon her.

Anna froze where she stood as the pitiless gaze of the gray werewolf seared into her. Blood and saliva dripped from its fangs and Anna thought she would wither under the burning heat of its soulless stare. And yet, there was something uncanny about the beast's gaze, a sinister intelligence that chilled Anna to the bone. Some part of this black-hearted creature was human.

Anna's eyes darted for the stairs, but they were too far away, the distance drenched in blood and strewn with body parts. She would never make it in time. The reddish werewolf bared its fearsome teeth at her, its maw dripping entrails as it stood over the mutilated remains of its gruesome feast. Movement in the corner of her vision snared Anna's attention as the third werewolf emerged from the tunnel. The immense creature was black all over and possessed the same sense of cruel malice as the others.

Anna trembled with panic. There was no way out; the beasts cornered her on all sides.

A low growl rumbled deep in the gray werewolf's massive chest as it began to stalk toward her. Even on all fours, its massive head was almost level with Anna's heaving chest. She could feel the primal power emanating from it in waves and was almost brought to her knees in terror-filled submission. It took all of her will and courage to retreat a step and ready herself to run. Escape was hopeless, but anything was better than allowing herself to be torn to shreds and devoured alive. The monster was only yards away now. If Anna was going to flee, she had to do it now. She wouldn't get another chance.

Just as Anna was about to bolt, something very unexpected happened.

As the merciless beast closed the distance to her, it rose on its hind legs and changed before Anna's eyes. Even as it strode toward her on two legs, its claws retracted and its whole massive frame shrank in stature. Its thick mane of silver fur receded and vanished, revealing the pale white skin of a slender body. The bloody fangs contracted as the werewolf's long snout flattened into a human face—a woman's face.

"You..." Anna breathed in disbelief.

Lucretia Stroud stood naked before her.

Chapter 13

Anna stood awestruck as the two other werewolves changed form and joined Lucretia at her side. The first was a slender woman in her mid-twenties. She had a round face, high cheekbones, and amber eyes that matched her blood-drenched mane of tawny hair. The other woman was a black-haired Indian who couldn't be more than Anna's own age. Blood ran in rivulets from their chins and over their bare breasts. It gleamed in the lurid light of the torches as it streamed down their naked bodies to the downy thatches of hair between their legs.

None of the trio of women appeared to be ashamed of their nudity. They seemed to revel in it, as if there were some forbidden power to be had in the shedding of their clothes and modesty.

Anna's gaze fell on the Indian woman and was thunderstruck by a revelation. "Tabitha?"

The young woman's dark eyes remained inscrutable as she stared back at Anna. But it was Lucretia who spoke.

"I am pleased to see you survived my husband's ritual, Miss

Bell."

Despite the danger she knew she faced, Anna's expression hardened with anger. "You knew what he intended to do?"

Lucretia gave a nod and a grim frown. "We knew what, but not *where*. Had we not been obliged to wait until moonrise, we might have spared you the horrors you endured at my husband's hands. As it is, you will be the last to live through his torment." Lucretia's pale green eyes glittered with malevolence as they wandered to the mangled heap of Virgil Stroud's corpse. His stomach cavity was a ragged crimson hole and what remained of his innards lay strewn about like shreds of bloody rope.

"I had my suspicions of Virgil while we still lived in New Haven," Lucretia went on. "I wondered why he would give up the prestige of Yale for a position here in Vermont. I now understand it was because of this place." She waved a hand around the hellish well. "This forgotten Tomb of the Crucible of Night."

"Crucible of Night?" Anna's brow furrowed. "Who are they? Some manner of cult?"

"Something far more insidious, as I fear you have now discovered for yourself. The Crucible is an ancient secret society of scholars and learned men. They have dozens of chapters across the globe, each dedicated to the veneration of the various demons of the *Key of Solomon*. It is through their unholy pacts that men such as my husband are granted the intellectual power and enlightenment for which they are esteemed. Their temples—or *Tombs* as they are known—are founded on powerful places such as this; cursed lands where rebel angels are believed to have fallen through the Earth on their way to Hell."

Lucretia drew her gaze away from her husband's mutilated remains and settled on Anna once more. "It wasn't long after I discovered the true nature of Virgil's vile secret that I sought out the Dominae who blessed me and initiated me into the Order, just as I have become the Dominae of the women here with me now."

Part of the mystery Anna had been pursuing had just been laid bare. Virgil Stroud and the twisted secret society he led had nothing to do with the women who had gone missing. On the night of a full moon, each of them gave themselves up willingly to Lucretia.

Anna's mind reeled as she tried to make sense of this unexpected turn of events. Though they were without mercy, these weren't the mindless, rampaging brutes she had envisioned from her mother's teachings about werewolves.

"I don't…" she stammered. "What is this Order you speak of?"

"The Order of the Lupamatri," Lucretia replied with an eerie coolness, as if she had not just torn her own husband to bits and feasted on his entrails. "A sisterhood of women such as ourselves."

"Werewolves."

Lucretia's eyes narrowed. Was it curiosity or suspicion? "You are familiar with our kind."

Anna cringed inwardly. If she had any hope of surviving this perilous encounter, she couldn't reveal just how much she knew about lycanthropes, or that she had been trained to hunt and kill them. "I have heard stories," she explained. "I thought them to be nothing but superstitious folktales of the

Old World."

A bemused smile played on Lucretia's lips. "For centuries, we have prowled the shadows, but our numbers grow with each full moon. We play the roles of dutiful wives and servants to some of the most powerful men in the nation. When the time is right, the Lupamatri will reveal itself and put an end to thousands of years of male dominion."

Anna's gaze swept over the mutilated and dismembered carcasses of the men who had abducted and assaulted her. The cloying reek of their blood and viscera overpowered her nostrils and threatened to turn her stomach. "You *chose* this accursed existence?" she wondered of the women who stood with Lucretia.

"We all did." It was the amber-haired woman who spoke, the one whom Anna now understood to be Catherine Abell. "And t'was no curse. It was a *blessing*. Before Lucretia initiated me into the Order, I was betrothed to a man of my father's choosing. He was of sufficient property and a good income, but he was also a cruel and loveless man. When I announced I would rather choose spinsterhood than share his marriage bed and bear his children, my father whipped me mercilessly for the shame I'd brought him. Still, I refused, and the beatings went on without end. Each day when my brother returned from classes at the university, my father would have him march me to the barn, where he stripped me naked to flay my flesh anew. My brother—who was to become a cultured scholar while I remained languishing among the pigs—seemed to take great delight in our daily ritual." Catherine's gaze slid to the shredded carcass of the red-robed acolyte she had been feasting on. "I have now returned the favor."

Anna understood the woman's meaning and choked back her own disgust. "Where is Cassie Byrne?" she asked with a quickening sense of apprehension.

"The girl is safe with her mother," Lucretia replied.

"Mary is one of you?"

"She is. Come midnight, her daughter will join us too."

Midnight.

Anna was about to ask what had happened to Kitty Hayes when another piece of the puzzle fell into place. While the full moon imbued a lycanthrope with the power to change at will, it was only when the moon was at its highest point in the sky—and its lunar power at its strongest—that they could turn a person into a werewolf.

On the heels of the revelation, the chilling horror of Lucretia's intentions crashed over Anna. "You're going to turn Cassie into one of you? She's but a child!"

"And already she has borne witness to the cruelties of men," Lucretia shot back. "When she was but four, her father made Cassie watch as he pressed her mother's hand to the hot iron of the stovetop. Even as Mary's palm sizzled and blistered and she cried out in agony, the bastard wouldn't allow his daughter to look away." An icy look came over Lucretia's serene face. "Our kind are not immortal. Though our lives may span many generations—centuries even—we age nonetheless. In time, Cassie will grow into a woman under the guidance and protection of the Lupamatri." Lucretia's eyes glittered as they pierced into Anna. "We may do the same for you if you but ask."

The audacity of Lucretia's repellant offer struck Anna like a slap. "You want me to join you? To become a monster?"

"Monster?" Tabitha spoke at last. There was a dangerous glint in her black eyes that hinted at the ferocious beast within her. "These men would have raped you and disposed of you to satisfy their own ambitions. And you dare to speak of *us* as monsters? Shall we speak of who is truly monstrous? Shall I tell you of the nights Virgil Stroud left his wife's bed and made his way to mine to force himself upon me? Of the way I stuffed my own fist into my mouth to stifle my cries for fear of what he would do to me should I wake Lucretia while he rutted me like a swine? No, we are not the monsters; *they* are. Men such as *he*. They are the ones who are massacring my people and building this country on the backs of slaves. They are the ones who wage war after endless war upon each other while they expect us to stand by and pray for their dead."

Tabitha advanced a step and Anna flinched, worried that the inflamed intensity behind the Indian woman's words might provoke a transformation back to her wolven form.

"In ages past, women were at the center of all things among my people. Women were the givers of life, and it was the natural way for women to hold positions of great power to defend life. The will and authority of our women was equal to that of men. Women chose our leaders and declarations of war required our women's consent. So it was until the White man came to rape and slaughter, and so shall it be again when the Lupamatri restores us to our rightful place of power."

Anna glanced askance at the human carnage strewn about and knew she should protest, that she should insist no man deserved to be made to suffer such unspeakable violence. At least, that is what her mother would have said.

But the words rang hollow even to herself. There was truth

in what these women were saying, wasn't there? Anna had lived through too much to deny it. Try as she might, she couldn't keep her thoughts from returning to that dark cavern. She remembered the feel of the brutish acolyte's hands slithering up and down her thighs as he forced them apart and fought to penetrate her. She could still hear his bestial grunts in her ear, feel the revolting heat of his sour breath assaulting her, see the rabid lust burning in his eyes. Part of Anna had enjoyed smashing his skull and setting him ablaze. How many other women hadn't had the strength or instincts to fight back against such men? How many had succumbed and been victimized to satisfy a man's desires?

"You needn't feel pity for these men, Miss Bell," said Lucretia. "You are familiar with my husband's interest in female hysteria, but he neglected to tell you how he acquired the subjects of his research. He preyed upon women who refused to acquiesce to male expectations, women who spurned marriage or spoke out against their abusers or took too much or too little pleasure in intercourse. He, like others, believed that such women needed to be locked up and hidden away for fear their *disease* might infect others." Lucretia's thin lips twisted in a bitter sneer. "To Virgil, the women he called his patients were as the insects in his collection: nothing more than specimens to be prodded and studied and catalogued in the name of science. Once a year, my husband invited some of the richest families in New England to gawk at the spectacle of the madwomen he would parade around the university hospital. Their donations afforded him the luxury of those pretty plants he was so fond of."

Lucretia's tone became soft and persuasive now as she gazed

at Anna. "You are still young, Miss Bell. In the prime of your womanhood. Do you not yearn for freedom? For independence? Do you not long for a time when you will not be defined by whom you marry? When the doors to all the world's wondrous possibilities stand open before you? Join us and it may all be yours. Among us, you will find unfathomable power."

An angry rejection sprang to Anna's lips, but it never made it out. She thought of her mother, of the life she was already running away from. Where exactly was she running *to*? And what would she find there? A life of hiding from her darker nature? Of hopeless struggle against her irresistible compulsions? As a woman, she would always be met with oppression wherever she fled. What would happen when she refused to conform? Even if she never spoke of the world of the paranatural, when Anna refused to marry or play the role of docile spinster, how long until a man like Virgil Stroud diagnosed such aberrant behavior as hysteria and had her committed to a sanatorium?

A booming blast of thunder erupted overhead, its force so powerful it vibrated the stone walls. The more Anna considered it, the more she wondered if she was really so different from these women. Like them, there was also a beast raging within her. Had she their power, wouldn't she have done the same thing to Stroud and his acolytes? Instead of running and hiding from the darkness in her nature, perhaps it was time to embrace who she really was.

Beneath these reflections lay an even darker truth, one so dreadful Anna was afraid to admit it even to herself: Part of her envied the fearsome power she had witnessed in these women. Horrifying as they had been, there was still something about them that had captured Anna's fascination. What must it be like to live with such wild abandon? To cast aside all notions of right or wrong and give herself over without shame to the simplicity of her primal instincts?

Anna already thrived on violence and danger. Dominating and imposing her will on her foes made her feel like she had some measure of control in a life that seemed fated for tragedy. It was the same perilous allure that drew Anna to the blackest arts of witchcraft, an unquenchable thirst for power that had simmered beneath her flesh for as long as she could remember. It was a quality that both enthralled and frightened her at the same time.

Yet for all their similarities, there was still something that separated these women from Anna. Abigail had raised her to be a ghost-hunting witch and a killer of monsters. It was a solitary life by nature. How could anyone else understand or accept what she did? From her earliest memories, Anna had learned to keep others at arm's length and remain stony-hearted. Friendships and relationships only led to vulnerability and dependency. What few family bonds Abigail still maintained with her stepfather and sister were begrudging and superficial. Anna had no one in her life but her mother and her lifelong obsession with vengeance. But what a contrast these women were! They had each other. They were a sisterhood united in their common cause of burning down society's patriarchy.

But they also intended to turn an innocent girl into a bloodthirsty beast.

Anna's thoughts drifted to little Cassie Byrne and was

reminded of her own childhood, of the hostility and resentment she carried for her mother for her part in turning Anna into the cold-hearted huntress she had become. Anna had never been given the choice of a normal life. If these women had their way, neither would Cassie. What would the future hold for such a girl? One tragically similar to Anna's? Or infinitely worse?

"The hour of the wolf approaches," Lucretia said. "The Hunter's Moon nears its zenith and we have much to do before midnight. Now is the time for your choice."

Anna opened her mouth to speak and a shiver of revulsion ran over her. She didn't know what was about to come out. Was she actually contemplating this? Why hadn't she spat out a rejection of Lucretia and accepted whatever grisly fate the werewolves intended to mete upon her? What they were proposing was unspeakably contemptible. And yet, something about them had kindled a fire in her that refused to be smothered. Anna had the strangest impression that the entirety of her life had been sweeping her forward to this one moment, to the fateful decision she was about to make.

At last, she swallowed and found a tremulous voice. "I…"

Whatever she was going to say next was lost in the thundering roar of a gunshot.

Chapter 14

Catherine Abell's head snapped back and a spray of blood spurted from the back of her skull. A flap of hairy scalp tore loose as her body jerked backward and she was ripped off her feet. She crashed onto her back in a sprawl of naked limbs on the bloodstained marble.

Anna spun around. Abigail stood at the mouth of one of the tunnels. Tendrils of smoke coiled from the muzzle of the double-barrel pistol she still held, aimed and ready to fire at anyone who moved. A split-second passed in utter confusion. How the hell had her mother found her? Then Anna remembered Gideon, the invisible Familiar that was tethered to her at all times. In the same instant, she realized Virgil Stroud hadn't lied. There *was* another entrance to the labyrinth—and Gideon had led Abigail to it.

For a frozen moment, Lucretia seemed oblivious to Abigail's presence. Her attention was riveted on her unmoving disciple, who lay shot through the eye at her feet. Anna knew her mother would have aimed for Lucretia herself, but Anna had been in the way of her shot.

When Lucretia tore her gaze away from Catherine, she levelled a venomous glare on Abigail that blazed with hatred.

"*Run!*" Abigail broke the spell that held Anna enthralled.

Anna darted for the stairs, even as the pair of women behind her transformed. Lucretia's ears extended into tall arrowheads sticking up through her silvery mass of hair. More gray hair sprouted from all over her naked skin. Beneath the thickening coat of fur, her back broadened to at least twice its normal size. Her muscles contracted and grew as tight as cannonballs laced together with thick cords of sinew.

Anna dodged and leapt over the butchered corpses strewn about the round chamber. She chanced a glance over her shoulder just as the transformation spread to Lucretia's face. She glimpsed the woman's eyes widening, the pale green irises turning the golden yellow of a candle's flame. Lucretia's face elongated into a snout and when her black lips peeled back, rows of jagged fangs broke through her gums.

Anna ripped her attention away and focused on the stairs ahead. From the corner of her eye, she saw Abigail with her pistol still trained on the transforming women. Anna had never seen such fear in her mother's eyes.

She pushed herself to move faster. One of her bare feet suddenly slipped in a pool of blood and she pitched forward. She hit the ground with a rib-shuddering *thump* and skidded, her momentum slewing her forward toward the steps. She scrambled to stand but slipped again, this time landing hard on one elbow. An electric jolt shot up her arm to her shoulder as she managed to clamber upright.

A soul-scorching roar filled the well. Anna didn't have to look back to see that the women had finished their transformations. Who would reach the stairs first?

Anna darted forward, not looking back, eyes locked on the stone steps ahead of her. She tried not to imagine Lucretia's monstrous form barreling across the chamber toward her, closing the distance with ease, hideous fangs bared and ready to rip her to ribbons.

Anna caught a fleeting glimpse of Abigail getting ready to fire, and her heart sank. She knew her mother wouldn't chance wasting her last bullet unless the werewolf was within striking range of her. Lucretia was only feet away from her. Anna braced herself for the roar of the gunshot when, against all hope, she reached the steps and scampered up.

Abigail fell in behind her just as the beast that was Lucretia vaulted across the remaining distance and landed at their heels. Abigail swung around and pulled the trigger on her remaining shot. Brilliant sparks sprayed from the pistol as it boomed and blew a hole in Lucretia's hairy breast. The blast spun the beast around and sent her crashing to the ground with a bellowing roar.

Tabitha wasn't far behind.

Abigail whirled and spurred Anna upward, bounding up the steps two at a time. Higher and higher, they fled up the spiral staircase. A bloodcurdling snarl erupted close behind them. Anna knew the enraged werewolf would overtake them at any moment. Another few steps brought them to the fifth of the seven landings. Abigail skidded to a halt, snatched a burning torch from its sconce, whirled around.

The werewolf's hideous face lit up not five feet beyond the flame.

Tabitha towered over Abigail, her malevolent eyes gleaming

with rage in the lurid light. Her black fur bristled like a furious dog's on the hackles of her broad back. Slather dripped in viscous strings from the sharp points of her fangs as she hovered just out of reach of the blazing torch.

Lightning flickered and danced through the gaping opening at the top of the well as Abigail brandished the flame to keep the monster at arm's length and retreated backward up the steps. She moved cautiously but with urgency, careful to avoid a fatal false step that would give Tabitha an opening to attack. The werewolf growled menacingly as she pursued on two legs, dodging to either whenever Abigail tried to surprise her with a sudden thrust of the torch.

A furious pounding erupted behind and above Abigail. But she didn't dare turn her back on the vicious creature stalking her up the steps.

"The door is locked!" Anna cried. There was a tremendous *thud* as she threw herself at the solid wood. It wouldn't budge. She tried again and again, still without success.

Abigail continued her backward ascent, the snarling werewolf shadowing her so closely she could smell the blood on the beast's breath. She kept the torch between them until her back came up against her daughter's. She had reached the final landing; there were no more steps to climb. With the merciless beast bearing down on her, Abigail could retreat no further. They were trapped. To their left, there was nothing but a solid granite wall upon which a torch burned in its sconce. The curved balustrade and a hundred foot drop to the bottom of the well was on their right. Behind them stood the locked door.

Tabitha sensed her inevitable triumph and let out a

gloating growl. Abigail knew she wouldn't be able to fend the beast off much longer. A dizzying glance over the balustrade revealed Catherine Abell, recovering from her gunshot on the ground far below. She had crawled onto her hands and knees on the marble floor and was in the midst of transforming into her wolven form. Abigail hadn't expected her bullet to kill the monster, but she had hoped it would buy her more time before the lycanthrope's uncanny ability to heal mended her wound and put her back on her feet.

A searing strip of pain raked across Abigail's upper arm as Tabitha seized upon her fleeting moment of distraction and lashed out with her black, dagger-like claws. Abigail winced and swiped the torch at her. Tabitha's lips wrinkled back, and she bared her teeth, but she didn't retreat. Her prey was cornered. It was only a matter of time before Abigail let her guard down and the beast ripped her limb from limb. Behind Abigail, Anna continued to pound at the locked door as if she believed she could actually break through the heavy wood.

Tabitha lunged. Her fearsome teeth flashed in the torchlight as her terrible jaws sprang wide open, intent on rending Abigail's flesh from her bones. In the same instant, Abigail feinted to the side and thrust her torch deep into the beast's gaping maw. Tabitha's jaws snapped shut, and she jerked backward, flailing madly as the flame from the still-burning pitch seared her throat from within. She clawed at the torch's handle, but it was buried so deep in her gullet she gagged on it.

Abigail didn't waste a moment. She seized the other torch from its sconce on the walled side of the landing and swung it around, catching the thrashing monster in her exposed side.

There was a quick sizzling and a foul whiff of burning hair before flames shot up the beast's torso. Tabitha let out a ululating wail that was eerily human as she recoiled and swatted at herself to extinguish the flames. But she only fanned them higher. They licked at her breasts, her muzzle, her ears; engulfing her from her head to her clawed feet.

The flames blazing from the burning creature were so hot they would soon envelop both Abigail and Anna. Abigail thrust her spent pistol into Anna's grasp and wielded the torch with two hands like a club, cracking the writhing werewolf's huge head again and again and again. Weakened and in agony, Tabitha rocked to the side and fell against the stone balustrade. Another blow to the head sent her toppling over. Abigail sprang to the balustrade in time to watch the burning werewolf hurtling like a flaming pinwheel through the air before crashing into a broken mass on the stone floor a hundred feet below.

A blood-freezing howl ripped up the staircase.

Abigail's gaze shot to the base of the steps far below. Lucretia and Catherine's glowing eyes stared up at her with murderous resolve.

"Take this!" Abigail commanded. She handed Anna the torch and elbowed her daughter away from the door. From her coat pocket, she produced the lock-picking tools she carried with her at all times. She willed her hands to remain steady as she inserted the instruments and worked the tumblers.

"They're coming up fast!" Anna urged.

Abigail tried to ignore the clock ticking in her head and remain focused on the task at hand. She felt the satisfying click of the tumblers falling into place, twisted the knob, pushed.

The door wouldn't move.

A sickening dread descended on Abigail. The door was barred from the outside.

She whipped around and her chest constricted. The werewolves had already reached the fifth landing. They were about a hundred steps below and ascending fast, bounding up the stairs five at a time. There were only seconds to spare before they reached Abigail and Anna.

Abigail grabbed the torch from Anna and shoved her daughter behind her. She couldn't bear the thought of being made to watch her daughter being torn to shreds. She'd rather be the first to die. Together, they shrank back against the door as the werewolves crested the final landing. The beasts' yellow eyes smoldered with malice as they glared balefully at the flame blazing in Abigail's hand. She couldn't hold them both off—and they knew it.

It was Lucretia who attacked first. Her fearsome jaws gnashed and snapped as she launched herself at her cornered prey.

In the same instant, the door swung outward with a whoosh of fresh air. Abigail and Anna spilled out into the storm-swept night just as Lucretia's jaws clamped shut on the empty space where they had stood.

Suddenly free from the well, Abigail kicked the door shut in the monster's snarling face and Anna hurried to throw a thick wooden bar in place. They scrambled back just as a terrible crash shook the door. The heavy bar creaked and flexed, but the door held. An enraged roar erupted from the other side. Another furious blow to the door followed it as Lucretia launched her massive body against it, determined to smash her way through. Still, the door wouldn't give way.

A strong wind howled and whipped at them as Abigail stood back. She kept a wary eye on the door as she took in her surroundings.

They were somewhere deep in a black forest. The wooden entrance to the Crucible's Tomb was camouflaged and hidden in the crags of a massive stone face. The upper rim of the giant well protruding from the earth was cunningly crafted to blend in with its rugged surroundings. To the birds who flew overhead, it would be a gaping black hole. But from the ground it appeared as nothing more than an enormous mound of granite so overgrown with foliage and moss, it would be invisible to anyone who wasn't looking for it.

Not that Abigail suspected many ventured this deep into the dense forest. There was no trail and very little signs of passage that she could detect in the darkness. Wind rocked and buffeted the emaciated boughs of the treetops high above. A fine drizzle filtered through and sharp streaks of lightning raked across the night sky.

Another thundering blow shook the door. The old iron hinges groaned but didn't break. Still, Abigail suspected they wouldn't hold forever. She grabbed Anna's hand and turned away, ready to flee, when they discovered their savior lurking in the shadows of the trees behind them. The tall figure was clad in a crimson robe that whipped and billowed in the wind. His hood was cast back, revealing a handsome and familiar face.

Nathaniel. The very man Abigail had invited to her bed the

night before.

Without warning, Anna balled her hand into a fist and launched herself at him. Her blow cracked him squarely in the mouth with a dull and wet smacking sound. He reeled away and clutched a palm to his lip, blood already seeping from between his fingers.

"Bastard!" Anna cried. "You knew what they would do to me and you left me down there with them!"

Nathaniel spit blood and struggled to speak with his split lip. "No! I... I came back to help you! I—"

Anna's fist shot out and struck him another staggering blow to the jaw. Her fist pistoned back, cocked again, but Abigail caught it before she could hurl another punch.

"We haven't time for this." Abigail's gaze darted to the door, still being hammered mercilessly by the raging beast trapped on the other side. It was as if a small army were using a battering ram to breach a fortress. Abigail felt confident there was little chance the heavy oak of the door would shatter, but she noticed with some alarm that the rusty hinges were shaking loose from their stone anchor with each powerful blow. She returned her attention to Nathaniel. "Where are we?"

"About eight miles northeast of town," he replied, still nursing his lip.

"Have you horses?"

Nathaniel nodded and motioned toward a spot obscured in darkness further away.

Abigail grabbed Anna's hand and led her away. When Nathaniel made to follow, Anna whirled on him with a dangerous glint in her eyes.

"No!" she growled. "If you remain in my presence a moment longer, I swear I will kill you."

"But I… I can help," Nathaniel protested. "I… I can show you the way back to the village!"

Abigail hesitated. She didn't know what had happened between this man and her daughter, but she had seen that same black look in Anna's eyes often enough to know he wasn't safe around her. She had every reason to believe her daughter would make good on her threat. Still, they needed to escape quickly. And if he could lead the way…

A teeth-rattling screech pierced the night as one of the door hinges ripped free of the stone. The door slumped and wedged in its frame. A single hinge was now all that held the raging werewolves back.

"Come on." Abigail plunged into the darkness.

A short distance from the well was a small grove where the horses Stroud and his disciples had ridden stood tethered to an ancient hitching rail. Bathed in the frenetic arctic blue of lightning, the animals bucked and strained at their lead ropes, driven wild with panic by the nearby monsters.

Abigail dashed to the nearest horse and untied the lead. It was a black mare with white ankles and a snowy smear on its forehead. The horse reared back the moment she was released, her huge eyes rolling in her head. Abigail feared it might bolt in terror. Her soothing touch seemed to reassure the animal enough let Abigail mount it and settle into the saddle. She gripped the reins and swung around.

Anna and Nathaniel were mounting their own horses just as a booming crash resounded through the forest. Abigail's skin prickled as a blood-freezing howl ripped through the darkness.

The werewolves were loose.

Chapter 15

The stinging wind brought tears to Anna's eyes as she charged on horseback through the sepulchral forest. Nathaniel led the way ahead of her, guiding them along the twists and turns of an almost imperceptible herd path beaten through the underbrush. Abigail rode about thirty yards behind Anna, bringing up the rear at breakneck speed.

A frenzied squealing of pain and terror rolled from somewhere in the darkness back near the Tomb. Nausea roiled Anna's gut. The werewolves were slaughtering the horses they had left behind. In their haste to flee, there wasn't time to free them all.

Ghostly shards of lightning flickered through the bare boughs of the giant trees as the trio raced to put distance between themselves and the beasts. A quilt of fallen leaves blanketed the forest floor, their warm hues now cast in monochrome blue in the unearthly light. The trail was a tight vein snaking through the dense forest.

Anna had to shield her eyes from the branches whipping at her face and legs. She stole a glance over her shoulder and glimpsed two massive shapes hurtling up the trail in pursuit. How far away were they? A hundred yards? It was impossible to tell in the gloom.

The path twisted unexpectedly, and she lost sight of the creatures. *They can't possibly outrace our horses*, Anna thought with mounting unease.

When the trail straightened again, she saw the werewolves gaining ground. Their monstrous forms winked in and out of the flickering light as they sprinted through the woods on all fours. A flurry of dead leaves whipped into the air in their wake. Anna remembered their cords of rippling muscles and the fearsome power she had witnessed back at the Tomb. It wasn't beyond belief that they could match even the fastest horse.

Anna returned her attention to the way ahead. The twisted shapes of the trees sped by in a blur around her. How much further were the village limits? Nathaniel had said the Tomb was about eight miles to the northeast. But did he really know the way back? Or had he just been bargaining to save his own skin? Anna guessed they had covered little more than a mile. She wished they could coax more speed out of their mounts. But even a well-conditioned horse could only manage two or three miles at this pace without rest. Even if the werewolves couldn't match their speed, they would very well run the horses to exhaustion before they reached the village. What would Anna and the others do then? The bloodthirsty beasts would pick them off like wayward lambs.

A thin branch shot from the darkness and lashed across Anna's eyebrows. She rocked back in her saddle, tears springing to her eyes. She wiped them away with her palm and felt a sharp sting from the cut the branch had left just above the bridge of her nose. Any lower, and it would have blinded her. More tears spilled from the corners of her eyes as her eyelids blinked and fluttered. Her blurry vision finally cleared, and she threw another nervous glance back over her shoulder.

The werewolves were gone.

A sinking feeling settled into the pit of Anna's stomach as she searched the empty trail unspooling behind them. The woods were eerily quiet except for the howl of the wind in her ears and the pounding gallop of the horses' hooves. Her gaze focused on the spot where the beasts had been only moments ago. Where had they disappeared to?

This isn't right, Anna thought. Lucretia and Catherine had been gaining ground. Why were they letting their prey escape? They couldn't have given up; this must be a trap. Anna noticed the trail they were on had been curving sharply toward the east, bending in an almost ninety-degree turn over a great distance. The foreboding gripping her gut tightened. What if the werewolves had left the path to cut through the forest? What if they were already waiting for them on the trail ahead?

With her stomach plummeting, Anna whipped her head around, squinted into the darkness, peered at her mother's galloping silhouette.

And saw the huge shape explode from the trees to her left.

Lucretia rammed into the side of Abigail's horse at full speed and took the animal down in a rolling tumble of terrified squeals and flailing hooves. Had the horse not thrown Abigail from the saddle, it would have crushed her beneath its great weight as it crashed to the ground and skidded across the forest floor. Abigail catapulted through the air and slammed into the underbrush. Scraped and bruised, she scrambled away for fear the panicking horse might roll on top of her. But one of the mare's hind legs had broken in the collision and Lucretia was now harrowing the poor animal with her razored claws.

Ribbons of black hide flew into the air as the mare thrashed and bucked under the werewolf's savage assault. Unable to stand, the horse squealed and gibbered with fright. Lucretia dodged and weaved around the animal's powerful kicks with preternatural agility. She snatched one of the horse's flailing forelegs out of the air with her claws and snapped the bone like an old walking stick.

The mare let out a pitiful and keening screech, her wild eyes rolling in her head, whites flashing brilliantly in the darkness. Lucretia lunged and clamped her jaws around the horse's throat with a stomach-turning crunch. Freshets of blood sprayed from the ravaged artery and drenched the werewolf's silver hide as she whipped her head, wrenching away a ragged mass of the horse's flesh. She gnawed all the way to the spine, leaving denuded bits of vertebrae visible in the gaping wound she left behind. The horse ceased her struggles and went rigid except for one hind leg still pistoning with death spasms.

Blood and gore dripped from Lucretia's fearsome maw as she swung around on two legs and leveled her burning eyes on Abigail.

Lucretia's surprise attack had happened so quickly Anna barely had time to react as she witnessed the slaughter from about twenty yards ahead. With the merciless beast now bearing down on her mother, she kicked her heels into her own horse's flanks and snapped the reins, urging her mare forward. The animal was too terrified to obey.

Panicking at the sight of the vicious monster, the mare reared back on her hindquarters and almost hurled Anna from the saddle. She dropped the reins and threw her arms around the horse's thick neck as the animal whinnied and bucked with unrestrained fright. With great effort, Anna managed to bring the mare back under control, but there was no way she could compel her to advance. The ferocious werewolf was only seconds away from gorging on Abigail's flesh.

A gust of chilly wind furrowed Anna's hair as Nathaniel thundered past her. Somehow, he had persuaded his horse to charge and was now barreling toward Lucretia. The werewolf whirled around, snout wrinkled back to reveal her rows of gleaming fangs. Nathaniel spurred his horse onward, galloping harder, closing the distance. Lucretia let out a rumbling growl, eyes slitted and flaming with hatred, eager for the chance to shed more blood.

Nathaniel yanked hard on the reins and brought his mare skidding around. Lucretia snarled and raked the horse's flank in the same instant that it shot a powerful kick at her chest. The mare's hind hoof was like a sharp stone fixed to the end of a heavy club driven by eight-hundred pounds of solid muscle. With a sickening crack of broken bone, it caught Lucretia just below the sternum. The impact jolted the werewolf around and sent her sailing into the thick trunk of a huge silver maple. Stunned, her lungs wheezing beneath her broken ribs, Lucretia struggled to stand. She made it to a teetering crouch before she toppled back to the earth.

Abigail didn't waste an instant. She dashed through the underbrush and swung herself into the horse's saddle behind Nathaniel. He stood in the stirrups and snapped the reins.

Anna found she could breathe again, her spirits leaping as Nathaniel and Abigail galloped up the path toward her. Behind them, Lucretia's monstrous figure lay slumped and struggling at the base of the tree. She wasn't dead—it would take much more than the horse's kick to kill her—but it had bought them some time.

A thought sent a cold ripple over Anna's skin: Where was Catherine Abell?

With a swift spike of alarm, Anna swung her horse around and saw the red werewolf's looming silhouette wreathed in lightning on the path ahead. Like a pair of predators working together, Lucretia had distracted them while Catherine circled around through the forest to cut off their escape.

"Run her down!" Abigail clapped Nathaniel's shoulder with one hand. Her other hand was wrapped around his waist as they pulled even with Anna.

"No!" Anna shouted, but Nathaniel had already spurred his horse into a charge.

Catherine bared her fangs and let out a throaty snarl as they raced at her, her lust for blood blazing in her one good eye.

Anna's windpipe tightened and her mouth went dry as she took off after them, barreling toward the immense beast in a deadly game of chicken. There was no way Catherine could withstand the charge of the two bolting horses, of the nearly two thousand pounds of raw muscle hurtling down the path toward her. But the werewolf showed no sign of backing down. She threw her clawed hands wide on either side, her tight bunches of muscle and sinew ready to be unleashed on the riders who dared to challenge her.

A terrible alarm flared in Anna as the distance to the looming monster shrank. She could still hear her own pounding heartbeat in her ears, despite the thundering of the horses.

Catherine bent her huge shoulders into a defensive crouch, muscles flexing, lips peeled back in a hideous rictus of viciousness.

Anna flung her arms around her horse's neck, readied herself for the devastating collision, for the flaying claws and snapping jaws.

At the last possible moment, Catherine leapt aside with impossible agility. Her black nails flashed as she lashed out and harrowed the horses' sides as they thundered by. Anna's mare let out a pitiful scream as blood ran in rills over her brown hide. The riders blew past the werewolf in a blur of pounding hooves. Catherine let out an enraged howl and leapt after them in pursuit. Too late, Anna realized the werewolf was drawing them in so she could cut them down from behind.

The beast was close now, chasing them on all fours. She was only a few yards away from running down Anna's horse as she trailed Nathaniel and Abigail. Anna leaned forward in her saddle, urging every ounce of speed out of her frightened mare. But terror would only carry the horse so far. Soon she would tire and slow. How long? Minutes? Even less?

Anna peered ahead, caught her mother's head swiveling back to face her and the pursuing beast. Was she thinking the same thing as Anna? That there was no way they were getting out of these woods alive?

Catherine leaped without warning and swiped an enormous claw at Anna's horse's hindquarters. Her nails whistled through the air like a scythe cutting down corn, but the mare was still out of reach. Again and again the werewolf lashed out, her sharp claws always missing by inches but creeping closer.

Something massive lay across the trail ahead, obscured in the gloom. Anna saw it was the enormous carcass of a fallen tree. A grove of forest surrounding her now appeared to be dead, the ancient trees having fallen victim to some terrible blight. Anna squinted into the darkness and saw Nathaniel's horse vault over the huge trunk. Seconds later, she was upon it. She clutched at the reins as her horse propelled herself into the air and came back down with a jolt that rattled the teeth in Anna's head. Having cleared the hurdle, the furious pace took its toll on Anna's mount. She felt the exhausted horse slowing beneath her. It was an almost imperceptible change, but one that flooded her with dread.

Catherine sensed her prey weakening and leapt, launching another furious swing at the horse. The powerful blow was meant to cut the mare's hind legs out from under her, but it caught her in the rump instead and sent her slewing sideways. Thrown off-balance, the horse skidded across the wet blanket of leaves and smashed broadside into the hulk of a dead maple about as thick as Anna's waist. It was almost entirely stripped of its bark and pitted with deep woodpecker holes in dozens of places.

An ear-splitting crack shot through the forest like musket fire as the tree's rotted trunk snapped from the tremendous force of the collision. The entire upper portion of the maple hinged forward, the trunk buckling and splintering as the twisted boughs came crashing through the forest canopy, plummeting toward the ground.

By some primal instinct for self-preservation, Anna's horse wheeled away in time to avoid being crushed. Lost in a red fog of bloodlust, Catherine reacted a split-second later. She lurched to one side, but it was too late. The collapsing tree clipped her mid-thigh, the blow from its enormous weight snapping her femur with an audible crunch of fracturing bone. The werewolf let out a bellowing roar of pain and fury as the tree hit the ground and shook the earth with its impact.

Catherine staggered to her clawed feet, as if oblivious to the cause of her agony, only to have her shattered leg give out beneath her again. With an enraged snarl, she attempted to stalk forward on all fours, but her useless hindquarters sagged back down to the earth, unable to bear any weight. Another enraged howl burst from her slavering mouth.

With the fallen tree now cutting across the trail like a barricade, Anna cast a nervous glance at the wounded werewolf. Catherine kept trying to stand and collapsing, as if her fury itself was enough to overcome her gruesome injury. Nathaniel and Abigail had circled around, and Anna spurred her spooked horse to join them. Together, they sped down the trail through the forest toward the village.

The trauma of the past few hours shook Anna. She was dimly aware that they had no plan for what they would do if they made it out of these woods. The werewolves might have been incapacitated enough to allow their escape, but the beasts would soon heal. Already their broken bones would be knitting together, the fractures healing themselves as if they had never happened. Soon, they would be free to prowl the darkness of the unsuspecting village and paint it red with blood.

And many hours remained until sunrise.

Chapter 16

It was cold in the cave. The air was heavy with moisture and the dank scent of minerals issuing from the ancient stone. A churning torrent of water cascaded like a white curtain just beyond the cave's mouth, hiding it behind the waterfall.

A day had passed since her old friend, Mary Byrne, had ambushed Kitty in the woods. She had awoken in this cave hours later and had since marked the passage of time by the quality of the light shimmering through the waterfall. She knew the sun had risen and set again and still Mary kept her captive here, guarding against her escape.

They had spoken little, not since Kitty had lost her patience and tried to storm her way out, shouting to be let go. There had been a scuffle. Shoves were exchanged and faces were scratched and Kitty had been about to throw a punch when Mary let out a low and inhuman growl that froze Kitty where she stood. There was a lethal glint in Mary's eyes that made Kitty's flesh bunch into tight knots. Something monstrous was lying in wait within her friend. Kitty caught a glimpse of it and knew something unspeakable had happened to Mary in the month since she had disappeared. If Kitty was going to get out of the cave alive, she would need to bide her time and wait for the right moment.

A torch now filled the cavern with an amber glow as Kitty sat with her knees drawn up to her chest and her back pressed against the cold stone. Across the cave, Cassie Byrne lay curled on her side, slumbering with her head in her mother's lap. Mary was still wrapped in the heavy bearskin that had fooled Cassie into thinking she was being pursued through the forest by some nightmarish creature. Little did the girl know about the true beast lurking *within* her mother. All the fear and confusion Cassie had experienced since Mary brought her here had now melted away under the blissful oblivion of sleep. Her little face was serene as Mary passed the time smoothing her matted, strawberry-blonde hair.

Kitty wasn't surprised to discover Mary had returned to reclaim her daughter. More surprising had been the fact that Mary had endured a month of self-imposed separation while she adapted to her new form and grew comfortable in her new skin. As she observed them together now, Kitty was struck by how much Cassie resembled her mother. Both shared the same heart-shaped face; the pointed chin and button-nose; the dusting of freckles and pale blue eyes.

Of course, there was now the inescapable fact that Mary looked more youthful than she had since she was a teenager. Though she was only in her early twenties, her face had been creased and worn from the strain of appeasing and enduring her abusive drunkard of a husband. But whatever dreadful change had happened to her in the month since she had vanished had somehow revitalized her. She now emanated a strange inner power and energy that flowed and pulsed just beneath her skin.

"It wasn't supposed to be like this," Mary said unexpectedly. They were the first words she had uttered in hours, and her voice startled Kitty out of her silent ruminations. Mary kept her voice low to keep from waking her slumbering daughter. "I was supposed to wait until tonight's full moon to come for Cassie. But when I learned Jericho had come back early from the camps…" She drew a deep breath and let it out again. "Did I ever tell you about George Dent? He was the overseer on the poor farm before you arrived, before Emmett and Martha took over."

Kitty raised her eyes and shook her head, but said nothing. She had spent most of her adult life trying to bury the memory of the childhood years she spent as an orphan in Burlington's almshouse. She and her parents had come over from Dublin when Kitty was a girl. Her father was an engineer by trade and had been engaged by the fledgling Lake Champlain Steamboat Company to help master engineer Jahaziel Sherman build steamships for the burgeoning cargo routes on Lake Champlain.

Less than a month after their arrival in America, both Connor and Maggie Hayes were dead of the tuberculosis they contracted on the ship on their way over. Young Kitty often wondered why God hadn't loved her enough to claim her as well when she found herself a seven-year-old ward of the almshouse. Located south of town on a farm on which the residents were expected to earn their keep, the county home was a god-awful dumping ground for the crippled, the mentally ill, the destitute, petty criminals, unmarried mothers, and orphans.

It was at the almshouse that Kitty had befriended Mary. The older girl had taken Kitty under her wing and became something like a big sister. Together, they weathered the dreary toil of the poor farm until Mary was old enough to get work as a barmaid at the Nobody Inn. She struck out on her own and took Kitty under her own roof. Soon, they were working at the tavern together.

All Kitty had left of those years on the poor farm was a silver hairpin that had belonged to her mother. Fearful one of the other unsavory residents of the almshouse would steal it, Kitty had buried it beneath a large oak at the farm's edge. It had remained there throughout Kitty's stay, hidden away until she could return for it. She still wore the pin to this day. Even now, it kept her wild tangle of red curls from spilling into her tired and pale face.

"George Dent was a widower with no children," Mary went on quietly. "He was a pitiless man, quick with the whip and keen on starving the poor farm's inmates if it would save the town purse a coin or two. After my father ran off on my mother, she said she would rather starve or freeze to death than go to that accursed poorhouse. We spent nearly two years suffering the shame of town beggars. Can you imagine that? Two years. My mother cobbled together a hovel in the alley behind where the American Hotel now stands on Main Street. She got us through the first winter by stubbornness alone, but the second one strangled the land and almost finished her. She finally changed her tune."

"Less than a month after we knocked on the almshouse door, George Dent let himself under my blanket for the first time. I was eight. He did it right there while my mother lay on her cot next to mine. You remember how we slept in the bunkhouse? All those rows of straw pallets lined up against the walls? My mother kept her eyes closed and pretended to sleep, but I knew she was awake. She knew everything Dent did to me and still she said nothing for fear he'd cast her out or hire her out at auction. And so, she just kept her eyes closed…" Mary choked on her words. Her eyes were glassy with tears as her gaze slid down to the girl sleeping with her head in her lap.

"I've seen the way Jericho looks at her," Mary whispered after a moment. Her eyes never left Cassie. "George Dent used to get the same vile look before he came to me in the night. When I learned Jericho was back early, I thought, *what if tonight is the nigh*t? I couldn't stand the idea of Cassie alone with him without me there, not even for one minute. I wouldn't betray my daughter the way my mother failed me."

Something about the look in Mary's eyes as she gazed at Cassie filled Kitty with dread. "Mary, what are you going to do?"

"I'll not keep my eyes closed."

"Mary…"

"Tonight I'm going to empower my little girl to defend herself…"

"Mary, no…"

"Not only against her father, but against *all* men."

A wave of horror washed over Kitty as Mary's intentions became clear. "No, Mary! You can't do this! Whatever monster you've become, you can't do the same to your own daughter. You think you're protecting Cassie? You're cursing her for life. You're no better than your mother!"

Something black and venomous flashed in Mary's eyes, and Kitty knew she had gone too far. But she didn't care. She might be at her friend's mercy, but she would be damned before she listened to Mary speak about turning an innocent child into a monster as if it were some act of heroism.

The look Mary gave her could have scorched the skin from Kitty's bones as she uncoiled and slipped out from beneath her daughter. Kitty's heart leapt in her breast as Mary crossed the cave to crouch before her. The cloying reek of rancid blood still clung to the thick black bear hide she wore.

"I slaughtered this bear with my bare hands," Mary said, her eyes simmering with spite. "It was the night of my Blessing. After my transformation, I had no fear when I came across the beast deep in the woods. She had cubs, and even as she reared up to protect them, I knew *she* should be the one to be afraid. I tore out her throat with my teeth before I feasted on her young."

Mary leaned in close, her face only inches away from Kitty's. Kitty felt an unnatural heat radiating from her, as if someone had thrown open the door of a blazing stove. She searched Mary's face, looking for some glimmer of her friend. Her thoughts travelled back across the years to when Mary had found her miserable and crying by the side of the creek that bordered the poor farm. They had sat there together for a time, two girls with their shoes cast off in the grass, united by heartbreak and sorrow, stealing a moment of honey-warm sunshine before the overseer noticed they were gone. Mary had plucked some reeds from the bank of the creek and shown Kitty how to weave them into a bracelet. Kitty had worn hers until it grew too brittle and cracked off her wrist.

The memory of Mary's kindness choked Kitty's heart and brought a lump to her throat. She searched for that warmth in Mary's face now, desperate for some shred of Mary's old self that Kitty could cling to like a faded cameo in hopes that her friend could be redeemed.

All of that was gone now. Only malice remained in Mary's expression. There was no saving her.

"Shall I show you what those cubs saw before I tore them open?" Mary asked, without a shred of humanity.

She shrugged off her bearskin and was naked beneath. This close, Kitty felt Mary's warm breath quickening with excitement. She saw the monstrous change in her eyes as they enlarged and melted from blue into yellow. She saw the wiry hairs sprouting from the skin of Mary's face and hands; the grotesque elongation of her nose and upper lip into a wolven snout.

Kitty's silver hairpin flashed as she swung it around and plunged it into Mary's throat.

Blood spurted from the punctured artery as Mary reared back and let out a bestial roar. She slapped a hand to the wound, her enraged cry jolting Cassie awake.

Kitty was already darting across the cave toward the girl. She scooped Cassie up in her arms and dashed for the cave's entrance. "Hold on to me, Cassie!" She felt Cassie's little arms clench tighter around her neck. "Keep your head down! Don't look back!"

Cassie buried her face in Kitty's chest and the last thing Kitty saw before rushing from the cave was a glimpse of Mary trapped mid-transformation. Not quite fully wolven, she was a grotesque abomination to behold. Sprouts of hair covered her skin, but her slim body had yet to swell and harden with muscle. Her face was elongated and misshapen, but still disturbingly that of a human woman. Her yellow eyes glowed with malevolence, but her teeth were not yet the fearsome fangs of a wolf.

Oh God, please don't let this little girl see her mother like this, Kitty pleaded silently. *Please spare her that horror. Please…*

The roar of the waterfall crashing down in front of her was deafening in Kitty's ears as she rushed from the cave. She skidded to a halt at the lip of the steep precipice. It was a nearly eighty-foot drop to the churning pool at the base of the waterfall. The rushing torrent cascaded just a few feet beyond where Kitty stood, a curtain of water she could stretch out and plunge a hand into. A soaking mist sprayed her face and plastered her red curls to her cheeks.

A rocky path stretched away in either direction behind the falls, the stones wet and slick with moss. Both ways led into corridors that yawned open like mouths of darkness. With her pulse thundering in her ears, Kitty went left by some wild impulse and fled with Cassie's chest pressed against her own. How much time had her surprise attack bought them? Enough to find a way out? How long until Mary recovered and came after them? Even now, Kitty thought she could hear pounding footfalls echoing in pursuit. A tremor of terror struck her racing heart.

The sound of the waterfall resounded in the dark confines of the passage, but its roar diminished as the tunnel zig-zagged away. The air felt dead and decaying the further Kitty fled. With Cassie's little arms and legs fastened around Kitty's neck and her waist, it was like running with an iron cannon in her arms. But she dared not slow down. She was fearfully aware she had no idea where the passage was leading her. To an exit? Or further deeper into this subterranean hell? A terrifying possibility gnawed at her, filling her with dread. What if there was no way out of here? What if it was just an endless underground labyrinth? The thought was so awful, Kitty pushed it from her mind. Still, it lingered. What a horrifying way to die, lost in this suffocating darkness.

With Mary still hunting them down, Kitty had no choice but to push ever deeper into the unknown. Cobwebs clung to her face and vermin scattered before her as she went. More than once, she slammed into a wall and ricocheted with a jolt. She never slowed, never pricked her ears to detect how close Mary was. It didn't matter; all that mattered was getting Cassie away from her mother. Kitty was already running as fast as she could; knowing the unholy thing that used to be her friend was gaining on her wouldn't help wring any more speed out of her.

"Bring me my daughter, Kitty!" Mary's furious roar rolled up through the darkness. "You can't escape me! I can *smell* you!"

Kitty's gut lurched into her throat and Cassie's head snapped up at the sound of her mother's inhuman voice.

"Mama?" she cried in a small voice. She struggled in Kitty's arms, only now realizing she was being separated from her mother again. "Mama!"

"No, Cassie!" Kitty shouted. "Keep your head down! Your ma's not well! She wants to hurt you!"

A gust of wind blasted Kitty in the face as she burst from

the passage into a black forest. The exit came upon her so suddenly she didn't see it coming. She pitched forward and lost her grip on Cassie. The girl tumbled from her arms as they slid down a steep incline, rolling away from the sheer rock face of the mountainside that encompassed the tunnel. Stones scraped at Kitty and sticks lanced into her sides until the ground leveled and she rolled to a rest among the dead leaves and withered ferns of the underbrush. She scrambled around and cast a glance upward.

Mary stared down at her from the mouth of the tunnel, her womanly shape now limned against the darkness of the passage. *Why kind of monster has she become?* Kitty wondered fearfully. *What could have done this to her?*

Cassie was now staggering to her feet a couple of yards away. Blood seeped from a cut on her left cheek. Kitty scooped her up again and rushed into the forest, racing through the trees across snarls of roots and underbrush. She caught fleeting glimpses of something shimmering ahead and realized it was a river rushing from the falls upstream. She darted in the water's direction. On this side of the mountains, all rivers drained into the great basin of Lake Champlain. She had to be close to the lakeshore. She would find people there —people and safety. But was anyone truly safe from the creature pursuing her relentlessly?

The frenzied storm had blown over and the full moon now cast an eldritch glow through a ghostly scrim of clouds. Its light danced across the river's surface. Whitecaps hovered like phantoms on the black current as Kitty reached the water's edge. Crazily, she wondered if the beast Mary had become could swim. Not that it would make any difference; the river was far too powerful to ford. It was perhaps sixty yards across to a dark wall of impenetrable forest on the other side. A slim path hugged the rocky bank.

Kitty skirted along the riverbank, heading downriver as fast as she could manage with Cassie clinging to her. Her energy was flagging now. Her cramped muscles were ablaze and her lungs screamed for air. She couldn't go on like this much longer. She chanced a glance over her shoulder, expecting to see Mary surging through the darkness toward her. But the woman was nowhere to be seen.

Where is she? Kitty wondered with growing trepidation. *Where has she gone?*

A rope suspension bridge spanning the river materialized from the gloom ahead. As Kitty drew near, the indistinct path she was on ended in a wall of dense fir trees. She slowed to a halt and set Cassie down on the ground, her muscles rejoicing at the merciful release. The only way to keep going was to cross the river.

But the bridge looked like it would collapse under the slightest weight. It was nothing more than three rope cables stretched across the rushing whitewater: one rope on which to stand and two to serve as handrails. The ends were lashed around thick trees on either shore. A tattered web of smaller cords linked the handrails to the lower rope. The bridge had to be almost a century old, all the cables green with age and rot. It was likely put there by the Iroquois ages ago and was since forgotten as the Indians were pushed out of the valley in the years after the War of 1812.

Kitty shot a glance backward, and a fist clenched her heart. Mary was about thirty yards away. Blood drenched her throat and chest, but she seemed unbothered by the gruesome wound Kitty's hairpin had opened as she stalked toward them along the river's edge.

"Get on my back!" Kitty crouched so Cassie could climb up. With Mary drawing nearer, Kitty approached the bridge and set her hands upon the rotting handrails. The ropes were cold and slimy in her palms. They shook and wobbled under her touch and Kitty wondered what help they would be to keep her from pitching over into the rushing flood of whitewater. The cables could barely sustain their own weight, let alone hers. But she didn't have any choice. If she lingered here any longer, Mary would inevitably reclaim her daughter and unleash a savage retribution on Kitty. It might already be too late.

Kitty inched her feet onto the bottom rope.

The entire bridge swayed dangerously as she stepped from the shore. Cassie let out a frightened yelp and clenched her arms around Kitty's neck so tightly she was nearly choked of air. Kitty's stomach lurched, and she froze in place, gazing fearfully at the way ahead. Sixty yards of rope remained and there was no turning back.

Kitty gripped the handrails for balance, careful not to put too much weight on either of them. The rope was slick as she slid one foot before the other, advancing gingerly across the length of the decrepit span. Ten feet below her, the river churned and surged over giant submerged boulders. A quick look over her shoulder revealed Mary drawing near the bridge. *God, it can't possibly support us all*, Kitty thought with dread.

She was past the halfway point now, nearer to the far side

of the river than the way she had come. The bridge sagged dangerously beneath her, the sodden ropes stretching and going slack under her weight. She secured Cassie's position on her back and crept forward, painfully slow but not daring to strain the already treacherous cables.

A tremor shot through the rope beneath her feet.

Kitty teetered and caught herself. She swiveled at the hip and saw Mary stepping onto the already drooping bridge. "Mary, no! Go back!"

Mary's pursuit was unrelenting. Painted silver in moonlight, her appearance had returned to that of a beautiful, naked woman. But there was still something baleful in her eyes as she glared at Kitty across the length of the bridge. Step after step, she advanced across the treacherous cable, one foot after the other like a ballerina, heedless of the peril she was walking into.

Kitty saw there was no dissuading Mary. Her only chance of saving Cassie was to make it to the other side and escape into the woods before the bridge collapsed. She started moving again with renewed urgency. She could feel the bridge vibrating and swaying beneath her as Mary got closer.

Kitty's right hand suddenly dipped through the air as the length of handrail snapped and dropped into the river. Kitty's heart leapt into her throat as she staggered for balance. She almost over-compensated and threw all of her weight upon the remaining handrail, but she caught herself at the last second. She swiveled around again.

"Go back, Mary!" she cried, pleading now. "Go back or you'll drown your own—"

The entire bridge gave way beneath her.

Kitty plummeted into the icy water and felt herself being torn in every direction. The ferocious current ripped Cassie away as they were both swept downriver. Kitty shot out a desperate hand for her, groping blindly in the frothing torrent of whitewater. Water filled her mouth and her lungs screamed for air as the river tossed her around like she was nothing more than a fallen leaf. Her muscles cramped and twisted from the freezing cold. The current shot her upward and, for a brief instant, her head broke the surface. She sputtered and gasped, gulping oxygen before she was pulled under again. She slammed into a rock and spun around in the water, her whole lower body going numb from the bruising impact. She tried to swim, flailing desperately against the current, but it was too powerful.

Kitty shot up again and saw she was rushing toward the black length of a fallen tree jutting across the water from the shore. It was snagged against two rocks and wedged in place. Water sloshed into Kitty's mouth again and she gagged. She would drown if she didn't reach the log. It was coming at her fast. She wouldn't get a second chance to grab it.

She kicked with all her strength and lunged in the water just as she was about to be swept by the fallen tree. Her hand slapped against the slick wood and slipped off. Her fingernails raked across the length of the log as the current propelled her downstream. With her strength failing, her fingertips caught the nub of a broken branch just as it was about to slip out of reach.

Kitty crimped her fingers and strained against the current. The black river rushed and frothed around her. With her last shreds of willpower, she threw her other arm around and got a good grip on the log. She heaved and managed to swing herself into an eddy about twenty yards from the shore. Her toes brushed against stones beneath the surface and she realized she could stand. The black water was up to her throat as she steadied herself and waded to the shore. Freezing and exhausted, she hunched over and retched gobs of water from her lungs. Her chest heaved, breath blooming white in the air, as she collapsed across the rocks of the river bank.

Movement on the other shore caught her attention.

Kitty's heart withered with despair as she watched Mary haul Cassie up from the river onto dry land. The girl lay motionless on the rocks, and Kitty was certain she had drowned. But then Cassie rolled onto her stomach and struggled to her feet. Mary wrapped an arm around her daughter's shoulder and pressed her tight against her own sodden body.

A gulf of whitewater stood between them, but Kitty could feel the malign heat of Mary's eyes upon her as she glared across the river. The connection lasted only an instant, but it was long enough for Kitty to know she would never sleep peacefully again. If she survived this harrowing night, she would live in dread of the moment her old friend hunted her down to make good on the pitiless vengeance her look promised. And until that fatal moment, the memory of having failed to save Cassie would haunt her.

Soaked and shivering all over, Kitty lay sprawled across the rocks and watched as Mary hefted her daughter in her strong arms and disappeared into the black depths of the forest.

Chapter 17

Abigail sat hunkered on an overturned log and reloaded her pistol. "A secret society of werewolf women," she mused incredulously as she packed the powder in both barrels and primed the pistol's twin flashpans.

They had taken refuge in the blackened skeleton of a large barn that had caught fire some weeks earlier. The hulking remains of the scorched beams and planks stood at crooked angles like the black bones of some massive rib cage splayed open beneath the night sky. The rain had ceased and a stiff breeze was now rising. It rustled across the vast and open pasture surrounding the barn's ruins and whistled eerily through the splits and cracks of its ravaged walls. The fire had eaten a gaping hole through the roof and the corpse-white face of the full moon flitted between the remnants of the storm.

The acrid stench of wet ashes and charred wood still tainted the night air and assaulted their noses, but it was exactly what Abigail was counting on to mask their scents from the werewolves. All three of them were cut and bleeding. If the beasts were still hunting them, they could detect the smell from miles away.

"The Lupamatri," Abigail ruminated to herself as she set the pistol down on a fallen plank and returned her powder pouch to a coat pocket. She had wrapped her cloak over Anna's thin cotton chemise to help keep her warm, but her daughter still lacked something for her feet. Nathaniel had offered his boots, but Anna had refused with a withering glare.

"'Tis Latin," Nathaniel offered. He sat on a toppled beam on the opposite side of the barn. "Roughly translated, it means *wolf mother*."

"My, my," Anna grumbled sarcastically. Illuminated in the cold and bloodless moonlight, her blue eyes were sharp points as she glowered at him with her arms folded across her chest. "Exactly what must you have offered up to your demon to have learned Latin? Dash the brains of an infant or two upon your altar?"

A guilt-ridden look crossed Nathaniel's face, and he stared into the dirt at his feet. "I was foolish to have joined the Crucible. I know that now, but I cannot undo what I have done. When I started at the university, I… I wasn't like the others. Mine wasn't a privileged family. After a time, Stroud approached me with promises of enlightenment and I…" Nathaniel shook his head and frowned. "I had no idea what horrors they were capable of. I admit I failed you in my moment of weakness back at the Tomb and it will forever be my shame. But I swear to you I came back for you. Only I was too late; you were already gone, and that is when…" His Adam's apple bobbed as he swallowed. "That is when those beasts attacked."

"How very convenient for you that anyone who could attest to your story is now dead," Anna said.

Nathaniel raised his gaze to meet hers. "I did rescue your mother back there."

"No doubt because you'd like to bed her again," Anna shot back. "Most men do once they've gotten a taste of something they like."

Nathaniel frowned. "I want only to help save the girl."

"There may be more than Cassie Byrne who are in danger," Abigail said, putting an end to their bickering. An awful picture was now coming together in her mind.

Anna's eyes still smoldered as she turned her attention to her mother.

"The legend of the Wolf Mother goes back to Roman times," Abigail explained. "A Vestal Virgin was raped by an unknown man, and to avoid punishment, she blamed the resulting pregnancy on divine conception with the god Mars. Nevertheless, her infant twins, Remus and Romulus, were sent down the Tiber River to die. Except they were rescued by a she-wolf known as *lupa* who suckled and sheltered them when their basket caught the roots of a fig tree. According to legend, Romulus went on to found the city of Rome on that very spot and the she-wolf became a venerated symbol among the Romans. One of their earliest religious sects was the Luperci, a cult of men dedicated to worshipping the legendary *lupa*. Once a year they celebrated the *Lupercalia*, a festival during which Luperci smeared with sacrificial blood would chase and whip women with strips of animal skin to increase their fertility."

Abigail paused as more of the picture became clearer. "What if this secret society of lycanthropes—the Lupamatri—were an opposing cult, one that empowered and celebrated women in the face of oppression and existed in secret by necessity? The eldest among their order may very well have descended from the Roman Wolf Mother herself."

"You believe it was suckling from this she-wolf that gave rise to lycanthropes as we know them?" Anna asked.

"We know little about the origins of such monsters, of this terrible mingling of man and beast."

"*Woman* and beast," Anna observed.

"There is something I don't understand," Nathaniel interjected. "If Lucretia Stroud and her followers have been lying in wait for months, why have they chosen *tonight* to reveal themselves and attack?"

"Because tonight is the Hunter's Moon," Anna explained with a scowl of annoyance. "A month earlier and the trees would still have had enough foliage to conceal their prey; any later and snow could impede their hunt. But under the brilliant Hunter's Moon—with the trees stripped bare and the farmlands cleared and empty—there is no place to hide." Her eyes narrowed ever-so-slightly as she gazed at him. "The night is just right for killing."

"Except their goal isn't to feed," Abigail added, her tone grim.

Anna looked at her for a moment until she picked up the thread of her mother's thoughts with dawning horror. "They intend to use the moon's power to turn *all* the village girls, not just Cassie Byrne. Just as the legendary Wolf Mother protected the weak and vulnerable infant twins, this ancient order of Lupamatri has resolved to safeguard young girls by turning them into werewolves."

Abigail nodded. This was the same disturbing picture that had revealed itself to her.

"Then what are we to do?" Nathaniel asked. "If all the village girls are in danger, where will these monsters attack first? They could be anywhere. How can we possibly defend against them?"

Abigail wore a strained expression as she chewed it over in her mind. It was safe to assume she had killed Tabitha Brant by setting her ablaze back at the Tomb, but there remained three more werewolves that she was aware of: Lucretia Stroud, Catherine Abell, and Mary Byrne, who was now somewhere with her daughter awaiting the midnight hour. Assuming they were right about Lucretia's sinister intentions, what was her endgame? Would she and her followers be content to claim young victims at random? No; after waiting this long to turn enough of the townswomen to put her insidious plan into motion, Lucretia wouldn't waste time. She would want to turn as many girls as possible at once.

A gust of wind whispered across the desolate field. Somewhere in the charred bones of the roof, an owl let out a lonesome trill. The passing of each second scratched at Abigail's nerves. She couldn't stand these moments of inaction. Even now, Lucretia and her disciples could be carrying out their direful designs. Where were they? What were they doing?

A moment later, it came to her.

"The orphans."

"What of them?" asked Anna.

"They are the ones Lucretia and her followers will come for first. The orphaned girls who are alone and need protection the most."

"What of the little boys?" Nathaniel ventured.

No one answered. The possibilities were too awful to imagine.

"We haven't a moment to lose," Abigail said. There was a nervous urgency in her voice now. "Has the village a foundling hospital or an orphan asylum?"

Nathaniel shook his head. "We've only the almshouse on the poor farm."

"How many children are there now?"

Nathaniel frowned, gave an uncertain shrug. "Perhaps a dozen."

Abigail fished in her coat for her battered pocket watch. "'Tis just past seven. We've five hours until midnight. If we —"

Without warning, Anna sprang and snatched the pistol from where Abigail had set it down. The swiftness by which she moved caught Abigail off-guard. It happened in a flash and she gaped in horror as her daughter stormed across the barn and raised the pistol to Nathaniel's head. He threw a hand up and shrank back against the charred wall. But Anna only pressed the barrel harder into his temple and cocked a hammer as she stood over him.

"*Anna, no!*" Abigail leapt to her feet. "If you kill him, all hope of saving the children dies with him!"

Anna didn't seem to hear or care. Her face was a chilling mask of murderous intent. Abigail's heart pumping at a frenzied rate as she waited for the inevitable boom of the pistol. Only now did she truly understand just how damaged Anna really was, that the darkness raging within her could very well engulf her completely.

Nathaniel seemed to recognize his defenseless position and the futility of putting up a fight. He squeezed his eyes shut and waited to die.

The gunshot never came.

A breathless moment passed as Anna stood with the pistol jammed against Nathaniel's skull. "Why exactly do we need him?" she asked in an icy voice. The gun's barrel never left Nathaniel's temple as she waited for an answer.

"There are but two ways to kill a werewolf," Abigail replied, her whole body thrumming with tension. "Burning or decapitation. Both are incredibly difficult. In all my years, I have encountered but one lycanthrope and it all but ended me. But *silver* acts as a poison to them. For a brief time, it will reverse a lycanthrope's transformation—and as a human, they are much easier to kill. I suspect there is only one place around these parts where we might find both silver and the means by which to forge it into bullets."

"The university," Nathaniel breathed through clenched teeth. He cringed as the cold iron of Anna's gun barrel pressed into his skin. "There is ore and a blast furnace in the new Middle College building."

"And you can gain access to it?" asked Abigail.

Nathaniel nodded. "There is already silver smelted for the school of dentistry. We need only mold it."

A riot of conflicting emotions surged through Abigail as she gazed at Anna and waited with bated breath for her next move. What would she do if Anna pulled the trigger? If Anna killed Nathaniel, Cassie Byrne would surely be turned into a bloodthirsty monster. Perhaps even worse, Abigail could no longer hold on to any shred of hope for her daughter's salvation. The killing of the servant girl at the governor's mansion hadn't been difficult to justify and explain away. But executing Nathaniel here and now? It would be nothing short of cold-blooded murder. Was this the pivotal moment that severed whatever bonds remained between Abigail and her daughter?

An even worse possibility reared in Abigail's mind, one so dreadful it chilled her to the core: What if there was no end to Anna's dark bloodlust? What if she grew to become the very sort of soulless monster Abigail had spent most of her life killing? Would Abigail have it in her to mete the same fate upon her own daughter?

The nerve-straining tension of the moment stretched on as Anna's face remained an unreadable block of ice.

At last, she released the hammer and lowered the pistol.

Nathaniel let out a shuddering breath. He raised his eyes and met Anna's hard gaze as she squatted before him.

"In my mind, you are already a dead man," she growled. "What you do this night may restore you to the living, but fail us and I will put you in a grave where you belong."

Anna's eyes were narrow slits as she stood and turned her back on Nathaniel. She flipped the pistol around in her hand and offered the grip to Abigail.

Abigail tucked the gun back into her belt. Adrenaline still surged through her veins. Anna's frightening eruption had rattled her far more than she let on. She wasted no time heading for the horses, eager to put some distance between her daughter and the young man.

"Nathaniel and I will go to the university to forge silver bullets," she said. "Anna, you go to the poor farm and see to the children. Secure the building and do whatever you must to keep them safe until we join you. We can only hope that we are not already too late."

Anna hesitated a moment as Abigail hustled across the barn toward where their pair of horses stood waiting in the shadows.

"Mother..." she called after her.

Abigail paused by her horse's side and turned.

"I... I must thank you for coming to my rescue back at the Tomb," Anna said with a hint of bashful reluctance.

Abigail stepped from the shadows and gave her a thin smile. "Of course, my dear. What kind of mother do you think I am?"

High above, the barn owl let out a haunting cry as Abigail swung herself up into the horse's saddle and motioned for Nathaniel to join her. "Not all men are monsters, Anna. Your father wasn't. Nor was your grandfather Jonas or your uncle Duncan." A humorless smile crossed her lips. "Perhaps when this is over, you might tell me what your decision would have been had I not intervened."

Chapter 18

Anna hammered on the door until a candle flickered to light in an upstairs window. She stood back and huddled against the wind, drumming her foot on the porch as she waited for the farm's overseer to come downstairs. A merry display of harvest gourds sat atop a bale of hay next to the front door. Anna took notice and thought it admirable that the overseer's wife had attempted to bring some cheer to such an otherwise dismal place.

The Burlington poor farm was on a lonely track about a mile from town, well out of sight of the burgeoning upper class who supported the almshouse begrudgingly with their taxes. The poor farm owed its existence to the mandates of state law, not the benevolence of the local citizens. Its isolation allowed the town to purchase the land at a cheap price. It also served as a deterrent to ensure only those in direst need of help would venture to seek it out.

The farmhouse was built in the Federal style with a flat façade and two brick chimneys rising at both ends of the steep roof. The whitewashed clapboard siding was now gray and weathered with the scars of Vermont's harsh winters. There were five shuttered windows on the upper floor and two on either side of the front door. A veranda stretched the length of the house and wrapped around one side. A pair of majestic elms separated the farmhouse from the road. With their crooked limbs now stripped of their leaves, they stood like two giant upended brooms reaching up to brush the black from the night sky.

Two other structures neighbored the farmhouse: a sizeable barn with a gambrel roof, and a long, squat building that Anna understood to be the poor farm's bunkhouse. It was there that she would likely find the orphans. Seventy acres of pastures, meadows, and crop fields surrounded the compound. It was late in the season, but rows of corn still marched into the distance. Otherwise, with the harvest now come and gone, the land lay barren in the windswept night.

The glow of the candle vanished from the upstairs window and reappeared moments later on the first floor. The man who flung open the door was wearing a pair of wool breeches and a crumpled undershirt.

Emmett Webster was in his early seventies, but his flinty eyes were those of a man half his age. Only the gray-white of his full beard and the timeworn creases of his skin betrayed how old he really was. While Emmett wasn't a particularly tall man, he carried himself with such easy confidence that most people he encountered would be surprised to learn his true height. The one exception was his massive hands. They were two of the largest Anna had ever seen on a man. They were so incongruous to the rest of his stature that they reminded her of the huge paws of a lynx she had once come across. She took notice because one of Emmett's palms was wrapped around the barrel of a rifle. He regarded her with the weapon standing at his side, the butt of the stock planted on the floor and the barrel pointed up toward the ceiling.

Emmett fixed Anna with a hard eye and said, "We're locked up for the night. If you're in need, you can come back in the morning." His voice was low and gravelly, as if his throat were permanently parched. There was nothing unkind about the way he spoke, but the rifle at his side warned that his patience wasn't to be tested at this late hour.

"I'm not here for charity, Mr. Webster," Anna said. "My name is Charlotte Cole and I've come to you because the orphans in your care are in grave danger."

Emmett's gray brows creased over his steely eyes. "What're you talking about?"

There wasn't any other way to explain it, so Anna told him everything. She left out the details of her own kidnapping at the hands of Virgil Stroud and the Crucible of Night; her tale was already too wild and incredible to be believed. As for the rest of it, she heard the words leaving her own mouth and imagined how she must sound to this man. Here was a bedraggled woman, streaked with blood, clad in nothing but a wet chemise and a cloak, banging on his door in the middle of the night while raving about secret societies and werewolves and plots to turn young girls into monsters.

Emmett's rifle wasn't aimed at her—not yet—but Anna suspected it soon might be after what she had to say.

When she was through with her fantastic tale, Emmett stayed silent for a long moment as he studied her. His eyes were narrow and shrewd. Anna could see his mind working as he tried to make sense of everything she had revealed.

"Wait here." He swung the door shut in her face.

Anna heard his heavy footsteps moving away from the door and imagined him fetching a pair of manacles with which to lock her up. Despite the rifle he bore, she had no doubt she could best him if it came to a fight. She had no desire to harm the aging man, but nothing was going to stop her from securing the children.

With another pounding of footsteps, the door swung open again and Emmett reappeared. This time he carried a pistol and an oil lantern along with the rifle he had slung over a shoulder. Anna took a step back, balled her hands into fists, ready to defend herself.

"Easy, lass," Emmett said. "I believe you."

He must have registered the astonishment on Anna's face and felt the need to explain. "'Fore I took this job as overseer, I was a ranger out of Fort Thompkins during the war. Spent months out there in the woods up and down Mohawk Valley, spying on the Indians. I seen things out there in the woods, alone on moonless nights with nothing but the darkness and miles of trees in every direction to keep me company. Seen things I can't explain, things that make my skin prickle just thinking about 'em, things that'd make you believe…" The old man seemed to shudder almost imperceptibly. He looked Anna in the face for a moment and she got the impression he wasn't seeing her, but some haunting memory he had pushed deep and tried to drown.

"Come on." Emmett stepped onto the porch. "Let's get to the bunkhouse."

Lantern in hand, he led the way from the farmhouse

toward the long and flat building standing some distance past the barn. The wind whipped across the pasture and moonlight spilled silver upon them as they went.

"How many people reside on the farm?" Anna asked as they hurried along. She had to shout over the howl of the wind.

"Eleven," Emmett replied. "We're still early in the season yet. Give it another couple of weeks and the first snowfall'll start chasing more folks our way. Right now there's nine kids, a tramp fallen on hard times named Finney, and ol' Quill."

"You said *our* way. Have you a wife, Mr. Webster? Is she still in the house?"

Emmett frowned and something sad flashed across his face as he slowed his pace and shook his head. "It's just a habit 'o speaking, I guess. My wife Martha passed three years ago."

Anna sensed his lingering grief and regretted bringing it up. She remembered the festive display of gourds arranged on the house's front porch and realized Emmett himself must have taken the time to put them there, not his wife, as Anna had presumed. Her respect for the gruff man crept a notch higher.

"Are all the residents now in the bunkhouse?" she asked.

"All except for Quill. He's out spending the night in the pest house."

"What is the pest house?"

"A shack where we used to quarantine folks with smallpox. Quill's a bit of a lunatic, you see. Nuttier than a squirrel turd, actually. Most times he's harmless enough, but now and then he gets to raving something fierce. I got a soft spot for Quill on account it ain't his fault his roof ain't nailed tight, but I can't tolerate him scaring the children. So I give him the choice to spend the night out in the pest house. He seems to like it well enough out there by himself. Usually comes back in the morning in time for eggs and sings songs to the children. Quill just loves the little ones."

Anna studied the layout of the bunkhouse as they drew near. It would be a hard place to defend. The only entrance was a heavy door that bisected the building in the middle, but there were far too many windows. Even if they had the time, Anna doubted Emmett had enough material on hand to board them all.

"We must move the children somewhere safer until help arrives," she said. "The farm must have a root cellar?"

Emmett nodded. "Underneath the house." The creases on his face deepened as another thought came to him. "There's also the cages."

"What cages?"

"Fore I took over, the fella who ran the place before me used to lock up people like ol' Quill in a coupla' cages he had built in the barn. I ain't ever used 'em 'cause that ain't no dignified way to treat a person. Those cages are solid steel, though, and they might be enough to keep the kids safe."

"Are they large enough to accommodate them all?"

Emmett thought about it, conjuring a mental picture of all the orphans gathered together. "No."

"Then we've no choice but the cellar."

They reached the bunkhouse and Emmett fished a ring of keys out of his pocket. "We keep the men and the women separated—for propriety's sake, you know. Women and children in the room to the left; men to the right. If you—"

From somewhere in the night came a blood-chilling howl.

It was distant and faint, but distinct enough to make the hairs on the back of Anna's neck rise. Emmett's eyes went round as frying pans and flooded with apprehension at the unearthly sound.

"We haven't much time," said Anna. "We must hurry."

"Shit," Emmett muttered. "I gotta go get Quill."

Anna shot him a look. "How far is the shed?"

"'Bout a quarter mile across the pasture."

"You'll never make it there and back in time."

"Might be you're right," Emmett said with a resigned sigh. "But I can't just leave him out there to be slaughtered. Quill might be crazier than an outhouse rat, but he's still a man." He pressed his pistol into Anna's hand. "You ever used one o' these?"

Anna nodded and inspected the barrel and hammer. She had fired her first gun at the age of six. The jolt of the recoil had nearly separated her little shoulder from its socket. Since then, she had learned to handle firearms with ease.

Emmett turned the lock and left the key ring hanging there for Anna. "You rouse the little ones," he said and handed her his lantern. As he unslung his rifle from around his shoulder, he noticed her bare feet for the first time. They were scraped and bruised and splattered with mud. "Might find a tolerable pair 'o boots in the chest by the door in the women's room. And don't forget Finney. He's a bit of a loner, but I know him well enough to say life ain't been too kind to him. Lost his wife and little girl within the same year and he… well, I guess he just ain't been the same since."

Emmett paused and glanced out toward the desolate

swathe of the pasture. "You'll find the door to the root cellar 'round back o' the house. I'll knock three times when we get back."

Anna gave him a grim smile. "Good luck, Mr. Webster."

Emmett nodded and drew a deep and shuddering breath, as if the cold air could somehow bolster his courage. "You keep those children safe. They're all the family I got left."

Chapter 19

The University of Vermont stood atop a hill with its back to the mountains, overlooking the slumbering town and the shimmering black lake beyond. After a fire destroyed the original building some years ago, celebrated builder John Johnson was hired to erect a new building between the existing North and South colleges. Modeled after Princeton's Nassau Hall, Johnson's design for the Middle College was a long and deep three-story structure in the Federal style with a hipped roof and brick walls. A massive golden dome crowned its central pavilion, rising high above the town like the shining sun of enlightenment itself.

Contained within the building's walls were the university's chapel, library, museum, recitation rooms, medical hall, and a small foundry for the college of engineering. The governor's ball was held last night in honor of Johnson and the inauguration of his grand and auspicious achievement.

In the sweltering heat of the foundry, Abigail now looked on while Nathaniel banked the glowing coals of the forge to stoke the flames.

"Witches?" he asked while he worked. "Both of you?"

"Necromancers, actually," Abigail replied. "We conjure and bind the dead to do our bidding."

"To help you kill monsters?"

"Among other things." Abigail's blue eyes twinkled with amusement. "You surprise me, Nathaniel. I would have thought an initiate of the Crucible of Night would possess a more open mind to the world of the paranatural."

The shame that flashed across Nathaniel's face gave Abigail a small measure of satisfaction. She studied him while he worked. He had removed his cloak and his linen shirt was now plastered to his lean frame. It was wide open at the collar and he had rolled the sleeves to his elbows. Sweat tickled down his forehead and his sandy blonde hair was smeared with soot and coal dust.

Flames sprang to life on the smoldering coals as Nathaniel pumped the bellows and let air into the forge. The university's foundry was on the ground floor at the extreme end of the building's southern wing. A vast assortment of founding, casting, and blacksmithing tools hung from its brick walls. The forge itself was at the far end of the room. It was about five feet wide and equally deep. A giant hood descended from the ceiling to vent the smoke from the bed of coals and flames that burned beneath. A long worktable stretched the length of one wall with a sturdy vise fixed to one end.

At the center of the room sat an enormous anvil upon which a big forging hammer rested. The long handle of a huge sledgehammer also leaned against the anvil with its heavy head planted on the floor. Though the foundry had only recently begun operating, the inevitable sooty stench of coal already clung to every surface.

Abigail and Nathaniel had hitched their horse some distance from the building to avoid being noticed by any of the students in the dormitory buildings that flanked the Middle College. They had crept across the grounds of the university's campus on foot, hurrying under the great white eye of the moon. Nathaniel led the way, and Abigail had picked the lock. A silent corridor stretching past the medical hall and chemical laboratory accessed the foundry. They had lit no candles, and though the orange glow of the forge suffused the space with a stifling heat, darkness still haunted the corners.

"I am familiar with the Crucible of Night," Abigail went on. She propped an elbow against the anvil while Nathaniel worked the bellows again. "Founded three centuries ago by a renegade pupil of the infamous John Dee himself, though even Dee would later come to disavow his disciple's fiendish order. Am I correct?"

Absorbed in his work, Nathaniel clenched his jaw with chagrin and nodded. He remained silent as he filled a clay crucible with lumps of smelted silver they had pilfered from the medical hall down the corridor. With his hands shielded by a pair of heavy gloves, he used a long pair of blacksmith tongs to nestle the crucible within the fire. He worked the bellows a few more times, the incoming rush of air spurring the flames to an even greater intensity.

"Truth be told, I am surprised it has taken this long for our paths to cross," said Abigail.

It would only take a few minutes for the incredible heat of the forge to melt the silver. While they waited, Nathaniel lined up a half-dozen bullet molds on the worktable. Each resembled a pair of scissors but with a square block for a head instead of blades. The spherical mold for the bullet was created when the two sides of the head pressed together. A rounded notch on each side of the block formed a small hole, and it was into this that the silver was to be poured.

"They are left over from the war," Nathaniel explained, glad to be changing the subject. "Now they are used to practice metallurgy and simple casting. The bullets are donated to the local militia."

"My daughter is going to kill you."

Nathaniel froze. His eyes flicked to Abigail and found her icy gaze staring back at him.

"I wouldn't stand in her way," she went on, "were I to believe you to be an evil man."

Nathaniel glanced at her from the corner of his eye as he resumed his work and removed the crucible from the flames. The molten silver within shimmered with a life of its own in the firelight. "That isn't what you believe?"

"No. I believe you are someone with an imperfect heart who failed to do the right thing when called upon." Abigail's tone dropped. "The same could be said about me. And it is for this reason that I must believe there is always hope for redemption."

"But not forgiveness," said Nathaniel.

Abigail let out a wistful sigh, and the slim crack that had appeared in her stony façade vanished. "No, not forgiveness. I would never hope for as much."

Nathaniel frowned but didn't argue. His face was dark and pensive as he dipped a ladle into the crucible and poured a small amount of silver into each of the molds, working carefully to avoid spills and air bubbles as he moved down the line. Within moments, it was done, and he set the ladle aside.

Abigail studied the row of balls now cooling in their molds. Though unpolished, the silver was more valuable now than it ever could have been. Six bullets. It wasn't a lot, but it was enough. They might stand a chance of surviving this bloody night if they could get to the poor farm in time.

"This isn't your first time working a forge," Abigail remarked, impressed by Nathaniel's unexpected skill.

"My grandfather was the town blacksmith," he replied. He had his back to Abigail as he closed the damper and scattered the coals across the bed of the forge to extinguish the flames. "You could say that he raised me. Watching him at work, seeing him shape marvels from raw elements with nothing but heat and strength, was what inspired my curiosity for engineering as a boy. I suppose it was what set me on the path that eventually led me… here."

By his rueful tone, Abigail understood him to mean the university, not the foundry. For a moment, she thought she might even pity the young man. She knew too well how it felt to have made mistakes that would haunt her until the end of her days. She remembered Nathaniel as he had been when she met him last night at the tavern. He'd possessed an easy self-assurance then, a certain devilish boldness that Abigail had found attractive before everything had gone so very wrong.

Nathaniel turned around.

And saw the forging hammer in Abigail's hand.

Nathaniel stared at her a moment until a look of horrified understanding dawned on his face. "You were never going to let me live. You just said those things so that I might help you forge these bullets."

"You're mistaken," Abigail replied. "I meant every word I said. I don't believe you to be an evil man, Nathaniel. But I fear my daughter may be guided by an evil hand, and I must never let her succumb to it. Though it leads me to damnation, I must do anything I can to protect her... even from herself."

With the weight of the lethal hammer in her hand, Abigail was reminded of those disturbing moments in the barn. Images of Anna with her pistol pressed to Nathaniel's head thrust themselves into her mind. Abigail had been able to talk her down then, but she had seen that dangerous look in her daughter's eyes before. Anna would never relent until this man lay dead before her. Abigail couldn't let that happen. She could never allow her daughter to be so consumed by the dark spirit within her. Better that Abigail should kill Nathaniel now than lose Anna forever.

She tightened her grip on the hammer. She still had her pistol tucked into her belt, but the blast of a gunshot coming from the university in the dead of night would bring unwanted attention. Though it filled her with revulsion, one swift strike of the hammer to Nathaniel's skull and it would all be over. He might try to escape, perhaps even put up a good fight, but he would be no match for her. Abigail would spare Anna from bloodying her own soul with murder.

And she would never know.

Nathaniel saw Abigail's icy, emotionless glare and turned his back on her again. His surrender only heightened her self-loathing. He would offer no resistance; he would force her to do the unthinkable, to kill a defenseless man in cold blood. She shuddered. Was there a viler crime?

The hammer quivered in Abigail's hand now. It was almost imperceptible to the eye, but she felt as if her entire arm were shaking. Her heart raced and a horrible, sick feeling clenched at her stomach so that she thought she would vomit. She tried to convince herself that she had done worse, but it was a lie. Yes, she had killed men before, but never like this. This was immoral, as evil as the spirits and monsters she hunted. And yet, Abigail saw no other alternative, not if there was any hope of her daughter's salvation.

She took a step forward. It seemed like a simple thing, but it felt as if her legs were unwilling to move, as if even her body was revolted by what she was about to do. She willed herself to draw closer still. Now she could hear Nathaniel's shallow breathing as he awaited the fatal strike. Though she had shared her bed with him, Abigail knew almost nothing about this young man whose life she was about to take. She thought of the innumerable choices he had made throughout his life, the myriad twisting paths that had led him here, to this place, and the moment of his ignoble death at her hands.

Abigail raised the hammer, ready for the kill, and had an image of Mary Byrne, a mother so determined to protect her child from monsters that she would turn her own daughter into one. Is that what Abigail herself had done? Was Anna right about her? Had she cursed her own daughter when she had initiated Anna into the ways of the occult? What might Anna's future have been had Abigail not made that fateful decision?

Abigail's hand stiffened in the air.

She lowered the hammer.

Terrible though her daughter's fate might be, Abigail could no longer shield her from it. Not like this. If she murdered Nathaniel now, anything redeeming in her would die with him. And all that she had suffered and bled for throughout her life—all that she had hoped and dreamed for her daughter to be—would be for nothing. Even if it led her into darkness, the time had come for Anna to walk her path.

Nathaniel heard the thunk of the hammer being dropped on the worktable and breathed easier. He felt dizzy as he turned around, frightfully aware that for the second time this night, she had spared him.

"If you value your life, you would be wise to leave this town when we are finished here," Abigail warned. "That would be best... for all of us."

Nathaniel flinched and his lips compressed as he nodded.

Then they heard the shattering of glass.

It came from a distant point in the building, but it reverberated clearly through the dark and empty corridors. Abigail's eyes locked on Nathaniel's and she saw the fear sweeping over his face.

They weren't alone.

Footsteps rang out, deep and booming in the silence of the empty building. But there was another sound as well, a strange clicking that accompanied each heavy step across the wide pine floorboards.

Claws.

Abigail felt a chill creep over her and her attention flashed to the bullet molds.

Nathaniel read her thoughts and shook his head. "They're

not ready," he whispered. "Silver takes longer to harden than lead. If we quench the bullets too soon, we will shock the metal and cause it to crack."

Abigail stared at him a moment, stunned by the realization that if she had killed him, she never would have known this vital fact. The bullets would have misfired in her pistol and all would have been lost.

Nathaniel's eyes darted around the foundry, searching for something to defend themselves with. He found nothing useful except for the hammers. He wrapped his hands around the big sledgehammer leaning against the anvil and hefted it. Its handle was nearly half the length of his body.

The furtive footsteps reverberated loudly from somewhere far beyond the door to the foundry. Did the beast already know they were in here?

"I'll draw it away," Nathaniel whispered. "Wait another five minutes, then crack open the molds and quench the balls in that water." He gestured toward where a pail sat near the vise at the end of the worktable. "When it is safe, take the bullets and leave."

"No, we can wait." Abigail drew her pistol. "Nathaniel, you don't have to—"

"Please," he interjected, silencing her objection with a raised palm. "There isn't time. If that monster discovers us here, all of this will be for naught, and the children will surely die." A grim smile crossed Nathaniel's lips before a haunted look settled on his face. "Besides, I'm already a dead man, remember? And there must always be hope for redemption."

Chapter 20

Emmett Webster's breath bloomed white in the night air as he hustled across the windswept pasture toward the pest house. *God damn it, Quill,* he thought bitterly. *Why'd you have to pick tonight to act up?*

With the barren expanse of the fields rolling away in every direction, Emmett had never felt so vulnerable. This must be what a starving rabbit feels when hunger drives it out into the open for the fox to find. Revealed for all to see in the moonlight, even the twin-barrel rifle Emmett gripped in his big fists provided little comfort. He eyed the jagged silhouette of the forest looming in the distance and could almost feel hungry eyes staring back at him. Were the beasts out there right now? Waiting for him to draw nearer?

Emmett still hadn't mustered enough volunteers to help clear the northern cornfield, and he had considered looping around through its dense cover to reach the pest house. But there wasn't time. Straight across the pasture was the fastest way to reach Quill. He just prayed it wouldn't cost him his life.

The wind swept unimpeded across the open field and stung Emmett's eyes. It flapped his undershirt as he pressed onward with brisk, sure-footed purpose. A wintry prickle of fear crawled up his spine and settled on the back of his neck the further he ventured from safety. There was no way he would hear anything creeping up on him over the wind's incessant howl. He shook his head and shot a nervous glance over his shoulder for the hundredth time. What the hell was he doing out here? Scared shitless and losing his breath on the word of a young woman who had showed up on his doorstep in the middle of the night?

But the way he saw it, either Charlotte Cole was telling the truth and the orphans were in real danger, or she was a madwoman. If that was the case, the townsfolk would send her Emmett's way anyhow. And yet, something deep within him sensed she wasn't lying. He remembered the chilling howl that had pierced the night, the one that had turned his insides into quivering slush. An icy finger of fear scratched at his heart. No creation of God had made that blood-curdling sound.

The squat form of the pest house was now visible in the gloom ahead. It stood like a lonely mausoleum where the pasture met the forbidding darkness of the forest. A square window of firelight glowed like a beacon in the night. Smoke billowed gray on black from the tin chimney and was whisked away on the blustering wind.

Even from this distance, Emmett heard Quill's singing resounding from within. At some point in Quill's childhood, a drifter on the farm had taught him a song that had stuck with him ever since. Now and then he might hum some other random tune, but he always returned to his old favorite. Quill's singing voice was hoarse and ululating and unnervingly loud in the night as it carried on the wind.

"Friendship to every willing mind, opens a heavenly treasure. There may the sons of sorrow find sources of real pleasure…"

Emmett cringed, eyes darting around as he approached the shack. Any chance of going unnoticed and stealing away quietly was out of the question. Whatever was out there prowling the darkness had surely already been drawn to the lunatic's gleeful, off-key song.

When Quill had a bad night and got like this, there were times when Emmett was tempted to send him down to the asylum in Brattleboro. Emmett had heard about what went on down there. Some of it didn't sit right with him, but the folks at the asylum could help the poor man more than what Emmett could offer on the farm. But whenever the thought had crossed his mind, Martha talked him out of it. Martha, of the kind spirit and compassionate heart, who always seemed to make Emmett a better man than he thought capable of being.

He had met her as a boy when her family had taken shelter from a hurricane in his family's cellar in the tiny coastal hamlet where they had grown up. As the storm raged through the night, young Emmett was tickled by the first butterflies of love. A few years later, he made good on the promise he made to himself that tempestuous night and married his sweetheart the first chance he got. They left the coast and moved inland, drifting around to where the work was good until Martha encouraged Emmett to put his woodsman's skills to use in the army.

When they eventually took over Burlington's poor farm, Martha found a purpose for her own warmhearted soul. In the years that followed, she often told Emmett that caring for the poor and orphaned was what God had put her on Earth to do. She continued to do His will until the cancer took her and He gathered her to His breast. Though Martha had never born Emmett a child of their own, he had never cared. She was all he had ever needed.

It was Martha who had reminded him that Quill had lived on the poor farm all his life. The only home Quill had ever known was the almshouse, where his blind mother died in childbirth. The cruelty of sending the pitiful man packing anywhere else would be like binding kittens in a sack and tossing them in the Winooski River.

The ten-by-ten shack exhaled a breath of warm air as Emmett unlatched the door and swung it inward. Quill's dreadful singing swelled even louder.

"Poor are the joys that fools esteem, fading and transitory; Mirth is as fleeting as a dream, or a delusive story…"

The shack was bare and spartan except for a straw pallet bed, a pitcher of water, a tin wash basin, and a dented wood stove that filled the tiny space with heat.

Quill's long face broke into a childlike grin at the unexpected appearance of the man in his doorway. "Emmett!"

Quill was shirtless, all skinny ribs and sunken chest, and the pasty white of his hairless flesh beamed like a fish belly in the firelight. Though he was lanky and almost Emmett's own age, Quill had the intellect of a toddler. It was as if some fairy tale hag had cursed him as a boy, freezing his mind in time while the rest of his body kept growing bigger and older around it. The only physical remnant of that boy now lived in Quill's eyes. They were the warm brown of springtime maple syrup and so full of trust and loyalty they often reminded Emmett of the black Labrador retriever he'd grown up with back in that tiny village on the coast of Maine.

A growth of gray beard sprouted from Quill's gaunt cheeks and his unkempt hair fell past his shoulders. Emmett had persuaded the town barber to visit the poor farm once a year, but Martha had insisted on keeping Quill trimmed herself. With her passing, Emmett had taken it upon himself to do the same, as if it had been some unspoken dying wish. After a week of deliberating and making his peace with the awkwardness of handling another man's hair, it had taken him an hour to coax Quill into sitting still long enough for the cut. With the first snip of Emmett's shears, Quill had become so agitated he'd needed to spend the night in the pest house. Since then, Emmett was content to wait for the barber's visit and not attempt a haircut again.

Quill's gaze darkened with unease as it slid down from Emmett's somber face to the rifle he carried. Emmett understood the threat he must present and relaxed his white-knuckled grip on the gun.

"Evening, Quill," he said as he stood framed in black at the shack's threshold. "You gotta come back to the house with me. It ain't safe for you out here tonight."

Quill's jolly face soured like curdled milk. His bony hands balled into fists at his sides and Emmett tensed, worried the man would lash out at him for ruining his fun. The only time Emmett had seen Quill become violent was the day Martha died. He'd been wild with grief then. But on nights like this, anything was possible.

"You know I ain't here to hurt you, friend," Emmett said.

Quill relaxed his fists and turned his back on Emmett. He retreated like a petulant child who didn't want to give up a forbidden plaything and resumed the awful braying he thought was singing. "*Learning, that boasting, glittering thing, scarcely is worth possessing; Riches, forever on the wing, scarce can be called a blessing...*"

Outside, the wind was a haunting wail. A powerful gust slammed into the side of the shack like a rogue wave and rocked the timber walls.

Dreadfully aware of the danger lingering behind every passing minute, Emmett heaved an exasperated sigh, stepped inside, and locked the door behind him. Quill wasn't going to make this easy. Precious seconds were slipping away. "C'mon, Quill. Don't do this now."

Quill shot him a dark look and raised his voice even louder in defiance.

"Quill! We can't stay here! It ain't safe. We gotta go. Now!"

Something scratched at the window.

Emmett's mouth went dry and his scrotum shrank tight. He wanted to believe it was a branch blowing in the wind, but there weren't any trees close enough to reach the shack.

Quill heard it too. His singing came to a merciful halt, and he swiveled to peer at the window as if he had never seen one before. He couldn't help his childlike curiosity; he took a step toward it.

"No!" Emmett lunged. "Quill, don't!"

Something huge and powerful slammed itself into the

door. It trembled on its hinges and rattled against its frame.

Emmett spun around. Leveled his rifle on the door.

Whatever was out there reared back and struck again. A chilly draft of wind stole through the crack above the door and tickled Emmett's beard. The thing struck again and again, determined to get in. Emmett's knuckles went white with tension as he aimed his rifle, expecting the door to explode inward at any moment.

Ignorant of the menace lurking just outside the door, Quill grinned at the excitement and resumed his merry song. *"Luxury leaves a sting behind, wounding the body and the mind; Only in friendship can we find pleasure and solid glory…"*

The assault on the door ended abruptly.

The eerie silence that followed filled Emmett with dread. From beyond the door came a low and threatening growl. Quill guffawed and clapped his hands with glee like a toddler at a petting zoo. Emmett trained his rifle on the door, squinted down the barrel, pressed his finger to the trigger.

And fired as the door splintered down the middle from top to bottom.

A monstrous creature came bursting through the wreckage. It was wolf-like, but more massive than any wolf Emmett had ever seen. His gunshot grazed the beast's hairy collarbone as it smashed its way into the shack and lowered into a crouch, yellow eyes smoldering with malevolence. Blood spilled from the gunshot wound, but the terrifying silver-gray creature seemed impervious to pain. Its large ears were plastered back against its giant head and its snout was wrinkled back, baring its dagger-like fangs.

Quill's song turned into hysterical shrieking as he shrank,

cowering against a wall.

The werewolf sprang.

Emmett fired again. Quill clapped his hands to his ears and gibbered with fright. This time, the bullet caught the beast in the upper chest, near the left armpit. The blast of the close-range shot jolted it aside as it lunged for Quill and sent it careening into the pot-bellied stove. The monster collided with tremendous force, driven by its wild momentum. There was a teeth-rattling screech of tearing metal as the stove sheered free of its tin chimney pipe and toppled over on its side. The stove door whipped open, belching blazing logs and red-hot embers across the timber floor.

The air itself seemed to ignite with a great and terrible whoosh as hungry flames sprang up between the men and the beast. The werewolf regained its footing and whirled on them, the leaping glow of the fire reflected in its evil glare. Emmett grabbed Quill by the waist of his threadbare breeches and yanked him toward the ruined door. The searing heat of the crackling flames licked at their backs. The trapped monster let out a furious roar as they spilled out into the night.

Emmett didn't look back. He kept one hand clamped on Quill, half-dragging the whimpering man as they scattered from the shack. Emmett didn't head for the pasture. There was no way he was leading that nightmarish thing back to the farmhouse and the children. Instead, he hauled Quill north toward the cornfield. Maybe they could lose the beast in the sprawling maze. Or maybe they'd keep heading north, through the corn and the woods beyond to the Jones's dairy farm over a mile away.

The first rows of cornstalks were within reach when a

tremendous crash erupted behind them. A flurry of sparks and embers sailed their way on the wind like a swarm of glowing hornets. Emmett allowed himself to hope the burning shack had collapsed and engulfed the monster in flames. But even as they plunged into the yellow-brown rows of corn, he knew the creature must have smashed its way out and was now stalking them as they ran. Though he dared not slow a step, he could sense the predator back there, gaining ground on them.

Desiccated blades of head-high corn slapped at Emmett's face as he dashed headlong through the stalks. His world shrank to the few inches in front of his nose. Quill squirmed and bucked in his grasp, driven wild with panic.

"C'mon, Quill!" Emmett gasped.

Quill's thrashing only became more manic, more desperate. A steady stream of raving whoops and yawps spilled from his twisted mouth.

"Quill, stop it! We gotta—"

Quill was gone.

One instant, Emmett was manhandling the pitiful man through the corn; the next, he lost his grip and Quill went racing away like a hound after a squirrel. Emmett fumbled after him, grasping for him like Quill was a hat blown out of reach by a powerful gust. Then the vast cornfield swallowed him up and he vanished from sight.

Emmett skidded to a halt. Gripped his rifle with both hands. There wasn't time to reload, but he'd use the weapon as a cudgel. Panic twisted his gut as the awful severity of the moment crashed down on him.

He had lost Quill.

Emmett turned in a slow circle. There was nothing but tall cornstalks in every direction. And no sign of Quill. He swallowed and found his mouth so parched it was as if it was packed with sand. The wind rustled the dried leaves around him, the cornstalks crackling as they swayed side to side like true believers at a revival. Emmett's blood thundered in his ears as he stood perfectly still, squinting into the darkness, listening for any hint of Quill. Long moments ticked by, scratching at his frayed nerves as they went.

Then he heard it. Another sound. A telltale rustling. Something moving, pushing through the cornstalks—something big.

"Quill!" Emmett hissed and instantly regretted his own stupidity.

What if it wasn't Quill moving out there? What if it was—

Another sound warbled loudly in the eerie silence.

Quill was singing.

He wasn't far off, maybe twenty or thirty feet—but he wasn't where the rustling had come from. He bellowed the same song he always sang and Emmett felt so sick with sorrow at the sound of his clarion voice, he thought he would vomit. *Oh hell, Quill*, he thought despairingly and heard the werewolf surge through the cornrows with a furious shredding of withered leaves.

Quill's song came to an abrupt end mid-verse and was replaced with agonized cries that drove daggers into Emmett's heart. He'd failed. Without thinking, he made a move to go to Quill's defense, but what could he do? It was already too late.

Emmet hated himself as he turned and ran for his life,

thrashing his way through the corn. A wave of mind-fracturing fear swept over him when he heard a shattering snarl come from somewhere behind him. He heard the pounding of heavy claws rushing his way, the *whump, whump, whump* of cornstalks being crushed beneath the monster's great weight. If Martha was looking down on him, he prayed she knew he had tried to bring Quill home safe. God help him, he had tried.

Chapter 21

Distant screams carried on the wind. Anna heard them and a black thread of sadness coiled around her heart. She thought of Emmett's selfless willingness to risk his own life for another man's sake. How many innocent people would die before the sun rose?

Anna stood with Emmett's pistol in hand at the head of a steep staircase that descended beneath the farmhouse. Along with a snug pair of boots, she had found an ill-fitting muslin shift in the women's barracks. She had been glad to change out of her damp and soiled chemise while the children threw on their clothes.

Behind her, a pair of thick double-doors now lay flat on either side of the coffin-sized hole in the ground behind the house. Anna had wanted to wait until the last possible moment for Abigail to arrive before she joined the others in the darkness of the root cellar.

With the tortured wails echoing from somewhere deep in the cornfield, that moment had come. Anna could delay no longer. With a heavy heart, she hurried down the stone steps into the narrow space beneath, heaved the surface doors closed behind her, and secured the oaken beam that kept them fastened.

It was about a dozen steps to the base of the stairs where a second door stood, insulating the root cellar from frost. Anna entered and swung the door closed behind her. She shot the bolt and turned around. Nine little faces stared back at her in the lamp-lit gloom. The orphans were a ragtag bunch, comprising six girls and three boys. The youngest was a girl named Lizzie, who had just marked her fourth birthday a week ago. Emmett had brought them all candied apples to celebrate, and it had been the happiest day of her life.

The eldest among them was a standoffish twelve-year-old boy named Jonathan. Anna noticed the knees of his threadbare breeches were patched recently. Emmett must have taught himself how to sew since his wife's death. She recalled her mother's insistence that not all men were monsters like Virgil Stroud and Jericho Byrne. But a voice in her head whispered that Emmett was just the exception to the rule.

As Anna emerged from the shadows into the sickly radius of the lamp, Finney's anxious gaze locked on hers. The drifter was a young man, in his early twenties, but the world-weary look in his gray eyes made him seem old and haunted. Slim and of average height, he had a head of mussed, dirty-blonde hair. He had narrow shoulders, thin lips, a pinched nose, and half-moon cheekbones. A layer of sandy stubble roughened his tapered jaw. Somewhere in the cellar, he had found an old hatchet and a rusted hunting knife Emmett must have misplaced and forgotten. Finney now gripped both in each hand.

The young widower was quiet and said little. When the orphans had been frightened at being roused in the middle of the night and made to throw on their clothes, it was Finney who had calmed them with the misleading story that they were playing a trick on Emmett. It was one that required absolute silence as they hid in the cellar.

Anna observed his friendly interactions with the children as they hustled from the bunkhouse, and she thought Finney must have been a good father to the daughter he had lost. She wondered how it must feel to love someone so much that their loss would send her life spiraling into destruction like the young man's had.

Though she dared not speak it aloud, the dark look Anna now gave Finney conveyed everything he needed to know about Emmett and Quill.

Heavy shadows obscured the stone walls of the cavernous root cellar. It was about half as wide as the house itself, and its low ceiling comprised the timber planks of the floor above. Fresh from the harvest, overflowing baskets of potatoes, turnips, carrots, and cabbages were lined up on rough-hewn shelves against the walls. Bushels of corn hung in rows from the ceiling, drying out to be used as cornmeal. The musty scent of earth and stone hung thick in the stale air. It was cold down here and ridden with an insufferable dampness that crawled through flesh and curled-up close to the bone.

Anna held a finger to her lips to hush the children as she snuffed the lantern's flame. The cellar vanished. Darkness engulfed them—black, absolute, and smothering. There was a quiet shuffling of feet as the orphans crowded closer together, searching for reassurance in nearness to one another. Anna could make out the dim outlines of the figures gathered around her. Emmett had left his candle burning in the room above and its faint glow streamed through the cracks between the wide planks overhead.

Minutes crawled by like a spider as they waited in the dark. Every sound was deafening in the deathly silence. Anna's nervous heartbeat pounded like a war drum in her ears. Where was Abigail? How long before she brought the silver bullets to escort them to safety?

Something jounced the outer doors at the head of the stairs.

A nervous ripple spread through the huddled children. Anna worried one might giggle at their prank and give away their presence. If they could keep it together just a little longer, just a few more minutes until Abigail arrived…

Another thud. Louder. More insistent.

Anna heard Finney fumbling through the dark to her side. "What if it's Emmett?" he whispered into her ear.

"It's not," she replied in a low voice. "Emmett's dead."

A loud *bang!* shot through the cellar like a thunder crack. Whatever was out there was shaking the outer doors violently now. The children jolted as one and a few startled gasps escaped them. Anna flinched and hoped they weren't loud enough to alert the beast lurking outside. She felt tiny hands encircling her thigh in the darkness. Lizzie was clinging to her in silent fear. With the girl's face buried in her overcoat, Anna raised a hand to the back of Lizzie's head and stroked her lusterless curls.

The furious assault on the door stopped abruptly.

The stifled sound of the children's fearful breathing filled the cellar. Anna gripped her pistol tight and tried to picture what was going on outside. She doubted the werewolf could smash through the double-doors on the surface; they were thick and sturdy and secured with a solid beam. Lucretia had waited patiently for this moment. She and her followers wouldn't let a simple locked door stand between them and the orphaned girls. What were they doing right now? What was their next move?

A shattering crash came from somewhere upstairs.

Broken glass skittered and tinkled across the floor above. The cellar's ceiling creaked and groaned. The werewolf was stalking through the house.

Anna sensed the fear spreading like an infection among the children. They knew something was wrong now—they could *feel* it. They knew the truth: This was no game, and that wasn't Emmett upstairs. It was something else, something so horrific they had been hidden away for their own protection.

Anna felt a trembling against her side. Lizzie was whimpering with fright. Some of the other children were crying too and Anna knew it didn't matter if the beast upstairs heard them. It already knew they were down here—it could *smell* them. All it needed now was a way in. Anna felt her own heart slamming at her chest. She was afraid now too, not for her own life, but for what would happen to the children if Abigail didn't arrive soon to rescue them.

A shadow passed across the slivers of candlelight streaming between the ceiling planks. A scattering of dust sprinkled down upon them. Finney's knuckles cracked as he tightened his nervous grip on his hatchet. The monster was directly above them now, less than a foot over their heads. And it had stopped.

The beast was so close Anna could smell the musk of its hide, the reek of its blood-matted fur. Her entire body went tense with adrenaline as she held her breath. *Where are you, Mother...?*

A sound broke the silence, a guttural grunting and furious scratching at the planks over their heads. Anna's heart leapt into her throat. There was a squealing whine of nails being pulled loose, and a crack of light appeared where two floorboards abutted.

The werewolf was prying the plank loose with her claws.

The crack of light grew larger. Screams erupted from the children. Many of them were sobbing openly now, crying desperately for someone to save them. Anna knew she had no choice; they had to flee the cellar. It was only a matter of moments before the beast ripped through the ceiling and dropped into the cellar with them.

"*Go!*" she shouted.

Finney leapt into action. Hatchet in hand, he whipped open the inner door and dashed up the steps. Anna heard him fling open the heavy double-doors at the surface as she kept an anxious eye on the ceiling that was steadily being dismantled.

Candlelight now beamed through a gaping hole where the werewolf was prying up the floorboard. The long plank groaned under the strain and bent nearly vertical before it snapped in half with an ear-piercing *crack!* of splintering wood. The beast tossed the jagged fragment aside with a ferocious snarl.

The children shrieked and scattered in mind-shattering

panic as the fanged face of their nightmares appeared in the narrow gap above their heads. A clawed hand shot through, swiping at them as they bolted for the open door and the cool night air flowing down from above. Finney was there at the base of the steps, gesturing for them to hurry.

The werewolf's claw twisted around, dug its nails into another plank from underneath. Its coarse hair was silvery-gray.

Lucretia.

A chilling thought struck Anna as the children streaked past her. Where was Catherine Abell? She remembered how the werewolves had worked together back in the woods, how Lucretia had acted as a distraction while Catherine got ahead to ambush them. Where was Catherine now? Was she waiting for them outside while Lucretia flushed them out of the cellar?

It was too late; the orphans were already scampering up the stairs. Lucretia yanked on the ceiling plank and ripped it free. She tore another and another loose and cast them aside in a savage frenzy.

Anna retreated toward the door as the werewolf dropped through the jagged hole in the ceiling and landed on all fours. A murderous growl rumbled from deep in her chest as she bared her fangs and fixed her merciless eyes on Anna. Something unmistakably human flashed across her hideous face, something eerily like a leering grin.

Anna aimed her pistol and fired from ten feet away. The gun roared, and the cellar lit up with a blinding shower of sparks. But even as the acrid stink of gunpowder filled the air, another angry snarl cut through the smoky haze and made

Anna's flesh crawl.

The pistol had misfired.

Panic churned Anna's stomach. She flung the useless weapon aside as she scrambled backward through the interior door. The werewolf surged toward her on all fours. Anna slammed back against the steep stairs, kicked the door shut, just as Lucretia's clawed fist came crashing through the wood, smashing a hole the size of a skull. Anna kicked hard at the extended arm and something crunched in Lucretia's wrist. She roared and snatched her claw back.

Finney was up on the surface now, ushering the children up the steps. Their little feet pounded the stones as they raced up and out into the night. Anna kept one eye on the damaged inner door and glanced up over her shoulder. Four children still remained…

Three….

A ferocious growl rolled from the darkness beyond the door…

Two…

Jonathan would be the last to exit…

Lucretia crashed into the door and smashed the entire thing right off its hinges.

Anna fell back against the stairs, rolled her knees up to her chest, and caught the door with her feet as it toppled toward her. She pushed upward with her legs to keep the fallen door propped upright in the narrow stairwell like a shield between herself and the snarling werewolf.

BAM! BAM! BAM!

Lucretia hammered at the door, punching jagged holes through the wood. Her sharp claws missed Anna's legs by a hair each time. She screamed in terror. Her years of training and killing were forgotten. She was nothing but a frightened young woman fighting for her life against an unstoppable monster.

The werewolf's weight on top of her was crushing. Its black nails swung through a gaping hole in the door with a *whoosh*, but Anna squirmed to one side. Her scrabbling hand brushed over something cold lying on a step—Finney's hunting knife. He had lost it in the mad scramble to evacuate the children. Anna snatched it, thrust up, stabbed the blade through Lucretia's hairy forearm.

Blood sprinkled down on Anna as the werewolf roared and reared back from the door with the knife still stuck in her flesh. Anna seized her chance and rolled onto her stomach. She scrambled up the slick stone steps on hands and knees. She got halfway to the surface when Lucretia burst through the yawning opening of the doorframe and grabbed her ankle. The splintered wreckage of the door still lay wedged between them, but the werewolf's grip was strong and crushing as she hauled on Anna's leg.

Anna screamed and kicked with all she had. She clawed for the black portal of the surface door. "Help me!"

No one came. Where was Finney? Fleeing with the children or abandoning them to save his own skin?

The werewolf snarled and slavered as she clawed at Anna from below. Anna's desperate thrashing deflected much of Lucretia's assault, but the beast's nails still raked bloody streaks across her calves and thighs.

Fingers brushed against hers from above. Finney, reaching down from the surface for her. Anna stretched her hand out for him. Their fingertips touched.

Lucretia jerked Anna back.

Anna kicked hard again, caught the werewolf with a wicked shot to the snout.

Lucretia let out a furious grunt and loosened her grip long enough for Finney to haul Anna up through the door.

The children were already scattering for the road. Jonathan brought up the rear. Heroic beyond his twelve years, he had gathered up Lizzie and now ran with her on piggy-back, her little arms and legs wrapped tight around his scrawny neck and waist. Anna caught up to them and swept another little girl into her arms. She looked over her shoulder for Finney.

He wasn't there.

Finney had stopped a few yards away from the cellar stairs. The young widower was now brandishing his hatchet and backpedalling as Lucretia stalked up the steps toward him.

"Finney!" Anna cried.

He didn't turn around, just kept his eyes on the monster bearing down on him. "Get them out of here! I'll slow it down!"

Anna understood his grim intention. She didn't look back, but as she and the children dashed into the night, she felt a terrible despair pulling her under. The young man's sacrifice would be meaningless. She had no plan, no idea which direction they should flee; just a vague notion that they might find safety if they headed for town. Finney might buy them some time, but they were still a mile away. The children would never make it on foot, not before Lucretia hunted them all down.

Chapter 22

Finney clenched the hatchet in his fist and squared off against the giant beast as it rose on two legs and advanced. He had been helpless against the wasting fever that had claimed his wife and child back in Massachusetts. But this beast… at long last, this was something of flesh and blood that he could fight.

The hellfire in Lucretia's eyes threatened to set Finney ablaze as she glared at him, this wretched man who stood between her and her escaping prey. Painted silver in the moon's light, her fur bristled and her black lips quivered, eager for the taste of his flesh.

The monster charged at him.

Finney rocked back on one foot and tore down with the hatchet. Lucretia feinted to the side at the last second and Finney's blade went whistling through empty air. The momentum of his swing overextended his arm and presented an unguarded target. Lucretia slashed with a claw and rills of blood spilled from Finney's shoulder. He grimaced and whirled with another desperate swing aimed at the werewolf's midsection.

Lucretia danced back and lashed out again, harrowing four deep lacerations across Finney's chest from his right collarbone to his left nipple. He let out a cry and tried to retreat, but Lucretia launched herself and plowed into him. Her slavering jaws snapped at his face as they toppled backward. Finney straight-armed a palm up into the underside of her chin and forced her head up toward the sky. They hit the ground hard, the werewolf's weight crushing the air from Finney's lungs. He rolled aside, gasping, and swung again. The hatchet screamed through the air and bit into the meat of Lucretia's huge shoulder. But the blade was too dull to sink very deep.

Lucretia roared and whirled and Finney lost his grip on the hatchet. He scrambled back and shot a glance over his shoulder. The orphans were nowhere to be seen. How far had they gotten? Far enough to reach a neighbor? To find help?

Finney's entire chest was slick with blood now. His eyes cast about for the hatchet. It lay in the grass about ten feet away, but the monster was in his path. She stood upright on two legs, muscles rippling, her hideous face grinning like a fanged demon's.

Finney made a desperate lunge for the hatchet, but Lucretia lashed out a claw and ripped a long gash from one side of his abdomen to the other. Finney's stomach split open and his insides spilled out as he crumpled forward to the ground. His hot blood and viscera steamed like incense in the cool night air. Finney was still alive when Lucretia seized him by the throat and crotch and hefted him over her head. Blood rained down upon her, painting her crimson, and she spread her fearsome maw wide to devour the vital organs that fell out of the ghastly tear in Finney's gut.

When she had finished glutting herself, Lucretia hurled his weightless body aside, threw back her bloody head, and let out a spine-chilling howl of triumph that echoed for miles across the land.

Lucretia turned toward the darkened road. Her snout crinkled and twitched as she smelled the night air. At first, she could detect nothing beyond the intoxicating iron of Finney's blood. But then… ah, yes, there they were. The children weren't far. Lucretia could smell the pungent scent of their sweat, their unwashed clothes, the grease of their hair—their *fear*. She started after them, excited by her bloody feast and ravenous for more. She would spare and bless the girls, but the boys…

The sharp *crack!* of a rifle tore through the night.

Lucretia jerked forward and blood spurted from her breast as she pitched onto one knee.

Emmett stood at the edge of the cornfield thirty yards back. Tendrils of smoke twirled from the barrel of his rifle before dissolving in the wind. He looked like a dead man risen from the grave. His face was corpse-white, and the flailed flesh of his back was scarlet ribbons from where the werewolf had run him down in the cornfield.

Whether it was her rage at being wounded or her supreme confidence in her ability to hunt the orphans no matter where they fled, Lucretia now drew herself up and swung her attention to Emmett. A gut-churning growl rumbled up from her chest and rolled from between her deadly jaws.

Even from across the distance, Emmett saw the fury

blazing in the werewolf's golden eyes. A frozen pit opened up in his stomach. Woozy from blood-loss, his mind spun in and out of a murky fog. But he wasn't done for. Not yet, not as long as he could still run. The children needed more time to get away. Somehow, Emmett had to draw the beast away from them.

He bolted for the barn.

Lucretia sprang after him with a bloodthirsty snarl, charging on all fours.

Emmett's rusty heart screamed in his chest as he pumped his legs. The barn was a little more than twenty yards away now, but the giant beast was shooting at him like a cannonball. If only he could make it there before the monster chased him down, he might lock himself away safely inside one of the old cages.

Emmett skidded to the barn door with only moments to spare. His wild momentum slammed him up against the wide planks. He hauled on the sliding door. The wheels squealed along the metal track overheard. Emmett's head spun and his strength failed. The big door was too heavy, and he had too little life left in him. The feverish pounding of claws grew louder behind him. He managed to inch the door a crack wider, just wide enough to slip through. Lucretia launched through the air and crashed into the empty spot where he had been standing.

Emmett teetered on his feet inside the barn. The animals in their pens were a frenzied riot of panicked screeches and wails. The pigs let out wild, high-pitched squeals that pierced the brain while Emmett's only horse thrashed and kicked at the walls of her stall. Lightheaded, Emmett grabbed the door handle and tried to slam it shut in Lucretia's snarling face, but her clawed hand swung at him through the crack. He recoiled and spun around, but his head kept spinning. A gray mist overcame him and he staggered, fell to one knee, dragged himself back up.

The cages stood in the shadows at the rear of the barn. There were two of them, one on either side, cube-shaped and seven feet high. The left one hadn't been opened in years. Its lock was now rusted solid. The door to the other stood wide open from the last time Emmett had used the cage as a birthing pen for a goat. His vision dimmed dangerously as he staggered toward it.

From behind came a terrible rending of metal and a shattering crash as Lucretia tore the door off its track and thrust her way inside the barn. The animals were hysterical now, driven wild with terror at the bloodthirsty predator in their midst. Lucretia's murderous gaze found Emmett in the gloom. He was almost to the open cage. She sprang at him just as he lurched inside and grabbed for the cage door. It was a self-locking mechanism; all he needed to do was swing it shut and it would lock him safely of reach behind the cage's steel bars.

Lucretia's clawed hand shot out and seized the door before it could lock. She flung it wide again and slammed it back against the steel bars with a teeth-rattling *clang!*

Emmett retreated into the furthest corner as the savage beast stormed into the cage with him. She was walking upright now, sharp fangs bared, wicked claws spread wide and flexing eagerly. Her hairy head brushed against the overhead bars and she seemed to fill the whole cage as she towered over him. Emmett shrank back up against the bars. *At least I've bought the children some time,* he reasoned. *Maybe they'll make it to town, maybe they'll—*

The cage door swung shut with a loud *bang!* The lock clicked.

Emmett's gaze shot toward the figure backing away from the cage in the gloom.

It was Quill.

How in hell the man was still alive, Emmett couldn't tell. Maybe he was too crazy to know he should be dead. Quill's face and chest were a ravaged mess from where the werewolf had mauled him with her claws. One arm was a pulpy sausage casing filled with blood and mangled meat. His breathing was wet and ragged and filled with more blood than oxygen. His mouth opened and closed in a spastic rhythm like a fish out of water, and Emmett realized the crazy bastard was still struggling to sing. Quill fell to one knee, then the other, weakened and gasping for air. With his dying breath, he choked on the last verse of his song.

"*Happy the man who has a friend, formed by the God of nature…*"

Emmett had time to wonder if the simpleton had intentionally imprisoned the werewolf in the cage or if he simply thought this was part of some exciting and elaborate game. Either way, he may very well have saved the children's lives. Quill had always been fond of the little ones.

Lucretia recognized they had trapped her and let out a soul-withering roar. She slammed herself against the steel bars. The entire cage shuddered and rocked under the impact. The bars wouldn't keep her caged for long. Eventually, the welds that connected them together would break under the beast's enraged assault. Emmett just hoped he had bought the children enough time to escape before the creature freed herself.

With nowhere to turn, Lucretia vented her fury on the bars. They shook and rattled until she relented and whirled on Emmett, baring her gleaming teeth. She'd make this old man suffer for tricking her into this cage.

She lunged for him with a twisted snarl.

In that instant, Emmett had an image of Martha in his mind, and he knew he'd made her proud. She gave him that crooked smile that had so captivated him on that long ago stormy night as children. She silently told him he would see her again very soon. Emmett clung to that smile as Lucretia's fangs tore deep into his throat and sprayed the air with his blood.

Chapter 23

Anna kept the children huddled together for warmth as she herded them past the sloops and trading schooners that rocked side-to-side in the turbulent water of Burlington's harbor. It was a Sunday night, and the waterfront was eerily deserted. The remorseless wind sweeping across the lake chased whitecaps ashore like foot soldiers fleeing before a cavalry of phantom horses. The skinny piers of the harbor scratched like a reaper's fingers across the water. Moonlight shimmered and danced in mesmerizing patterns over the rolling waves. The sky was a blizzard of twinkling stars.

Behind Anna, at the north end of the harbor, the banners atop the twin flagpoles at Courthouse Square billowed and whipped in the night. The sharp *cracks!* of the fabric echoed like gunfire on some distant battlefield. Across from the lakefront, the warehouses, lumber mills, and mercantiles that lined the muddy track of Water Street were silent sepulchers drenched in silver moonlight. Enshrouded in the windswept darkness, the slumbering town now felt like a place abandoned and haunted.

Anna cast fearful glances in every direction as they went. Out here in the open with nothing but water to one side, it would be harder for Lucretia to take them by surprise. Still, there were too many shadows, too many hidden spaces where the terrible beast might lie in wait.

The harrowing flight from the poor farm had been among the most terrifying moments Anna had ever experienced. Her last vision before tearing her gaze away from Finney to shepherd the children away had been of Lucretia's monstrous form bearing down on him. The hatchet he wielded looked sad and pitiable in his hand as he confronted the monster, and Anna knew deep down he didn't stand a chance of survival. How many minutes had his sacrifice bought them? Five? Ten? Not enough to outrun the merciless werewolf.

And yet, the minutes somehow strung together one after another, with no sign that they were being pursued. Had Finney somehow prevailed against the odds? Or was Lucretia stalking them unseen at this very instant? It was in these moments that Anna had been most afraid, when the darkness seemed to have a life of its own and she waited in breathless anticipation of the beast's savage attack. Would she see it coming? Or would she find herself mauled and bleeding in the mud before she knew it, gasping her dying breaths while Lucretia feasted on the boys and made off with the girls? The ghastly thought spurred Anna onward.

More darkened farmhouses and cottages flew by with greater frequency as they drew closer to town, but Anna had insisted they keep moving. She remembered Lucretia's ruthless determination to reach the children back at the poor farm; the werewolf's fearsome power as she ripped through the farmhouse floor to get at them. There was no point in taking refuge anywhere else, not if the beast was still pursuing them. Seeking help would only result in more lives lost. Anna's only hope was to hole up with the children somewhere where they might disguise their scents from the werewolf; somewhere crowded, even on a Sunday night.

Somewhere like the Nobody Inn.

Now, with the crooked windows of the tavern glowing warm in the night at the southern end of the harbor, Anna wondered if she had made a terrible mistake. Was there truly any safety in numbers from these monsters? If Lucretia did hunt them down, there was nothing that would stop her from claiming the orphan girls, even if it meant turning the inn into an unspeakable bloodbath. Had Anna just led the devil right to their unsuspecting door?

Another chilling thought crept into Anna's mind: Where was Abigail? Anna was dreadfully aware that Lucretia had been alone in her attack on the poor farm. Had Catherine Abell gone after Abigail and Nathaniel? Or was she somewhere else, enacting some part of Lucretia's diabolical plan that had yet to be revealed? Even if Abigail was successful in forging silver bullets, she had no way of knowing where Anna and the children were now. She would be on her way to the poor farm, unaware of her daughter's whereabouts.

Nervous tension clenched Anna's insides like minced meat in a butcher's fist as she threw yet another uneasy look over her shoulder.

There was a figure behind them.

Anna felt the hairs rise on the back of her neck. She brought the children to a skidding halt. Obscured in the distant gloom, the figure huddled against the wind and shivered as it staggered toward them. Anna eyed the indistinct shape warily. Was it some drunk? Wobbling through the night toward another drink at the Nobody Inn? Or was it something else? Anna's pulse leaped as the figure drew nearer. She swept the children behind her, putting herself between them and the advancing figure. Then she glimpsed a youthful face illuminated in the moonlight.

"Kitty!" Anna rushed forward.

Kitty's clothes were damp and her fiery hair was a bedraggled mess. She was dreadfully pale as she squinted through the windswept darkness and peered at Anna in bewilderment. "Ms. Cuthbert?" she rasped.

Anna had almost forgotten the fake name she gave the barmaid the night before. God, had it only been twenty-four hours? It seemed like ages ago. Heedless of her own comfort, Anna shrugged out of her overcoat and wrapped it around Kitty's trembling shoulders.

"Where have you been?" Anna asked. "Where is Cassie?"

Kitty's voice was hoarse and her teeth chattered as she gave a hurried account of Mary's abduction of her daughter; of being held hostage in the cavern behind the waterfall; of her escape and failure to rescue Cassie; and of her terrifying flight through the woods along the meandering course of the river until it led her to the northern limits of town.

"How far was this cave?" Anna asked.

"Hard to say." Kitty frowned. She had lost all notion of time on her journey back to town. "Perhaps an hour upriver?"

Anna cast a look up at the moon's angle in the sky. She guessed they had only a couple of hours until midnight. Time was running short if they had any hope of rescuing Cassie.

"I… I didn't know where else to go," Kitty went on. "I couldn't go home; Mary knows where I live. I thought if I could make it to the Nobody, I could at least warn them about that monster."

"*Monsters*." Anna corrected her with an emphasis on the plural. "There are more than one—and they are after the children. We must get them somewhere safe."

"The Nobody?" Kitty suggested and nodded toward the inn. "It'll be as bustling now as any other night."

Anna shook her head. "I had thought the same, but I fear more people won't mean more protection from these beasts, just more victims."

Kitty's lips pressed into a grim line and they both went silent. Many of the children were shivering now as bitter gusts tore across the lake. Lizzie had sidled up to Anna's side and trembled against her hip. The oldest boy, Jonathan, had his skinny arms wrapped around the shoulders of a pair of forlorn children named Timothy and Anabelle. Wind-blown waves crashed against the thick pilings of the piers and sloshed onto the weather-beaten planks. The eerie clinging of ship bells rang through the unnerving quiet of the harbor as the boats rocked in their berths.

The haunting sound gave Anna an idea.

"The *Franklin*," she said.

Kitty's gaze flicked to where the great bulk of the steamboat swayed at the end of the long stretch of pier known as the Pine Dock. "You want to hide the children on the steamboat?"

Anna's eyes gleamed. "I don't want to hide on it… I want

to steal it."

Kitty gave her an incredulous look.

"The storm postponed today's departure," Anna explained. "And the ship couldn't sail past nightfall because the Narrows to the south are too dangerous to navigate in the dark. The captain will want to leave at first light, but he'll need to keep the boiler warm through the night. Am I correct?"

Kitty nodded. "On nights like this, Billy Miller goes out every hour to stoke the fire. He's likely killing time in the Nobody right now."

"So if we can get the children aboard, we can fire the ship's boiler and steam out into the middle of the lake, where we can wait until sunrise to be rescued." Anna looked at Kitty. "The deckhands and crew spend most nights at the Nobody. Surely you must have learned something about how the ship operates? Nothing so complicated as docking in a berth, but enough to head out to open water?"

Kitty bit her lip and a sly twinkle appeared in her green eyes. "Aye. Billy Miller stokes more than just the steamboat's fire while he's at the Nobody, if you take my meaning. He and I steal away to the ship when we're in search of a quick place to be alone. I've seen how the boiler and engine work. I suppose t'wouldn't be too much for the two of us to handle, really. We simply need to raise enough steam, weigh anchor, and steer straight ahead. 'Course, there's always the chance the boiler could explode should we cock it all up."

"Then it's a good thing we haven't any cocks, isn't it?" Anna threw another glance at the huge ship. She knew her plan was ludicrous. But it was the only one they had. "Come on." She ushered the children toward the *Franklin*.

The big steamboat bobbed in the water about seven or eight feet away from the end of the Pine Dock. At the pier's edge, the gangplank stood pointed skyward like a raised drawbridge. Anna threw open the winch. The timber plank hit the boat's deck with a sharp *bang!*, bridging the distance across the turbid water. Anna scooped Lizzie into her arms and led the way.

The gangplank hitched and swayed dangerously beneath her as she teetered across. A powerful gust slammed into her and almost blasted her off her feet. Her stomach clenched violently as she lurched and wobbled with the little girl's weight in her arms. Reeling on the brink of the plank, she somehow managed to regain her balance and hurried across the final few yards.

On the safety of the ship's deck, she motioned for the other children. She doubted any of the orphans knew how to swim. She held her breath, ready to dive into the freezing water should one of them pitch over while they shambled across the treacherous and unsteady gangplank.

Kitty was the last to board, following close on Jonathan's heels.

"Go fire the boiler," Anna said. "I'll find somewhere to shelter the children."

Kitty nodded and skirted along the port-side railing while Anna herded the children toward the cabins. When Kitty reached the service door accessing the boiler room, she found it locked. Undaunted, she returned to the enormous stacks of firewood mid-ship and found the hatchet Billy Miller left there. The last time she'd seen it, she had been so aroused by the sight of Billy's rippling muscles as he split the wood that she'd enticed him to bend her over right there by the firewood.

Now she brought the heavy axe head smashing through the boiler room door with a flurry of splinters. She swung again and punched another fist-sized hole in the door. Jagged fragments of wood gouged her wrist and forearm as she reached through and released the latch.

The boiler room swam in inky darkness. And it was hellishly hot. Kitty had been freezing, tip-toeing on the verge of hypothermia ever since she had dragged herself soaking wet from the river over an hour ago. The heat of the steamboat's massive boiler was a welcome comfort, even as beads of sweat sprang to her forehead.

It took a moment for Kitty's eyes to adjust enough to locate the oil lamp and spark the wick. Feeble yellow light spilled through the room as she crossed to the iron door of the boiler's big furnace. She swung it open and a molten glow suffused the space from the red-hot embers within. A stack of split hardwood stood nearby. Kitty filled her arms. She couldn't remember how many armloads it took to raise enough steam to power the ship, so she crammed the firebox until she could fit no more. The wood wasn't entirely dry, but within minutes it caught and Kitty swung the door closed on the blistering inferno raging beneath the enormous cylinder of the boiler.

Through the ceiling, Kitty could hear the pounding of little footsteps overhead as Anna led the children down the cabin corridor. The cabins were likely locked. Kitty resolved to bring the hatchet with her when she was done.

But first, she needed to know if the boiler needed water.

While the fire blazed below, she brought her ear as close as she dared to the boiler cylinder and heard a telltale rumble coming from deep within, like that of a pot bubbling on a hot stove. A high-pitched sound would indicate there was too much empty space, and the boiler required water, but the noise Kitty heard was low and resonant. Billy must have adjusted the water level on his last rounds of the boat. As she found the damper valve and spun it wide open to release steam into the engine's pistons, Kitty marveled how she remembered any of this given the torrid circumstances of her visits. How many times had she accompanied Billy here in the middle of the night? A dozen?

And then it struck her like a thunderclap, a realization so powerful it was paralyzing: Her father had designed ships exactly like this one. It was what had drawn him to America, the enticement that had led him to set foot on that disease-ridden ship that had ultimately claimed his life. As a girl in Dublin, his wondrous tales of engineering and the marvels of combustion and steam had fascinated Kitty. Those stories had faded over time, painted over by the years of hardship and privation on the poor farm. But they came rushing back to her in a flood now. It was hard not to wonder if her whole life had been preparing her for this moment when so many lives hung in the balance. She wished she believed in such things as she returned to the main deck and found Anna emerging from inside the ship.

"The children are gathered in the saloon," Anna said. "Come, help me with the anchor."

She led the way along the ship's rail to the bow. There, she inserted a wooden bar into the drumhead of the iron capstan around which the thick anchor rope was wound. Pulled taught by the weight of the anchor below, the rope stretched sideways across the deck before disappearing down a hole in the deck near the gunwale.

Kitty grabbed another bar opposite the capstan from Anna and they both leaned and pushed with all of their weights. The huge upright spool creaked and groaned as it inched clockwise. The exertion was staggering, the process painstakingly slow. The anchor wasn't deep, but the rope was as thick as Anna's wrist and sodden with water. It would normally take a crew of deckhands to haul up the weight.

Anna grit her teeth as she strained. She noticed the children watching them from the windows of the forward-facing saloon. Seconds stretched into minutes as the women toiled, revolving in slow circles around the capstan. Blisters surfaced in Anna's palms. The muscles of her thighs and back screamed for release.

The winch lurched, and Anna's head snapped up from where it hung between her shoulders. Jonathan had joined them. The boy had inserted a bar and was lending whatever strength he could muster to their efforts. Anna was about to scold him for leaving the saloon when she heard the heavy clank of the anchor dangling against the boat's hull.

They released the bars and staggered away, hearts pounding, breaths short and rapid.

"I told you to remain with the others," Anna huffed.

Jonathan glared back at her with a hard and defiant look. "You needed help… and I'm not a baby."

An angry rebuke sprang to Anna's lips, but she suddenly saw something of herself in the boy's fierce insolence. Except

Abigail had never treated her like a baby. She had never allowed Anna much of a childhood.

"If you want to be a man, look after the others," Anna said, her tone softening. "Lizzie's afraid. She needs you to make her feel safe." Her words seemed to work because the sharp look left the boy's face. He spun on his heels and trundled away toward the saloon door.

Anna turned to Kitty. "Have you an idea of a heading?"

Kitty nodded and motioned toward where the Juniper Island lighthouse glowed like a candle a little over three miles to the southwest. "To the left of the light is Shelburne Point, but if I stick to the right, there is nothing but open water."

Anna nodded. "How long will it take to raise enough steam to sail?"

Kitty shrugged. "Ten minutes? Maybe less?"

"I'll cast off the lines and raise the gangplank. Leave as soon as you can." Anna turned to go.

"Wait! Where are you going?" Kitty demanded.

"To save Cassie."

Kitty stared, her face aghast. "No! You can't go after her alone. You'll—"

"I know where to find help. But right now, I need to know if you can pilot this boat and get these children to safety by yourself."

Kitty bit her lip and thought it over. "I suppose I could get the boy to help me."

"Good." Anna turned again and headed for the gangplank.

"Miss Cuthbert…" Kitty called after her. "Good luck."

"Anna," was the reply. "My real name is Anna Jacobs."

Kitty gave her a quizzical look.

"I'll explain in the morning," Anna said. "When this is all over."

Anna scrambled across the heaving gangplank to the pier. Three taut hawsers kept the *Franklin* moored to the Pine Dock. Anna unfastened the thick lines from the iron cleats one after the other and hurled the ropes back over the rail onto the ship's deck. Kitty was gone now, having disappeared into the boat's interior to fetch Jonathan. All that remained was for Anna to raise the gangplank. For the first time in many hours, she took hope. This just might work. If Kitty could just get the children out onto open water, they would be safe from Lucretia and her werewolves.

Anna launched the last of the ropes across the water and turned around.

Right into the leering face of Jericho Byrne.

"Evenin', bitch," Jericho growled. "We was wondering when you'd come back."

Chapter 24

Nathaniel had always dreamed of being admitted to the prestigious halls of academia. Now he wanted nothing more than to escape alive. He swallowed as he crept down the silent corridor, but what little spit there was only scraped down his throat. His mouth had gone dry and his tongue felt parched and swollen. The muscles of his arms knotted from the weight of the big sledgehammer he carried. Perhaps the unwieldy instrument had been a mistake, but it was better than defending himself against a werewolf with his bare hands.

Somewhere in the building ahead, he could still hear the muffled thump of footfalls on wide pine planks. This was just what he wanted. The Middle College was laid out like a "T" with a large, circular pavilion sitting below the grand dome where the two perpendicular corridors met. If he could get to the pavilion before the beast came his way, he could lead it away from Abigail and the foundry.

Nathaniel was perhaps twenty yards away now, but he still couldn't discern from which direction the ominous footsteps were coming. His heartbeat quickened with his breathing as he drew nearer to the pavilion. He would be trapped between the beast and the foundry if it appeared before he arrived. He'd have no choice but to fight… and likely lose.

Nathaniel drew to a wary halt.

He could no longer hear the werewolf moving around. The heavy footsteps he'd been tracking had stopped.

Goosebumps prickled at Nathaniel's skin. Where had the monster gone? He strained his ears, listening for even the slightest hint of the beast's whereabouts.

Nothing.

The heavy silence of the building weighed on him like it was a physical force.

The creature could be anywhere.

Cold sweat slicked the nape of Nathaniel's neck as he steeled his nerves and crept into the pavilion. He had passed through this vast space countless times as a student; had stood in admiration beneath the vaulted dome that soared up to a point above him. This place made him feel like he had escaped the lowly confines of his impoverished village. Through hardship and toil, he had raised himself up to a rarified status worthy of respect. It was here, gazing up at the majestic frescos, that Nathaniel felt like he had done justice to the many sacrifices his grandfather had made for the sake of his future.

Cloaked in darkness, the ominous silence of the sepulchral pavilion now gave him a shiver. He swept a glance around the giant, shadowy ring. The way ahead led to the university's Museum of Natural History. To the right was the chapel. And to the left…

The front door.

Nathaniel stared at it and it struck him that he could simply leave. He glanced up and down the darkened corridors. There was no sign of the werewolf; nothing stopping him from walking right out that door. He owed Abigail and her daughter nothing. Both had almost killed him already tonight. Why shouldn't he escape with his own life? The door was locked, but from the inside. He could easily slip out onto the campus green and put his back to this night of horrors.

And what of the orphans? Nathaniel was reminded of what his grandfather would have said. Would his grandson condemn innocent children to die—and worse—simply because he was too much of a coward to stand and fight? Nathaniel gritted his teeth, disgusted with himself for even considering the idea of abandoning Abigail and leaving her unguarded and unaware. He had already shamed his grandfather's memory once tonight; he wouldn't do it again.

A floorboard creaked in the foreboding silence. Ahead. In the museum.

Nathaniel's heart jolted at the sound. His knuckles were corpse-white as he clenched the sledgehammer. What exactly was his plan? Every moment the monster remained distracted bought Abigail more time to escape with the silver bullets. Maybe she was already gone? Nathaniel could keep waiting in the pavilion, ready to sprint in another direction if the werewolf emerged.

But that wasn't good enough.

Nathaniel hadn't been able to stomach the silent pleading in Anna's terrified eyes back at the bottom of the Crucible's

Tomb. He had turned his back on her then, knowing what was to come yet still walking away to spare himself the terrible guilt. He had now spent every minute since that moment feeling spineless and ashamed. It was an awful feeling, one that gnawed at his gut with blunt teeth. When Anna and Abigail had both threatened to kill him, he had almost welcomed the end of his torment with relief.

He now had the sledgehammer. It might not kill the beast, but he could damn well cripple it before it slaughtered anyone else.

He headed for the museum.

The great double-doors waited in the gloom as he drew near. One door already stood open a crack. He gave it a soft push. It inched inward soundlessly on well-oiled hinges.

Nathaniel's blood hammered in his ears as he slipped through the gap, careful not to accidentally strike anything with the sledgehammer on his way in.

Moonlight illuminated the vast hall of the museum. It was two stories high, with an elegantly curved ceiling. Rows of tall glass cabinets marched away from the door on either side of a wide central aisle, displaying the museum's extensive collections of natural history. A diverse assortment of stuffed animals stood frozen in timeless silence behind the protective glass.

Larger specimens were positioned up the middle of the aisle, including a fearsome polar bear from the far north. A trio of stuffed Timberwolves were arranged in lifelike postures upon a pile of boulders at the center of the room. A second-floor mezzanine wrapping around the hall housed the geology and insect displays, including a special collection donated by

Dean Stroud himself. At the far end of the hall was a huge arched window.

There, silhouetted in the spectral light, was the werewolf.

Nathaniel darted behind a large display cabinet, but not before he got a good look at the beast's hideous face. One eye socket was nothing but a scorched hole—it was Catherine Abell. Why had she followed them here? If the orphans at the poor farm were indeed the werewolves' intended prey, why hadn't she gone there instead of hunting him and Abigail down to this place?

Nathaniel could think of only one explanation: Vengeance. Abigail had shot out the werewolf's eye and burned one of their kind alive. This beast wouldn't relent until she had torn her to pieces.

It wanted to make Abigail suffer.

A collection of osprey stared at Nathaniel with cold, dead eyes as he hid behind the giant glass display, waiting for his chance to ambush the monster. He willed himself to think clearly despite the red fog of terror that had overcome him. The floorboards creaked at the far end of the room; the werewolf was moving again, stalking the unexplored shadows. Nathaniel readied himself, but another question tugged at his brain: If the beast had tracked them this far, why was she still prowling around looking for them? Why hadn't she gone straight to the foundry?

The forge, Nathaniel reasoned. The werewolf hadn't been able to detect their scent through the stench of coal and soot.

But now that he'd left the foundry…

Nathaniel's gut twisted.

The cabinet behind him exploded in a hail of glass.

Catherine's huge reddish body crashed through and landed on top of Nathaniel before he could get out of the way. He hit the floor on his back with the sledgehammer wedged between them. The werewolf's hideous face was so close to his, hot drool spilled from her jagged fangs and landed on his cheeks. Her snout wrinkled, inhaling his fear, and she opened her jaws so wide Nathaniel could see down her throat. Seconds before she could bury her teeth in his face, he gripped the sledgehammer handle and thrust up with all of his strength. The massive head smashed into the underside of Catherine's elongated chin, and her mouth snapped shut with a loud click. Nathaniel pounded her again. She sagged a little to one side, just enough for him to scurry out from beneath her.

Catherine's black nails flashed out and slashed across his ribs as he escaped, furrowing four long slits through his flesh. He grimaced as blood poured in crimson rills down his side. Catherine dropped to all fours and Nathaniel swung the sledgehammer like a lumberjack trying to fell a tree. The blunt head whipped through the air and collided with Catherine's skull with a sickening crunch. She skidded sideways and ploughed into another cabinet. The glass exploded beneath her and the skeleton of the cougar within smashed to pieces. A shard of glass flew up and a hot flash of pain bloomed on the side of Nathaniel's head as it sliced through his ear. Blood sluiced down the side of his neck, but he kept both hands wrapped around the sledgehammer handle.

Catherine wasn't moving.

Nathaniel kept his eyes on her, breathing so hard his chest

burned from heaving, not allowing himself to believe for an instant that the beast was dead.

Her good eye flicked open.

Catherine slowly extracted herself from the glass and bones of the smashed cabinet and shook her bestial head from side-to-side, like a dog shaking off an injury. She let out a menacing growl and stood up on her legs, rising almost as tall as the polar bear that dominated the hall.

Nathaniel swung again, putting all of his strength into the blow. But Catherine's hand flashed out and caught the sledgehammer before it could do damage. She yanked it from his grip and tossed it aside like it weighed nothing.

Nathaniel backpedalled as the beast stalked toward him. The scattered bones of the cougar crunched beneath his feet. He swooped low and snatched up a sharp fragment just as Catherine lunged. He dodged at the last second and lashed out with the bone, pumping the spear-like tip into the werewolf's hairy torso and ribs. Blood spurted from the wounds and Catherine roared with pain and scalding rage.

Nathaniel knew this close-combat was a losing battle. His only hope was escape. With Catherine still reeling from his unexpected counterattack, he spun for the door and tore into the pavilion, sprinting for the front door. If he could just get the beast to follow him away from the building…

Catherine loped after him, still stunned and sluggish from her wounds. She read his intentions and took a sharper angle toward the door, cutting him off. He veered to the left, toward the chapel, changing direction so quickly he nearly broke an ankle. He hit the door and threw it wide.

The chapel yawned before him: a giant, two-story place of

shadows and echoes. At the far end was the ornate wooden altar, carved from white oak and waxed to a gleam. Beyond it, moonlight streamed through the stained glass of the enormous clerestory windows and painted the sanctuary with an otherworldly radiance. Rows of pews stretched toward the altar and arched columns on either side of the nave supported the galleries above.

Nathaniel slammed the door in the werewolf's face and dashed down the aisle toward the altar. He heard the thundering crash of the door exploding behind him, but he didn't dare turn around. The clattering of the beast's claws on the stone floor reverberated off the walls and climbed toward the vaulted ceiling as she bounded after him. Nathaniel raced past the altar, the effigy of the Savior seeming to stare down at him in mockery from the giant crucifix. He had made pacts with demons and left a woman to be raped; there was no hope for his salvation.

Nathaniel swerved to the left, darted behind the vestry to the crisscrossing staircase that led to the gallery. He reached the middle landing, turned, sprinting upward two steps at a time. The werewolf was so close he could feel her fetid breath hot against his ears. He was almost to the top when Catherine snarled and leaped at him, raking the flesh of his calf. A flaming agony raced up his leg. He stumbled up the remaining steps, pitching forward across the marble floor of the gallery. He pistoned his other leg and smashed his heel into Catherine's hideous face. She reeled and fell back, tumbling back down the steps to the middle landing.

Nathaniel dragged himself to his feet and fled through the gallery, toppling votive stands behind him and spilling candles across the floor as he went. Blood spilled from his shredded calf and left a long scarlet stain along the floor. Catherine came roaring up the stairs behind him, the heavy votive stands in her way barely slowing her as she tossed them aside.

Panic swept over Nathaniel as he burst through the door at the end of the gallery into the second-floor corridor beyond. Up here, there was nothing but lecture rooms and recitation halls. The werewolf charged after him as he bolted down the lightless corridor. The monster was getting closer and closer, and he could feel it. He turned a corner, slammed into another door. He whipped it open. Another set of steps ascended into darkness. Except these were so steep and narrow, they more closely resembled a ladder.

Nathaniel faltered as he gazed up into the gloom. He had no idea where the stairs led. Straight into a dead-end trap? But there was no turning around now. Catherine's huge shape rounded the corner and caught him hesitating by the open door. There was nowhere to go but up. He would rather throw himself from the roof than be devoured alive by this foul monster.

Nathaniel darted through the door and threw it shut. It shuddered on its hinges as the beast slammed into it at full speed. The darkness was smothering. Dust filled his lungs as he climbed hand-over-hand up the rungs. Strangely, the ladder seemed to curve beneath him. *It's tracing the contour of the great dome,* he realized. *I'm in the dome's framework, climbing up toward the cupola...*

Nathaniel's stomach clenched with terror. There was no way off the cupola. He was ascending to his own doom.

The door shattered below and the scrabbling of claws on wood rose up through the darkness. The cramped confines of the dome's wooden framework were slowing the enormous beast's ascent, but it was still gaining ground. Nathaniel's head rammed into something solid and he pushed up, cracking open the trap door that accessed the cupola. He climbed through and slammed the door.

The wind screamed and whipped at Nathaniel's hair and bloody shirt as he spun in a circle in the cupola high above the college and the town below. The space was perhaps eight feet in diameter, barely large enough for a fight. A wooden railing encircled it. Nathaniel peered over, saw the curve of the dome, the slopes of the college's roofs below it, the flagstones surrounding the building almost two hundred feet down.

This was it. There was nowhere left to run.

The trap door burst open behind him and Catherine came surging through. Spittle dripped from her fangs. She flexed her claws eagerly as she stalked toward him.

Nathaniel backpedalled, retreating before the advancing monster until he could go to further. He laid a hand on the railing, glanced over at the fatal drop below…

And then noticed a shape moving behind the merciless beast.

Abigail rose unseen from the trap door. Nathaniel's heart went cold at the sight of her. What was she doing here? Why was she risking everything to save him? Then he saw the steel in Abigail's eyes as she levelled her double-barreled pistol and aimed it at the back of Catherine's skull. He knew then that she wasn't here for him. Nothing mattered more to her than killing the monster.

Something in Nathaniel's eyes must have given Abigail away as she cocked the hammer. She fired just as the beast whirled around and batted her hand aside, almost knocking the pistol from her grip. The gun roared, but the silver bullet missed and shot harmlessly into the night.

Catherine slashed at her with a snarl, but Abigail skipped back, out of reach. The backs of her thighs banged up against the wooden railing that encircled the cupola. There was no more room to retreat. Catherine's fanged maw twisted in a triumphant leer. Abigail shrank back, cocked the hammer on the pistol's second barrel. She wouldn't get the shot off in time.

Nathaniel saw it happening. Abigail was going to die. With a wild bellow, he launched himself and crashed into the werewolf. He rammed his shoulder into her lower back, pumping his legs to drive her sideways.

Right over the railing.

Nathaniel and the monster toppled together, cartwheeling through the air as they shot downward. The college's great golden dome was much wider at its base than at the cupola from which they had fallen. Nathaniel completed a careening revolution and saw the outcropping where the wood dome joined the building's brick rushing up to meet him. He raised his hands in a futile gesture to protect his head, but he flipped over one more time in the air and the base of his skull collided with the stone with horrific speed.

The dull crunch of the impact was audible even to Abigail, high above. Nathaniel's head snapped forward on his broken neck and he went limp, dropping like a boneless doll.

Catherine tumbled next to him until they both slammed into the steep slope of the college's roof. Nathaniel's body bounced off the shingles and slid down, down, down over the edge into space again. He plummeted another sixty feet like a lead ball and hit the ground head-first like a hammer to an anvil. A spout of bone shards and brains burst across the flagstones from the top of his shattered skull.

From where she stood in the cupola high above, Abigail saw Catherine cresting the top of the building's huge western gable. The beast had scrabbled up the shingles and leered up at Abigail with her one good eye.

Abigail aimed the pistol. This time, she wouldn't miss.

A howl tore through the night.

It was distant, emanating from somewhere far down the hill and across town, near the waterfront. Still, Catherine's wolven head swiveled around in response.

They're communicating, Abigail realized with amazement. *Even over great distances, they're communicating... But for what purpose?*

The werewolf bounded across the length of the roof, moving with a preternatural agility Abigail had never witnessed in a monster so large. She aimed the pistol again, but she had missed her chance; the beast moved too fast, her zigzagging too unpredictable as she bounded around the bend in the hipped roof. Abigail squinted into the night, but she'd lost sight of the monster.

Catherine was gone.

Abigail's hand dropped into the pocket of her overcoat, felt the cold silver of the round bullets in her palm. It was time to find Anna and end this waking nightmare.

But first, she had to raid the university medical hall. Where they kept the amputation knives.

Chapter 25

Anna cocked a fist and fired it straight into Jericho's tobacco-stained teeth. His head snapped back and there was a brittle crack as blood spurted from his mouth. Anna had known men like Jericho all her life, men who only responded to fists, blood, and violence. To gain an advantage, you needed to strike fast and hard. There could be no hesitation.

Anna could only guess at how Jericho had tracked her down. Perhaps he'd been biding his time at the nearby Nobody Inn until he could make good on the beating she had put to him that morning. If it wasn't for the dire urgency of the moment, Anna might have been glad he had found her. After hours of being on the defensive, of fearful running and hiding, she finally relished the opportunity to hit something and make it bleed.

It was only when Jericho staggered away, spit out a broken tooth, and cupped his palms around the blood gushing from between his lips that Anna noticed he wasn't alone. Three other men lurked in the shadows behind him. One was possibly the largest man Anna had ever encountered. He stood like a granite monolith at well over six feet tall. His hair was long and greasy, and he had a bulging brow ridge and undertaker eyes. Anna noticed a bone-handled bowie knife strapped to his belt, but what chilled her even more was the horrid grin spread across his wide face as he eyeballed Jericho. It was as if the big man was taking some sick pleasure in his companion's pain, like a child pulling the wings from a moth.

Another of the men was of average height and was missing an eye. The empty socket was nothing but a murky black hole as he stood glaring at Anna. The third man was short of stature and thick with muscle. His eyes were black ink spots and his bushy black beard was streaked with white across his chin and jowls like the face of a badger.

Jericho's cruel eyes seethed with venom as he drooled blood and whirled on Anna. But it was the Badger who grabbed for her first. She shocked him with a slashing chop that shattered his wrist with a dull crunch. She followed up with a hammering uppercut to the jaw that clicked his teeth together so hard, he almost bit through his own tongue. He bellowed and reeled backward to the edge of the wharf, windmilling his arms to keep from pitching over into the dark water.

Anna scrabbled away, but powerful arms encircled her shoulders and chest. The enormous man had her wrapped tight in a crushing embrace. Anna struggled desperately against him, but the big bastard wasn't human; he was some immense juggernaut intent on grinding her bones to dust in his arms. She whipped her head back, aiming for his jaw with the crown of her skull. But the man was so massive, the back of her head only rebounded off his broad chest. She thrashed in his arms, but he kept her pinned tight as she kicked and swore.

Dirch grinned wickedly and swung Anna around as if she were weightless. Jericho was there, waiting. Blood dribbled down his chin and through the wiry sprouts of his goatee as he hauled back the fist of his good hand and hurled it at Anna's jaw. A blinding supernova of pain exploded in her head. Sensing she might lose consciousness and spoil his fun, Jericho went to work on her torso, hammering her with left-handed blows. Bright bolts of agony shot up from Anna's stomach and ribs as Jericho pounded her raw. The pain was numbing, debilitating, and there was a shameful part of her that yearned for the blessed solace of unconsciousness.

"Hey, Dirch!" said One-Eye. His good eye had a lustful gleam as he nodded toward a darkened space between two buildings across the lane.

Even through the mist of pain that had enveloped her thoughts, Anna caught his meaning. The shuddering panic it inspired roused her from the verge of blacking out. Even at this late hour, a witness could walk by at any moment out here on the waterfront. But if the men dragged her into that dark alley...

Anna thrashed with renewed vigor as Dirch manhandled her away from the pier's edge. His grip on her was vise-like, unbreakable. He hadn't drawn his big knife yet—he hadn't needed to—but what would he do with it once they got her into the shadows? Anna screamed, but the howl of the wind carried her voice away. And there was no one around to hear it. The Nobody stood almost forty yards away, but it was too raucous at this time of night for anyone to notice. Icy dread twisted Anna's stomach when she pictured the atrocities these men were about to let loose on her.

Without warning, Kitty appeared and cracked the back of Dirch's skull with a rowboat oar.

The giant crumpled to his knees like a dropped grain sack and released his grip on Anna. His eyes rolled back and blood sluiced down his neck as he toppled over in a senseless mound.

All at once there came a teeth-grinding screech of twisting metal and a tremendous splash of something big hitting the water.

"Kitty!" Anna gestured at the steamboat. The twin paddlewheels were turning, the boiler now giving off enough steam to power the engine. Unmoored, the *Franklin* was chugging away from the pier with no one at the helm.

Kitty ditched the oar and made a dash down the length of the Pine Dock. The moving ship had sheered the gangplank from the pier. The gulf of water between it and the boat was expanding by the second. Kitty hit the edge of the pier at full speed, vaulted out over the water, arms windmilling, fingers stretching for the boat's deck rail…

And missed.

Kitty's mad leap fell short. Her outstretched palm slapped against the boat's gunwale and she would have splashed into the black lake if she hadn't tightened her grip at the last second. She now dangled precariously from the side of the boat, her feet swashing through the waves as the *Franklin* picked up speed and steamed from the harbor toward open water.

A body slammed into Anna and tackled her to the ground.

One-Eye landed on top of her with a grunt and held her pinned. One powerful hand clamped tight around her throat and clenched her windpipe while the other found her breast and squeezed at her nipple. Anna gasped and flailed at him, scratching for his good eye. But his stiff arm kept her nails out of reach. Pinpricks of light burst in her eyes as he choked the breath from her. She felt herself plummeting into a black abyss as the man held her down and groped her. She was aware of Jericho and Badger looming over her, waiting their turns.

A ferocious snarl ripped through the harbor.

Something huge tore One-Eye away.

Anna's eyes snapped open. She gulped air down her bruised throat as she rolled from her back to her side.

Lucretia held One-Eye pinioned to the wharf beneath her claws.

He was shrieking madly, the white of his one good eye gleaming as it rolled in his head. Saliva dripped into his face from Lucretia's great wolven jaws as she pressed him flat beneath her. She lowered her head, lips curled back, her terrible fangs inches from his nose. She lingered there a moment, exulting in his terror. Then her maw hinged wide and crunched down on his face.

The man's shrieks dissolved into a wet gurgling as his jawbone shattered and blood invaded his windpipe. His legs jerked and spasmed as if he was being shot-through with electricity. Blood bubbled around Lucretia's lips as she clamped her teeth together and whipped her head savagely from side to side. With his flesh torn away, all that remained of One-Eye's face was a ruined scarlet skull.

Jericho and Badger were backing away now, staring wide-eyed at the ghastly scene as if it was unfolding too fast for their brains to transmit the signal to run. Anna saw her chance and took it. She dove for the oar Kitty had discarded and swung it with all she had. The staggering blow caught Badger in the temple and his head spun around with a sharp and sickening *crack!* Neck broken, he twirled on his feet like a drunken ballerina and pitched over the edge of the wharf into the dark water below.

The *Franklin* had steamed beyond the lights of the harbor now. Smoke belched from the tall stack and blotted out the stars, stealing their light from their sky. The ship still reflected the moonlight, but Anna couldn't tell if Kitty had managed to haul herself aboard or if she had plunged into the lake. With no one at the wheel, the children were alone on an unmanned steamboat charging at full speed into the black reaches of the lake.

Dirch had now regained consciousness. Incredibly, he was lumbering toward the beast who stood hunched and feasting on his friend's mutilated corpse. He still wore a twisted grin —Jesus, the evil son of a bitch really was insane.

Lucretia reared up on two legs as he approached. The two were nearly the same height. Blood dripped from her lips and there were scraps of flesh caught between her jagged teeth as she faced him, her muscles rippling beneath her thick silver hair. With a powerful swipe, she tore down at him with a claw, but Dirch knocked her swing aside with his club of a forearm. He balled a meaty fist and pounded it into the side of Lucretia's snout. She rocked back.

Again and again Dirch struck, bashing Lucretia in the face

with his hammering blows. She pounced at him again, but Dirch ducked just in time to feel the whoosh of her nails whistling over his head. His palm flew to the big knife on his hip and he sprang up from his crouch, stabbing downward at the same time. The blade plunged deep into the thick cords of muscle where Lucretia's shoulder met her neck. She let out a furious roar and swiveled away, ripping the knife away from Dirch's grasp.

Lucretia's eyes were fiery slits as she bared her teeth and flew at him with claws outstretched. Dirch's hands shot up and caught both her of wrists in his crushing grip. They stood locked together, pressing into each other like an unstoppable force meeting an immoveable object. Dirch's thick arms quivered under the strain of resisting the werewolf's inhuman strength until, lightning-quick, Lucretia snapped her jaws and clamped down on his right arm, severing it at the elbow.

The maniacal grin vanished from Dirch's face and he let out a hoarse wail. Blood spewed from the ragged stump of his arm as he wobbled backward. Lucretia lashed out with a claw and clenched him around the throat. Her other claw punched into his stomach and tore through the flesh into his guts. Blood spilled from the hole in his belly and splattered the ground at his feet as Lucretia twisted her claw, reaching up inside him, shredding his vitals. She drew him toward her, her nails now somewhere up behind his ribs. More blood bubbled up from between Dirch's lips. His arms and legs flailed and his body jerked spasmodically as the beast pulled him even closer. With a flash of her wicked teeth, Lucretia bit down on his larynx and tore a gash in his throat all the way through to his spine.

Anna and Jericho had scattered in opposite directions. Jericho was bolting from the wharf with as much speed as his scrawny legs could muster. Lucretia dropped Dirch's corpse like a sack of rancid meat and sprang after him, bounding on all fours, incredibly fast as she ran him down.

He didn't get far. Lucretia launched herself and landed on Jericho's back. They hit the ground together in a tumbling heap. Jericho rolled away but Lucretia was already on her feet, towering over him as he knelt in the street before her like a penitent begging for absolution. Tears poured from his swollen eyes and his shoulders quivered and shook with unrestrained sobs.

Lucretia's clawed fingers were like five scythes as they sliced through the air and ripped through his throat, cleaving flesh and tendon and spine. Jericho's head tumbled from his shoulders as if he'd been guillotined. Blood sprayed from the severed artery as his decapitated body toppled forward at the werewolf's feet. Soaked in blood, Lucretia unleashed a rapturous howl and swung around, lusting for more carnage.

Anna was already gone, vanished into the night.

Chapter 26

Kitty was losing her grip. The cold lake-water was up to her calves as the steamboat dragged her along with her clinging to its side. The ship's gunwale was slick and her fingers were slowly slipping. She tried to tighten her already white-knuckle grip, but the increased pressure only made her fingers slip even more.

Stinging wind lashed at her face and billowed her sodden overcoat. Ten yards to her left, the ship's massive paddlewheel churned through the water and soaked her with spray. The waves tugged at her from below and she was too drained from her exhausting ordeal to resist them. The numbing sensation in her fingertips was excruciating. How easy it would be to let herself slip below the water's surface and find serenity deep in the icy darkness.

A face appeared over the rail. Jonathan was there, peering down at her with wide brown eyes. He bent over the rail, stretched his hand out for her, but his arm was too short to reach. He vanished from sight for a moment before returning with a length of mooring rope. He flung it over the side, but the wind caught it immediately and blew it out of Kitty's reach. Jonathan swung the rope around so that it would blow into Kitty and not away from her. It now dangled about a foot away from her face, writhing in the air like a snake enthralled by a charmer.

Kitty hesitated. What was the rope tied to? And how long was the line? Would she let go of the gunwale only to plunge deep into the lake? Her fingers were cramped claws as they slowly, slowly lost their hold. It was now or never. With her last shreds of strength, she grabbed the rope with one hand. *God, let it be tied to something sturdy!* Her heart slammed in her chest as she let go of the deck with her other hand.

The rope jerked under her weight. For one heart-stopping instant, Kitty felt herself plummeting into the lake. She had enough presence of mind to snap her mouth shut before it flooded with icy water.

But the rope held.

The water was up to her knees now as the big ship steamed ahead at full speed. Kitty bounced and splashed through the waves like a fish at the end of a line. Hand-over-hand, she climbed the rope, hauling herself upward. Jonathan did his best to help, pulling on his end until she had climbed even with the rail. She swung a leg up and heaved on the rope until she spilled over onto the ship's deck.

Jonathan crouched before her, his boyish face staring into hers as she lay sprawled in a heap, struggling to catch her breath.

"Christ A'mighty, boy," she gasped. "Don't you ever listen? You were supposed to stay with the others 'till I got back."

Jonathan looked wounded and was about to snap back

something sharp and cutting when Kitty managed a wry smile and clambered to her feet. "C'mon. We've got a ship to right."

The *Franklin* rocked beneath them as she led Jonathan to the smashed door of the boiler room and into the sweltering chamber beyond. Part of Kitty just wanted to remain here, soaking in the heat, letting it sear the numbness from her bones. But there wasn't time.

"You see this? This is the damper valve," Kitty explained, indicating the iron wheel protruding from the boiler. "It controls the ship's speed. I'll be in the wheelhouse right above you, but there's a bell up there that I need you to listen for. Every time you hear it chime, I want you to turn this valve a quarter of a turn counter-clockwise. Four chimes mean one full revolution. Like this…" Kitty demonstrated before opening the valve wide open again. "Do you understand?"

"Yes, ma'am." Jonathan tried to project confidence, but the look in his eyes betrayed how daunted he was at the responsibility being thrust upon his shoulders.

"Listen carefully for the bell," Kitty warned. "You'll know it when you hear it. And for God's sake, *do not* leave this room, no matter what."

Jonathan nodded again, and Kitty left him. The wind howled and swirled around her as she ascended the ladder to the pillbox of the ship's tiny wheelhouse. Her stomach tightened into a knot when she peered out the window.

With no one at the helm, the lake's strong current had veered the ship southward. It was now steaming straight toward the fingerlike peninsula of Shelburne Point.

Kitty laid her hands on the big wheel and was struck by the

uncanny sense that her father was there in the wheelhouse with her. A chill tingled up her spine to the base of her neck as she heaved on the wheel, steering the ship hard to starboard. The sudden shift in direction threw her sideways into the wheelhouse wall. Somewhere below, dishes and crockery flew from their cabinets and crashed to the floor. Kitty hoped the children were alright as she recovered and retook the helm.

The ship changed course toward the northwest, but it was still moving too fast. Juniper Island lighthouse stood directly ahead, perhaps a little over two miles away. The squat block of the island jutted from the lake like a tombstone. At the northern end, sheer cliff faces slanted straight down into the water from the trees above. But the eastern side leveled off to the pier where Malachi Corning, the lighthouse keeper, moored his boat at the southern tip.

The island wasn't wide, only about a quarter mile from end to end, but at their current speed, they would never clear the land in time to keep from crashing ashore. Kitty thought about swinging south again. The distance between the island and Shelburne Point was about a mile, but she had no idea how deep the water was. With a ship this big, it would be like threading a needle. The only real option was to slow the ship and hope the current wouldn't keep pushing them toward the island. Kitty reached for the bell to signal Jonathan.

A shrill scream tore loose from somewhere in the ship below her.

Kitty's blood ran cold. Something was wrong with the children.

But she couldn't leave the helm, not again. She needed to

keep the ship hard to starboard if they had any hope of missing the oncoming island.

Another shriek. Terrified. Laden with panic.

Kitty knew she didn't have a choice. With a fearful glance out the window at the approaching hump of land, she left the wheelhouse and scrambled down the ladder to the main deck. She raced forward, dashing up the ship along the rail toward the bow and the outside entrance to the saloon.

Through the windows, a monstrous sight brought her to a dead halt.

The children were huddled up against the glass, screaming hysterically as an enormous beast stood on two legs on the other side of the big room. Kitty had never beheld a werewolf before—her silver hairpin had halted Mary's transformation before it was complete—and what she saw now stole the breath from her lungs.

The huge beast's hair was the coppery-red of a slaughterhouse floor and it was missing an eye, the socket nothing more than a blasted hole. The beast must have stolen aboard during the chaos of the melee back on the pier and waited, biding her time until the ship was far away from the safety of land.

Now, there was no escaping her.

Catherine Abell's good eye blazed hungrily as she stalked toward the children, tossing aside the tables and chairs that stood between her and her prey. Behind her, the narrow cabin corridor stretched back into the heart of the ship.

Caught on the deck outside, Kitty dashed to the saloon entrance and found it locked. She didn't hesitate. Shielding her eyes with a forearm, she brought her other elbow crashing through the pane of glass. Shards fell over the screaming children as Kitty reached through and swung open the door. The orphans spilled out onto the foredeck and scattered in all directions.

Catherine let out a bone-numbing growl and bared her fangs in a hideous grimace. Kitty saw death coming in the beast's merciless glare.

All at once, the werewolf roared with pain and crumpled to one side.

Jonathan stood behind her at the mouth of the corridor. He clutched Kitty's forgotten hatchet in his hands. He heaved another swing and hacked at the beast's enormous arm. The blade sank deep into the meat of the werewolf's rippling bicep and chunked into the thick bone. Blood poured from the horrific gash as Catherine wheeled away and ripped the hatchet free of her arm. She tossed it aside and swung around. But Jonathan was already fleeing, sprinting away down the length of the cabin corridor.

Catherine dropped to all fours to run him down, but her wounded arm gave out beneath her. The boy hadn't had enough strength to sever the limb, but he'd still crippled her enough to force her to walk on two legs. She was slower upright, but still fast enough to give chase and devour his young flesh.

She stopped, her cunning intelligence flashing warnings. The boy was leading her away for a reason, drawing her into the cramped confines of the ship's interior. But her real prey was somewhere outside on the main deck. She turned to where Kitty was retreating through the door and sprung, landing short of the door. Kitty threw it shut in the beast's face, but Catherine crashed right through, landing on the main deck of the bow.

Kitty scrambled backward and slammed into the cold iron of the capstan. She dashed around it, keeping the big cylinder between her and the snarling werewolf. Catherine stalked after her, razor-sharp claws gleaming in the moonlight as she circled around. They exchanged positions as they revolved and the monster now lurked with her back to the lake and the ship's prow.

Kitty took a step back, daunted by the beast's towering height and powerful muscles. And that's when she noticed the bars. She and Anna had never removed them from the capstan. Three four-foot lengths of heavy timber still jutted out from the drumhead parallel to the deck. Kitty's eyes flicked to the winch lever.

Catherine read her intentions and lunged across the capstan for her, but it was too late. Kitty kicked the winch release and dropped flat against the deck. The capstan went whipping around, releasing its tension as the great weight of the anchor fell and splashed into the water. A bar whizzed over Kitty's head and slammed into Catherine with bludgeoning force. Already reeling from her wounded arm, the blow sent her flying into the deck rail and she pitched over into the lake.

Kitty dashed to the rail and peered down at the moonlit waves. There was the beast, tangled in the length of anchor rope and thrashing in the water. Except the anchor was never intended to be dropped while the ship steamed ahead at full speed on open water. Instead of sinking downward and dragging the monster into the black depths with it, the anchor was now trawling alongside the ship back toward the giant paddlewheel.

Kitty saw what was coming and a sickening feeling swept through her gut.

The anchor took the werewolf with it as it struck the spinning wheel. One of the iron prongs hooked a paddle, and the rope was snared instantly. The giant wheel continued to churn, spooling the anchor line around itself like a twenty-foot-tall fishing reel.

Tangled in the rope and bound to the wheel, Catherine plunged into the water and reappeared a moment later with each revolution. The entire length of the anchor rope was soon wrapped around the paddlewheel and its crankshaft. Stretched impossibly taut between the capstan in the bow and the wheel mid-ship, the rope ripped out of the hole in the gunwale and tore a gash in the deck. It quivered in the air, the capstan groaning dangerously under the incredible tension.

Snarled with rope, the paddlewheel strained to keep turning but failed. Its crank seized and its revolutions came to a shuddering halt. Catherine's cycle of immersion ended with her hanging in the air a few feet above the waves. A length of rope was wound tight around her dripping torso, chest, and throat. It cut deep into her hairy flesh as the wheel stretched the line even tighter, as if she were lashed to some medieval torture rack. Blood ran in rivulets down her chest. Her yellow eyes bulged in their sockets and filled with the scarlet spiders of burst capillaries as the rope cut through her windpipe. An instant later, it crushed her spinal column and severed her neck. A gout of blood shot into the air as the werewolf's fearsome head rolled from her shoulders and splashed into the water.

A sickening squeal of grinding machinery tore loose from somewhere in the ship's bowels. The strain on the paddlewheel was too great; the crank linking it to the engine snapped. There was an ear-splitting screech of rending metal as the gigantic wheel tore free of its mounts and fell into the lake with an immense spray of water. It bobbed like a giant buoy in the waves for a moment before it sank beneath the surface and disappeared into the fathomless blackness. With the engine still chugging at full steam, a broken connecting rod whirled around wildly in the engine room and punched a hole in the ship's hull just below the water line.

Horror washed over Kitty. She spun from the rail and made a mad dash for the ladder to the wheelhouse. Water was already sluicing through the hole in the hull. They were going to sink—soon. She had only one option: She had to run the ship aground.

The remaining paddlewheel continued to churn at full steam, spinning the ship northwest toward open water. Kitty heaved the helm hard to port, aiming for Juniper Island. The lighthouse stood dead ahead, less than a mile out. Kitty angled the ship toward where Malachi Corning's small boat bobbed alongside the pier at the southern tip of the island. If only the *Franklin* could remain afloat long enough to reach the island's rocky banks…

Kitty strained at the helm and shot a glance over her shoulder through the wheelhouse window. The children huddled together on the open deck of the ship's stern. Jonathan was there with them, doing his best to comfort the young ones who were crying. Kitty swung her attention back to the island. It was half a mile out now, but they were moving too slow against the headwind. Under the power of just one paddlewheel, they would never make it before the ship took on too much water and sank.

A terrible shudder rocked the ship. The engine let out a tortured rumble somewhere down below. Water had flooded the huge pistons. The remaining paddlewheel ground to a sudden halt mid-turn.

They were dead in the water.

Despair crashed over Kitty. They were going to sink and drown here, only a quarter of a mile away from the island. At this distance, she could make out the moonlit spires of the trees, the brickwork of the lighthouse, the weathered clapboard of the lighthouse keeper's cottage.

Momentum kept sweeping the ship onward toward the shore. Kitty kept her hands on the helm, pointing the prow toward the island's pier. The water below decks was weighing the ship down and it was sitting lower in the lake now. Waves sloshed over the gunwale onto the main deck as the ship rocked and swayed, drifting ever nearer to the island.

Closer…

Closer…

Kitty stuck her head out of the wheelhouse, shouted down at Jonathan and the other children. "Hold on to something! We're going to crash!"

Suffused with silver moonlight, the trees of the island loomed like jagged teeth ahead. Without warning, the ship rose and there was a splintering groan as the hull scraped over the submerged rocks that guarded the island. It surged onward, closing the distance to the pier and the banks beyond.

Yards…

Feet…

Kitty gripped the helm and braced for the impact.

With a booming roar, the ship's bow crushed the pier and smashed ashore.

The impact threw Kitty forward into the helm as the big ship plowed ahead onto the island. One of the helm's wooden handles punched into her ribs and she felt something crack. The air burst from her lungs and a blast of pain exploded in her side, one so excruciating it blinded her to the trees that were toppling across the main deck as the steamboat crashed through their midst. A haze of agony clouded her vision as the careening ship came to an abrupt halt. She peered out the window.

The bow had come to rest about twenty yards inland. What used to be the point of the ship's prow was now a blunt ruin. The bow had crumpled inward as it furrowed a deep trough through the rocks and mud before butting up against the unyielding stone of a steep ridge. The back half of the ship from mid-ship to stern still sat submerged in the shallow water and the other paddlewheel had sheared free of the hull as it collided with the land. It now lay on its side in the shallows. Waves washed over it in the darkness.

There was a pounding in Kitty's head and, for some strange reason, it sounded like a voice shouting for her. She became dimly aware of a lantern glowing in the darkness below. There was a figure there on the ground. It was hopping up and down atop the ridge and yelling something. Kitty realized it was the lighthouse keeper, Malachi Corning. And then she understood what he was shouting.

The ship's boiler was going to explode at any moment.

Icy panic gripped Kitty as she abandoned the wheelhouse and shambled down the ladder to the main deck. The searing pain in her side was so intense, bile leaped into her throat and she thought she would vomit. The children were already evacuating the ship, clambering over the smashed prow and leaping to the firm ground of the ridge. Malachi ushered them away, urging them to get clear of the wrecked ship as fast as they could.

Still on deck, Jonathan rushed to Kitty as she staggered toward across the bow. Her head swam. She didn't know how, but she found herself on the ground with Malachi Corning's arm supporting her as he hustled her away from the wreckage.

Malachi was a wiry war veteran with a craggy face and a bushy gray goatee. He steered Kitty up the ridge toward the lighthouse and the keeper's cottage, rushing as fast as she could manage. Every ragged breath was a searing flame in her chest.

The children had already reached the top of the ridge and were racing across the plateau there. The lighthouse loomed ahead, its array of lamps and reflectors beaming their light from thirty feet over the clearing. Only Jonathan trailed behind. He cast furtive glances back at Kitty as she and Malachi struggled up the rise. A strange whistling reached Kitty's ears, and she realized it was coming from the wreck. It was growing louder, more intense, more insistent.

They crested the ridgeline just as a shrieking roar erupted behind them and shook the earth beneath them. The darkness of the island lit up a hellish orange as an enormous fireball unfurled and bloomed in the sky. A concussive wave deafened Kitty's eardrums and then she was flying. She and Malachi were ripped from their feet and thrown through the air with a scorching gust of wind at their backs. For a split-second, Kitty glimpsed her own shadow blasting across the ground beneath her as she sailed weightlessly. Then she crashed back down and tumbled in a mass of flailing limbs. Shrapnel and wreckage rained down around her.

Everything felt broken. The world was absolute silence. Kitty lay on her back, unable to move. *This is death*, she thought. Her mouth was full of the rotten taste of grit and blood. She caught a glimpse of shadowy flames reflected on the trees and wondered if this was what Hell would look like. Black smoke curled into the night sky, obliterating the brilliance of the moon and stars. An acrid reek invaded her nostrils, and when the air made its way to her burning lungs, it made her want to stop breathing. A gentle snow had started to fall. Kitty closed her eyes and let it collect on her eyelashes until she realized the snow was actually falling ashes.

When Kitty opened her eyes again, Jonathan's face filled her vision. His wavy hair spilled into his eyes as he stared down anxiously into hers. Blood trickled down his forehead from a cut on his scalp. His mouth was moving, but she couldn't make out what he was saying. Her ears felt like they were stuffed with cotton. She blinked, swallowed blood, nearly retched. Jonathan slipped his hands beneath her and lifted her back off the ground, cradling her in his thin arms. She could make out some of his words now. They were indistinct and reverberating, as if uttered from behind a stone wall. He was pleading with her not to die, over and over again.

Please don't die...

The other children gathered around them. From the corner of her eye, Kitty spied Malachi staggering to his feet. Perhaps she would not die after all. Perhaps she should listen to the boy who obeyed no one.

To Jonathan's great surprise, Kitty reached for his face with a weakened hand and kissed him. The blood on her lips left a stain on his, but it wasn't nearly as red as the blush that rose to his cheeks.

"Boy," Kitty groaned as she dragged herself upright. "If only you were a few years older..."

The ringing in her ears crippled Kitty's balance. She wobbled as she took in her blasted surroundings. The *Franklin* was gone, its flaming wreckage slowly sinking beneath the wind-blown waves. All that remained now were far-flung pieces of smoldering timber and twisted iron. The trees around the site of the explosion had been levelled in all directions. Jagged tusks of tree stumps now sprouted from the earth in a huge semi-circle from the shoreline. The steep ridge had shielded Kitty and the others from the worst of the blast.

They had made it. Unless Malachi Corning was a bloodthirsty monster, the children were safe on the sanctuary of the island.

All except for one.

Kitty's thoughts went to Cassie. Smoke burned her eyes as her gaze travelled across the moonlit gulf of water to where the town of Burlington lay slumbering in the distance. Here and there a lantern twinkled in the night, but otherwise the town was cloaked in darkness.

"May the road rise to meet you, Miss Jacobs," Kitty murmured. "Whoever you are."

Chapter 27

The black hole of the tunnel's entrance stared at Abigail like an empty eye socket from the side of the mountain. "How fitting," she remarked as she dismounted the horse by the river's edge. "In the myth of Remus and Romulus, the Wolf Mother suckled the infant twins in a cave next to the Tiber River."

Anna was already moving away through the darkened forest. She had found Abigail kneeling over Nathaniel's shattered corpse at the foot of the Middle College building. His limbs were splayed at awkward angles and he was facedown in a crimson lake of blood oozing from his ruptured skull.

Anna's gaze had travelled from Nathaniel's ruined body to her mother's stony face. "You?"

"No," Abigail replied. "He died so that I might escape with these." She held up a silver bullet that glinted in the moonlight. Maybe she was looking too hard for it, but she thought she detected the slightest hint of disappointment in Anna's expression.

After retrieving the horse from its hitching post, Abigail had listened intently to Anna's terrifying account of the night's horrors as they sped through the forest along the riverside toward the waterfall and the secret cave it concealed.

Now Abigail left the horse behind and threaded through the trees to join Anna. She could hear the steady roar of the waterfall upriver and around a bend. The lustrous orb of the full moon was nearly directly overhead now, throwing ghostly rays through the treetops. The forest was deathly quiet around them, the silence of a place holding its breath and hiding from danger.

"We'll need light," Abigail said, eyeing the shadowy tunnel.

Anna tore a strip from the hem of her threadbare shift and Abigail wrapped it around the end of a thick branch. She then produced a vial of ether she had lifted from the university's chemical laboratory, sprinkled some on the muslin, and sparked it with a flint. The flammable liquid ignited, but the light of the makeshift torch was feeble.

"I don't like this," said Anna. "Walking into a den of werewolves with only a few silver bullets and a couple of knives?"

"Nor do I," Abigail conceded. "But we haven't any other choice, have we? This is where Kitty said they were holding Cassie. We must go in there after her and we must do it now. Look at the moon; we've only minutes until midnight."

Abigail brandished the flickering torch and turned for the yawning tunnel that would lead them through the mountain's shoulder to the werewolves' cave. As she entered and left the lambent moonlight behind, she was reminded of the inscription above the gates to Hell in Dante's *Inferno*:

Abandon hope, all ye who enter here…

Abigail led the way into the gloom, pistol in one hand and torch held high in the other. Anna followed close behind, gripping long amputation knives in each of her palms. The gleaming blades were wickedly curved like handheld scythes.

The tunnel was cramped but wide enough for them to walk shoulder-to-shoulder. Still, they kept in a line, their footfalls reverberating off the stone. The ceiling was low but high enough that neither had to stoop. The dim glow of the torch illuminated a radius of only a few feet, just enough so that they weren't wading through absolute darkness. Beyond the light, the black unknown seemed to pulse with a life of its own, warning them of the deadly threat that lurked deeper within the mountain.

Inside this tunnel of stone, no wind ruffled Abigail's blonde hair. The air was dead and smelled of ancient rock and mildew. Now and then, rats would flit through the torchlight and graze the women's feet as they crept further and further. Gossamer stands of cobwebs floated in the air like disembodied spirits and whispered across their faces.

Abigail saw the webs had recently been disturbed. Kitty had fled through here with Cassie, but did the werewolves travel by this passage too? She knew they were cunning. If they intended to bring the orphans to the cave, would they have left this approach unguarded? Abigail slowed and cast a wary glance over her shoulder, peering into the darkness behind her daughter. Were they being stalked at this very moment?

There was nothing there. The tunnel stretched away into silent darkness in either direction.

"What is it?" Anna whispered.

Abigail shook her head but lingered a moment longer, straining to discern any sign of movement in the gloom. She strained her ears, listening for the clacking of sharp claws on stone.

Still nothing.

Abigail's tongue felt parched and swollen and her stomach knit into an uncomfortable knot as they ventured on. Even as she shivered from the chill in her bones, a trickle of cold sweat crawled down the back of her neck. She had undertaken hundreds of perilous hunts and banishings over the years, but never had she felt more uncertain of survival. A new kind of fear walked with her now, one that had been born in the same instant as her daughter.

Until that moment seventeen years ago, Abigail had been fearless, reckless even, often uncaring if she lived or died. But now the thought of harm coming to her child filled her with terror. She tried to remind herself that she was a powerful occultist. She had been younger than Anna was now when she had vanquished the undead spirits who guarded Sarah Bridges' Book of Shadows in Salem's cursed Northern Woods. In the decades since, she had defeated and slain all manner of spirits and monsters and demons.

But this? How could they possibly survive this? How could anyone? Abigail had seen with her own eyes what savage horrors Lucretia and her followers were capable of. Perhaps they couldn't be stopped—perhaps *no one* could stop them.

And yet, there was no retreating now; they had to try to save Cassie. Abigail would never allow the innocent girl to be damned as a monster, even as a quiet voice in her head told her she and Anna wouldn't be leaving these caves alive.

Time seemed to lose its substance in this subterranean maze. They had to stop more than once to strip another scrap from Anna's dress to keep the torch alight. As the minutes crawled by, a wintry sense of foreboding gnawed at Abigail. What would they find when they arrived at the cave? Were they already too late? Had Mary already done the unthinkable to her daughter? And what about Lucretia and Catherine? They had last been seen at the harbor and university, but where were they now? Waiting for them ahead or some place else? Abigail stole another fearful glance into the impenetrable darkness behind her.

The passage was still empty.

An awful reek seeped through the air and poisoned their nostrils as the passage widened into a small cavern. Abigail couldn't see the walls beyond the shallow glow of the torch, but she could sense that the narrow confines of the tunnel had expanded around them. The cloying stench of the underground chamber was pungent, musty, acrid.

Abigail thrust an arm out and brought Anna to a skidding halt.

There was something in here.

Something alive.

Abigail could hear it rustling and suspiring in the murky darkness above their heads. She held her breath and raised her torch, letting the light penetrate as far as it could.

The ceiling was moving.

For a heart-stopping moment, Abigail had the wild idea that the werewolves could climb walls. Then she caught glints of torchlight reflecting off beady little eyes in the darkness.

Bats. Hundreds of them. Clinging to the ceiling overhead.

A chill crawled up Abigail's spine as she stared up at them. There was something very wrong about their presence here.

"What are they still doing here?" Anna whispered in her ear, giving voice to Abigail's own misgivings. "Nightfall was hours ago. They should be out hunting."

There was only one explanation Abigail could think of. "They sense danger out there."

The entire colony suddenly moved as one, launching from their roosts in an undulating mass of furry black bodies. A furious flapping of wings ruffled Abigail's hair and made the torch flicker in her hand as the bats shot from the cavern. They squeaked and clicked as they went, heading not back toward the mouth of the tunnel, but ahead into the unexplored darkness.

Abigail's guts turned to ice. She knew where the werewolves were.

Right behind them.

Abigail whirled around and fired just as Lucretia roared into the torchlight on a snarling storm of teeth and claws. The wild gunshot went wide and the silver beast smashed into them, slamming Anna back into her mother.

Lucretia's black lips rippled back and her deadly fangs flashed in the lurid light. Before she could strike, Anna slashed down with a curved blade and sliced a nasty gash across the top of the beast's snout. Lucretia roared and tore at her with a claw. Strips of fire raced across Anna's chest from her shoulder to her breast. Hot rills of blood spilled from the slits.

Abigail swung the torch around, but the flame was too

weak to repel the ferocious monster. Lucretia batted it aside with a snarl and knocked it flying from Abigail's grip. She lashed out a claw and clamped it tight around Abigail's throat. The beast's nails pierced her skin and narrowly missed her jugular as it drove her back and hammered her into the wall, lifting Abigail from her feet and pinning her to the stone.

Abigail choked and thrashed, beating at the monster with her free fist. The awful stench of Lucretia's rancid, blood-drenched fur washed over her. Lucretia barely flinched under her victim's desperate assault. Her golden eyes smoldered with bloodlust. Abigail still held the pistol in her other hand, but it was pinned between their bodies and pointed sideways at a harmless angle.

Anna threw herself onto Lucretia's muscled back, hacking and slashing with her knives, ribboning the werewolf's thick hide. Blood flew from the wounds but it was as if Lucretia's bloodlust numbed her to pain. Nothing would deter her from her savage onslaught. Anna got an arm hooked beneath her pointed chin and hauled back on her huge bestial head to clamp her jaws together. She swung a knife around to Lucretia's throat and sliced, opening the monster's windpipe in one swift motion.

Blood sprayed across Abigail's face as Lucretia fell back, relinquishing her hold on Abigail's throat. Her claws flew to the gruesome gash that was spilling scarlet down her chest. She let loose a blood-choked roar and snapped viciously at Anna, who skipped aside barely fast enough to keep from losing an arm.

Abigail gulped air and managed to twist the pistol around

between her and the injured beast. Her finger fumbled for the trigger.

An instant too long.

Lucretia reared her head, threw open her slavering maw, and lunged. Her teeth sank deep into the flesh between Abigail's shoulder and neck. Abigail screamed at the burst of white-hot agony. She heard the gruesome crunch of her collarbone snapping under the immense pressure of the werewolf's jaws.

Delicious blood filled Lucretia's mouth as her fangs scraped against Abigail's bones. But before she could tear away the tender flesh clamped between her teeth, Abigail pumped the pistol's barrel into Lucretia's hairy stomach and fired. The roar of the gunshot was deafening in the hollow cavern. Sparks and smoke filled the air as the bullet blasted the werewolf backward into the opposite wall.

The silver worked quickly. The change was sudden.

Within moments, the vicious werewolf was gone. A human woman lay naked on the stone. Lucretia's long gray hair was a wild mess, and she was letting out a reedy wheezing sound as her sinewy muscles tremored. She gurgled on the blood bubbling in her throat and clutched at the scorched bullet wound in her gut. More blood pumped from between her slender fingers.

The pain was unlike any Abigail had ever known as she slid to the ground and peeled back her overcoat to examine her bite wounds. Blood seeped from the ragged ring of punctures and lacerations. Her skin and flesh were pierced to the bone. She grimaced in pain as she retrieved her powder kit from her coat pocket and handed it to Anna, along with the pistol and two more silver bullets.

"Take these and reload," she said. "We must go quickly."

"Go?" Anna glanced over at Lucretia gasping and writhing on the ground. "But we have to finish her! The silver won't poison her for long. She'll—"

"We must go find the girl!" Abigail snapped through gritted teeth. She reached into her pocket again and produced the vial of ether. "Reload! Now!"

Anna retrieved the torch from the ground while Abigail sprinkled Lucretia's body. "Mother, we must decapitate her. It's the only way to be sure."

"We haven't time!" Abigail grimaced with pain as she snatched the torch away.

"But she'll turn again soon."

"Just reload!"

"But she'll—"

"It's already midnight!"

"But—"

Anna's protest fell from frozen lips as the awful implications of her mother's words slammed her in the gut. She stared at Abigail's wounded shoulder, at the bloody teeth marks oozing crimson in the firelight. Her eyes flicked up to Abigail's face and found her mother gazing back at her with a strange sort of sad surrender.

"I can feel it already," said Abigail.

Anna's insides went cold. She tried to speak, to say that everything was going to be alright, but nothing came out. Her mouth just opened and closed soundlessly.

They both knew what it meant.

Abigail had been bitten.

And it was the midnight hour.
"Let's go," said Abigail.
She threw the torch and set Lucretia ablaze.

Chapter 28

Mary Byrne beckoned for her daughter to join her at the cliff's edge behind the thundering wall of water. "Come, my little blossom. See how beautiful it is…"

Deeper in the cavern's gloom, Cassie sat with her back to the cold stone and gazed back at her mother with pale and fearful eyes.

Mary gave her a warm smile, one that had dispelled countless childhood nightmares in the cheerless nights of their cottage. "Come to me, Cassie. There is nothing to fear."

Cassie obeyed. She uncrossed her legs and stood up. Mary extended a hand from beneath her bearskin and held it out as her daughter padded across the stone to her side. Cassie slipped her little palm into Mary's and they stood together in silence, admiring the awesome majesty of the waterfall.

Midnight had come.

The full moon was at its zenith in the sky. The surging torrent glowed with an otherworldly radiance in its brilliant light. Fat droplets of water twinkled like prisms as they fell.

"Close your eyes, dear," Mary whispered. She released

Cassie's hand and held her own arms up, palms out to the surging cataract. "Feel it against your skin."

Cassie's eyelids slid closed. She raised her hands as her mother had done, palms-up and fingers splayed, as if offering herself up to the primal forces of nature. The cool sparkle of the mist tingled her face and palms. Her pale cheeks dimpled with the faintest delight.

Mary took in the moment, wishing it were timeless. Her sweet and innocent little girl. Glistening with purity.

She started to change.

Mary felt the searing heat building within her; embers igniting into flames that raced from her core to her extremities. Molten blood simmered in her veins. Her flesh burned as the hair came through, growing thick and coarse. The fire reached her fingertips. Her nails turned black and curved into wickedly sharp points. The bearskin strained around her swelling muscles and she shrugged it off, glorying in the wild abandon of her nudity. Her breasts hardened and burned like brimstone. The heat scalded her face as her mouth elongated. Fangs sprouted from her gums in the newly empty spaces between her own teeth.

Mary's whole being was engulfed now, ablaze with the primeval power of the transformation. The steady beating of Cassie's heart was cannon blasts in her ears. She could smell Cassie's sweat beneath her unwashed clothes, the electrifying iron in her blood as it pumped through her veins.

Cassie still stood at the precipice, chin raised and face upturned to the waterfall. Her eyes were closed and her hair shimmered with dewdrops. Mary fixed her huge yellow eyes on her daughter's exposed throat. There would be pain, but it would be mercifully quick. And then it would be done. They would be together forever. Safe…

She spread her jaws wide.

Cassie opened her eyes.

And screamed.

A fanged nightmare stood in the place of her mother.

Mary lunged for her, but her jaws snapped shut on empty air. Cassie squirted away, backpedalling dangerously close to the cliff's edge, too wild with mind-shattering terror to heed the deadly drop. Stones and gravel crunched under her heel and fell away into the swirling abyss below. Mary whipped out a claw to grab her daughter, to keep her from plummeting to her death. Cassie jerked away…

A booming roar erupted and set the side of Mary's bestial head on fire.

Anna stood at the mouth of the tunnel with the pistol still raised. She had been aiming for Mary's head, but the hastily forged silver bullet hadn't been true and blasted off the beast's ear instead. Anna hadn't seen the little girl hidden behind the huge werewolf, the one who was still inching off the cliff…

Pain tore through Mary's head as her claw seized on Cassie's overcoat with a desperate grab. Her nails punctured the threadbare wool and there was an awful ripping as the seams split. Cassie windmilled her arms, her blue eyes huge with panic now as she teetered on the brink. The murky depths yawned far below her. Mary's claw clenched into a fist and yanked. The coat tore to pieces in her grasp. Her other claw flashed out, snatched Cassie's wrist just as she fell. With a powerful tug, Mary jerked her daughter back from the brink and flung her to safety.

Weakened from the change surging through her blood, Abigail slumped against the tunnel wall while Anna cocked the hammer on the second barrel. But Mary was already charging. The werewolf swatted at the pistol before Anna could get a shot off. Anna lost her grip, and the gun went spinning across the ground toward the cliff, skidding to rest just inches away from the edge. Mary slashed at Anna, but she dodged and scampered around with her knives drawn, putting herself between the beast and Cassie.

Mary stormed at her, head low, a battering ram with teeth, ready to strip the flesh from Anna's bones and feast on her marrow. A claw came tearing through the air, aiming for Anna's stomach, swinging so hard it would cut her in two. Anna saw it coming and feinted to the side at the last second. In the same motion, she fired a powerful kick into the beast's extended knee.

Mary crumpled forward, but Anna wasn't done. Her knife gleamed and whistled through the air as she slashed at the back of Mary's leg. The sharp blade sliced through the hairy flesh, all the way to the vital tendons and ligaments beneath. They were so thick it was like sawing through ropes, but Anna didn't relent until they were severed.

Bellowing with unearthly fury, Mary whirled and backhanded Anna in the chest. The blow hit her like a club and blasted the wind from the lungs. She flew back against the wall and her skull ricocheted off the unyielding stone. Stars exploded before her eyes and the knife clattered to her feet as she folded, her legs feeling buoyant beneath her as if she were floating in water.

Mary swung around, fixed her hellfire eyes on Cassie, and

started hobbling toward her.

A woozy moan escaped Anna's lips as she wobbled on unsteady legs. Her vision undulated before her eyes. Blood ran in rivulets from the back of her head down the nape of her neck. She urged herself to move, but she was too dazed to find the strength. An awful nausea roiled her stomach.

Mary would get to Cassie before she did.

Cassie retreated from her mother's slow advance, eyes wide with terror. There was nowhere to run. She was cornered.

Abigail lurched from the tunnel and snatched the pistol up from the ground.

Mary let out a ravenous growl. Her jaws hinged opened. Slaver spilled from her demonic fangs…

Abigail aimed for Mary's head, pressed her finger to the trigger.

A blazing figure came screaming from behind and crashed into her. The pistol tumbled out of reach as Abigail hit the ground with Lucretia on top of her. Flames still licked at the naked madwoman's blackened flesh. Her long gray hair had burned away and her scalp was a ravaged dome of blistered skin. She raged and failed, scratching and biting at Abigail as if she were still a werewolf. They struggled inches away from the precipice, Lucretia's skin sizzling as the mist and spray of the waterfall roaring next to them quenched the flames.

With Abigail pinned beneath her, Lucretia didn't need claws to dig her nails deep into the raw flesh of her foe's puncture wounds. Abigail screamed as Lucretia clenched and ripped down, tearing a gash through the muscle tissue of her upper chest. Blood welled up and pumped from the wound in time with the beating of Abigail's heart. She shot a fist up and hit Lucretia with a straight-arm to the jaw. At the same time, she rolled sideways toward the cliff.

The momentum of the roll sent Lucretia tumbling, and she flipped over the brink. Her blackened hand shot out before she plummeted and grabbed Abigail's ankle, dragging her off the cliff with her. The nails of Abigail's good hand raked across the stone as the rest of her disappeared over the edge.

They hung there together for an instant, Abigail clinging to the crumbling cliff's ledge with one hand, weighed down by the scorched woman gripping her ankle from below, her strength failing, fingers slipping, slipping…

Anna shook off her dizziness and scrambled to the cliff's edge to seize her mother's wrist. Abigail's palm wrapped around hers and Anna heaved with all her strength, feeling the joints of her mother's arm popping from the strain. The weight of the two women dangling in the air was too great; Anna couldn't haul them up.

From the corner of her eye, she saw Mary stalking toward Cassie, dragging her crippled leg, backing the girl deeper into the cave. Cassie was shrieking now, hysterical with terror. Anna shifted back to her mother's pale face, staring up at her.

"Let me go, Anna!" Abigail cried.

Anna ignored her. The pistol had fallen just a few feet away. She kept one hand clamped around Abigail's wrist and stretched for it. It was just out of reach. She leaned for it, stretching, stretching, torn between the pistol on one side and the immense weight of the women on the other. Anna felt she would split in two as she strained and reached. Her fingers brushed the grip, but the pistol remained maddeningly beyond her grasp. She couldn't stretch any further; she would have to let go of Abigail to reach it.

She couldn't save them both. She would have to make a choice.

"Anna, let me go!" shouted Abigail. "I've been bitten in the midnight hour; there is no saving me. Go rescue the girl…"

"No!" Anna's fingers still stretched for the pistol. A crust of rotten rock crumbled from the cliff's edge beneath her planted foot. She glanced down again, and a pit opened in her stomach.

Abigail's eyes had melted from icy blue to pale yellow.

"*No!*" Anna screamed. "Hold on to me, Mother!"

"It's alright, Anna. Let me go…"

"No! Hold on!"

"Walk in the light, my precious girl…"

"Mother, hold—"

Abigail released her hand.

One moment, Abigail and Lucretia were falling together, Abigail's yellow eyes locked on Anna's as she plummeted. Then the crushing force of the falling water struck her and sent her pinwheeling head over heels. It all happened in an instant.

Abigail was gone.

Anna stared after her in horror, so numb with shock she couldn't even scream. Her wide eyes scrambled over the swirling mists that had swallowed her mother. There were no signs of life.

A wild, strangled wail ripped from deep within as Anna tore herself away from the precipice and snapped up the pistol. Mary had backed Cassie up against a wall now. Her claws were dug into each of the girl's frail shoulders. Cassie was shrieking madly as she kicked and thrashed against the monster that was her mother.

Mary roared triumphantly and tossed back her fearsome head. She bared her fangs, snarling as she aimed for her daughter's throat.

Anna pulled the trigger.

The silver bullet blasted a hole in the center of Mary's breast and spun her away from her child. She smashed into the stone wall and slid to the ground, leaving a long streak of blood behind her.

Anna exhaled. The pistol trembled in her hand as she lowered it. Her whole body vibrated with wrath.

Mary was already a human woman again—sprawled naked and bloody across the ground—when Anna strode over to her.

"Look away, Cassie," she said with the pitiless voice of an executioner.

The girl did as she was told.

Blood frothed through Mary's lips as she gazed up at Anna with an unfocused gaze. She saw the knife in Anna's hand, the cold killer in her eyes. Her voice was a gurgling croak. "Protect her."

Anna slit her throat and didn't stop cutting until the blade sliced through her spine. When she was done, she gripped Mary's severed head by the hair and hurled it over the cliff into the waterfall.

Anna's chest heaved and burned as she stood there, dripping blood and so flush with adrenaline she nearly convulsed. When Cassie started to turn around, she took the girl's cheeks in her palms and stopped her. "No, girl. You don't want to see her. Just close your eyes."

With Cassie's face buried in her shoulder, Anna swept the girl up into her arms and hustled her out of the cavern, out of sight of the headless corpse within.

"Listen to me, Cassie," Anna said as she set the girl down on safe ground near the entrance to the tunnel. "I'm going to leave you for a time, but I need you to stay here."

"No! Please..." Cassie sobbed miserably.

"I'll come back for you, I promise. But for now, just remain right here and sing a song. Sing it over and over again until I return. Just sing a song and don't go back there. *Never* go back there. Do you understand?"

Tears streaked Cassie's cheeks and her lip quivered, but she gave a slight nod.

Anna could hear the girl's forlorn singing as she returned to the cliff behind the cascading curtain of water. Through the spray and mist, nothing was visible of the dark pool below. If it was rocky and shallow, Abigail's body would be found dead and broken. But if the water below was deep enough, she could have survived the fall.

Anna didn't have time to wind back through the tunnels to the water's edge. If Abigail had survived the drop, then she would too. And if Abigail hadn't survived... well, what happened then didn't matter.

Anna closed her eyes and leaped.

Chapter 29

Anna hit the cold water hard. The crushing weight of the waterfall pummeled her mercilessly as it sucked her under. She flailed and tried to swim, but she was only pounded deeper into the seething maelstrom of the pool. Her limbs were pulled in all directions like a rag doll flailing in an angry dog's jaws. Icy water churned around her and flooded her mouth. She was tossed up to the surface, sputtering and gasping for air, only to be hammered under again beneath the punishing cataract crashing down upon her. She opened her eyes and saw nothing but froth and bubbles.

Moonlight shimmered through the water above her and cut through the blackness like a ghostly beacon. But without oxygen, Anna was weakening now. Her lungs were aflame and screaming for release. The moonlight grew fainter as she was pushed ever lower into the seething black cauldron. How deep could she possibly sink?

She resisted the urge to panic as her toes scraped across the rocky bottom. There was a crushing pressure in her chest as her deflated lungs suffocated. Pinpricks of light burst before her eyes as she gazed up at the diffuse orb of moonlight. Her strength was fading and along with it, her will to struggle. Already, an irresistible drowsiness was descending upon her. How long since she had last drawn a breath? Seconds? Minutes? It wouldn't be long before she lost consciousness. If only she could break free of the waterfall's pummeling force, she still had a chance of survival.

Summoning whatever scraps of strength she had left, Anna kicked desperately against the bottom of the pool and angled herself forward. At the same time, she spread her arms and swam. If this didn't work, she would drown.

Anna began to rise.

Hope rose with her and one swim stroke led to another and another. She kicked her legs, propelling herself ever upward, the moonlight growing more distinct—more *reachable*—with every motion. A momentary darkness fell over Anna's vision as her consciousness shuddered, but she still did not give up. Her arms failed her, but she had enough strength left in her legs for one more kick...

Cold air kissed her face as she broke the surface. Her mouth blew open and vomited water as she gulped air into her tormented lungs, feeling them devour the oxygen. She felt her strength slowly returning to her limbs as she bobbed a few yards from where the cascading torrent pummeled the pool. She had survived the fall—and if she still lived, Abigail might as well.

Anna spun around in circles in the water. Her chest heaved with shuddering breaths as she scanned the moonlit rocks that cradled the plunge pool.

She stopped. Her eyes were vast with horror.

Abigail's sodden body lay crumpled across the boulders at the water's edge.

Anna's heart constricted and she lunged forward, swimming desperately until her feet brushed against the shallow bottom. She splashed through the water to get to Abigail, hoping against hope that it wasn't already too late. She stumbled, dragged herself back up, staggered to where her mother lay.

Abigail's eyes were a lifeless stare.

Anna stood trembling over her mother's corpse, so numb with shock her limbs were boneless. Parts of her were breaking inside, fragile parts she never imagined she possessed. They were crumbling and shattering and falling to pieces, leaving nothing behind but a hollow emptiness that filled rapidly with grief. She had a wild urge to call Abigail's name, to wake her from this dreadful slumber, but she couldn't find a voice. There was nothing in her throat but a suffocating lump. All she could do was stare, willing her mother to draw a breath, to come alive again somehow. But there was nothing there but cold, white skin and a terrible stillness. This was how it ended.

Blood still seeped from the ragged gash in Abigail's upper chest. It was spreading across the boulder beneath her. She hadn't been here long; might even have been dragging herself out of the freezing pool just as Anna made the leap after her. She had died with one arm outstretched across the rock over her head. There on the granite slab where her bloody fingertips rested was an arcane sigil scrawled in her own blood. Anna's unfocused gaze found it through the tears welling in her eyes. In her dying moments, Abigail had cast one last spell.

A rustling in the forest jolted Anna from her grief.

She wasn't alone.

She turned around in a slow revolution, already knowing what she would find there.

Lucretia leered back at her through the mist from the shadows of the trees. She had transformed again, an unholy abomination on two legs. Any trace of the fire that had nearly consumed her was gone, effaced by her preternatural power of healing. The werewolf's yellow eyes were hate-filled slits, and her lips rippled back over her sharp fangs. She let out a rumbling snarl, dripping with ferocious loathing. Her claws were splayed out in the air, eager to shred the flesh and glut herself on the blood of this hateful woman who had ruined everything.

A whirlwind of heartbroken rage swept through Anna as she rose and stood between the merciless beast and Abigail's corpse.

Destroy her! A furious voice screamed in her head. *She killed your mother! Spill her foul blood and delight in her suffering! I will help you if you but release me!*

The werewolf advanced, a towering nightmare of teeth and claws cleaving through the mist.

Yes, Anna thought. *Live through me, my wrathful guardian...*

In her grief and despair, she called on the darkness within her.

And the darkness answered.

There was a simmering in her veins, a coursing rush of dark energy invading her being. Anna let it take hold of her, giving herself over to it, exulting in its black power.

Arcane words spilled from her mouth in a voice that wasn't her own, chanting the serpentine language of conjuring. The spell was unfamiliar, but the presence inside her made her to know that it required blood. She raised her wrist to her lips and sank her teeth into her own flesh. Blood filled her mouth, and she was flooded with the most intense feeling of rapture. A force was gathering within her, an ancient spirit born of torment and baptized in the fires of Hell. Anna had felt its presence her whole life, a constant companion lurking in the shadows of her soul. She heard its voice whispering in her ear in her earliest memories, enticing her to acts of remorseless violence.

Now she surrendered herself to it, let herself become a willing vessel through which it might take form. She felt a shuddering warmth, like the blissful release of a climax as the dark presence seized control and surged up her body from her belly to her throat. She arched backward and threw her head back, her jaw hinging wide as a thick white mist burst from her gaping mouth. It shot straight into the air above her, swirling and writhing with a life of its own. The unearthly mist went from an ethereal white to gray and then to an unholy black as it drew itself together and took shape.

The ghostly image of a woman in a tattered linen dress…

A face hidden behind a dreadful black veil…

Rebecca Hale.

Anna collapsed alongside Abigail's body as her great-great-grandmother's shadowy spirit filled the air above her. The baleful apparition's eyes were two flaming embers blazing in the fathomless abyss of her black veil. Alive with a black and forbidding energy, Rebecca fixed her burning gaze on

Lucretia.

For the first time, something like fear flashed in the werewolf's golden eyes, a glinting vestige of the human woman within the heartless beast. She lowered to all fours and retreated a step into the trees, hackles raised into tall spikes along her spine, snarling like a dog being backed into a corner.

The black mist surged.

Lucretia let out a ferocious roar and sprang up, slashing with her claws and snapping her vicious teeth as if the unearthly apparition were something she could actually rip and kill. The mist engulfed her like a black tornado, and the werewolf vanished into its swirling depths. Ghastly howls of agony burst forth and shattered the night, drowning out even the roar of the waterfall. Blood and viscera splattered the rocks below the roiling black mass as the apparition that was Rebecca Hale tore at Lucretia's hairy flesh and stripped it from her bones.

Anna staggered up to one knee on the rocks. Through the writhing mist, she caught a fleeting glimpse of Lucretia's ravaged face. Her pointed ears were shredded to ribbons and one eye-socket was a mutilated ruin. A strip of flesh had been flayed away from the top of her scalp to the tip of her wolven snout, exposing the long white skull beneath. What remained of her lips were ragged flaps of skin that no longer covered her long rows of jagged fangs. More flesh was torn away before Anna's eyes until the werewolf's horrid face vanished into the mist again. But Lucretia's piercing shrieks carried on, rising to a frenzied pitch before dissolving into a wet gurgle and dying into silence.

The werewolf was gone, her flesh torn apart and shredded, her remains scattered about in hundreds of broken pieces.

Anna exhaled, letting the air from her lungs as if she had forgotten how to breathe.

Then the mist coiled around and focused the orange flames of its eyes on her.

Anna felt the searing heat of Rebecca's glare pierce her heart from behind the shadowy veil. In that horrific instant, she knew with dreadful certainty that her dead ancestor intended to possess her for her own. A shiver of terror swept over her. Now that she had released Rebecca from her fiery prison, the spirit had no intention of returning. She had waited all of Anna's life for this moment, to live anew in Anna's flesh and do the devil's work wherever she went.

Anna realized her dreadful mistake in the same instant that the mist shot at her.

The force of the spirit slamming into her rocked her back on her heels. She felt Rebecca's venomous presence invading her veins. This time, there was no euphoric thrill; she was no longer a welcome conduit for Rebecca's dark energy. This time, Anna herself was the target of the hanged witch's undying longing to live again. She gasped and dropped to her knees as a tightness gripped her chest, as if the malevolent spirit had coiled around her heart and was squeezing the life from it. Rebecca was overtaking her, consuming her, insinuating herself into Anna's flesh and seizing control of her being.

There was only one hope for her deliverance from the spirit's insidious invasion.

Anna strained to move limbs that no longer felt like her

own and crawled on hands and knees to Abigail's corpse. Her whole body was wracked with shudders as she fought to regain control. Visions flooded her mind; terrible memories of a life that wasn't her own: She saw Rebecca trembling and wretched in the black squalor of Salem's witch dungeon. She saw seven little children hanging by their necks from a gallows tree. She saw Rebecca being led toward her own noose and the terrible black veil that awaited her before her hanging…

Anna clenched her jaw, her teeth grinding against each other painfully. The pressure in her chest was so intense she was certain it would burst wide open. Her nerveless hands shook as she fumbled at her mother's throat, searching for the iron talisman that had hung there since Abigail was a girl. The viselike grip on her chest crawled into her throat. Her breath became a saw rasping through wood and her eyes strained in their sockets as her grasping fingers curled around hard metal. The unpolished iron was cold to the touch and radiated an unearthly chill in her palm.

With her last shred of free will, Anna slipped her mother's charm around her own neck.

A soul-shredding shriek erupted in her head, one so powerful and full of fury Anna was certain her ears would bleed. Deep within her, she felt Rebecca's spirit recoiling from the rune like a viper from a flame. There was a painful writhing in her flesh as the trapped spirit raged and seethed.

"Hear me, Rebecca Hale!" Anna shouted aloud, her voice firm and commanding. "I am my own and none other's!"

A mocking laughter filled her ears, loud and cackling like that of a demon fiend delighting in the torments of Hell.

Ungrateful wretch! You are but a mewling child without me!

"No, accursed spirit! *You* are the one who needs me," Anna swore. "I am your only vessel between this world and the fiery damnation to which you condemned yourself years ago. In time, I will uncover a way to sever this infernal bond that unites us. Until that day comes, know that I am your master to be served and obeyed!"

Rebecca chortled her diabolical laughter again. But at the same time, Anna felt the spirit's hold on her withering under the power of the protective talisman pressed against her breast. She felt Rebecca's presence draining from her flesh and blood, retreating to the dark recesses within her where it had lived since the moment she was conceived. The terrible laughter grew quiet, then went silent. But Anna knew Rebecca Hale was still there somewhere within her.

She would always be there.

The eerie stillness of the night settled over the forest and the water's edge. Tears sprang to Anna's eyes and spilled down her cheeks. Bathed in moonlight, the roar of the waterfall drowned her wretched sobs as she sank to her knees on the rocks and curled like a child against her mother's body.

Epilogue

A jack o' lantern still burned in the parlor window of a stately row house in Boston's posh Beacon Hill. The revelry of All Hallows' Eve had long since ended and fallen leaves now whispered their forlorn song as they swept through the dark and empty lanes.

Any other year, Anna and Abigail would have risked their lives banishing one of the malign spirits who slipped through the Veil on this night when it was at its thinnest. It was an annual tradition as common as candied apples and spiced pumpkin pie.

But on this All Hallows' Eve, Anna had stood by the window as the fiery hues of sunset died in the sky and yielded to the indigo blue of twilight. She had spent the evening hours giving soul cakes to the costumed visitors who came to her door. And when the hour grew late, and the revelers deserted the streets, Anna had bolted the lock and wandered into the parlor.

She remained there in a moment of silent reflection, letting her gaze tip-toe over her mother's collection of cherished possessions—the payment and gifts she had received from the grateful multitudes whose lives she had saved over the years. This room had practically been Anna's nursery. Part of her still expected her mother to sweep in at any moment to draw her daughter's attention to some item she might find fascinating.

As a child growing up in this house, none of these treasures had been off-limits to Anna. The exquisite paintings, the rare volumes of poetry, the wondrous carvings and exotic curios; all had been Anna's playthings to explore and kindle her curiosity.

Abigail's most deadly and forbidden items were locked away deep beneath the house.

It was there that Anna had gone when the witching hour tolled on All Hallows' Eve. Beneath a secret door in the cellar floor, a stone staircase spiraled deep into the bedrock of the city itself. At the bottom, far beneath the surface and hidden away from the world above, was Abigail's *arcanium*—the clandestine laboratory and library where her vast collection of the occult and paranatural was stored.

Huge oaken beams supported the stone ceiling of the immense catacomb. An entire wall was lined with deep wooden shelves laden with books of all sizes and ages. Some were so old they had no bindings and were kept together with braided strands of human hair. Others bore pagan runes and titles scratched in dead languages.

Against another wall stood rows of cabinets bearing a vast array of skulls and effigies and jars of spices, graveyard dirt, bone-dust, and other, more ghastly components of witchcraft. A gigantic table stood at one end of the room. Knife wounds scarred the stone surface, and it was blackened with the stains of sacrificial blood. At the center of the chamber was Abigail's Scrying Pool, a placid stone well drawn from the water that flowed deep within the bowels of the coastal city itself. Its still and unbroken surface gleamed black, like a mirror held up to a starless night.

The smell of the arcanium had risen to greet Anna as she descended the steep and narrow steps. The scent was both enthralling and direful, a complex mingling of earthy spice, musty leather, and a sour trace of decay. When she reached the landing, Anna paused and swept her eyes around the chamber.

Dozens of candles, their wicks misshapen with an accumulation of wax rivulets, illuminated the cavernous space. But they failed to penetrate the sepulchral shadows that gathered in the corners. Their flames gave off no heat, as if an unearthly chill was emanating from the occult books and objects themselves.

Everything in this imposing chamber now belonged to Anna. All of it—from the rare and beautiful to the macabre and ghastly—was hers. Even the ancient book that now sat open upon an intricate lectern, its deep crimson binding gleaming like blood in the candlelight.

Her mother's Book of Shadows.

Anna cast a glance at the open page as she moved to one of the many cabinets. There, she withdrew a very special bottle —not a potion or elixir, but one of Abigail's rarest bottles of whiskey. She found a crystal tumbler and poured herself a goodly amount. She would need courage for what was to come.

Glass in hand, Anna had turned to the iron door cloaked

in shadows at the far end of the room. Beyond that door was Abigail's Conjuring Chamber, a special cell designed for communing with the dead and fortified with powerful warding to prevent their escape.

Anna had been surprised at the cautious trepidation she still felt as she approached that forbidding door. For a fleeting instant, she felt like a small child again, fearful of what lay beyond. Such were the lethal dangers of necromancy that it wasn't until well into her apprenticeship that Anna had been invited to join her mother inside the Conjuring Chamber. Such phenomenal things she had witnessed within, such phenomenal and terrible things that had filled her childhood dreams and nightmares.

As always, there was an excited tingle in Anna's blood as she drew nearer. She was now the Mistress of this unholy place. And there was now something else to be found within the stone walls of the chamber, something far more precious than anything in the whole of the arcanium.

The air had grown colder as Anna approached the door. When she grasped the handle, it was freezing to the touch. She pulled and an icy breath whispered across her face as the heavy portal groaned open. The chamber within was large and circular, measuring exactly twenty-two feet in diameter. Its ceiling was so high it was lost in the murky darkness above. An elaborate pentagram had been chiseled into the stone floor itself. Charmed torches burned eternally in their sconces and ornate, black-framed mirrors hung on the walls at the five points of the pentagram.

Abigail's body lay beneath a shroud at the center of the chamber.

Anna's breath had puffed white in the cold air as she crossed the threshold. She was immediately knocked back by an unseen force. A shadowy figure materialized before her eyes—the undead Guardian she had conjured to guard her mother's body. The spirit's unending presence, and the otherworldly chill of the grave that followed it wherever it went, would preserve Abigail's corpse for as long as Anna demanded it.

But Anna was no longer certain it would be necessary.

Something very peculiar had happened on the long journey home from Burlington to Boston: Abigail's body had shown no sign of decay. Though she gave every outward appearance of death—her chest still and breathless, her eyes vacant and unseeing, the ragged wound in her shoulder now bloodless—Abigail's cold flesh remained an alabaster white, unblemished but for her numerous scars. Days went by and Anna's thoughts returned over and over to the spell her mother had cast with her last breath.

Immediately upon her return to Boston, she had set herself to deciphering the arcane sigil Abigail had scrawled on the rock in the moments before her death. She found no reference to it in Abigail's Book of Shadows. It could only mean one thing: Whatever spell Abigail had cast was ancient, older even than the earliest spells inscribed by the generations of witches who had possessed the grimoire before her.

Anna had continued her search for days. Locked away in the subterranean crypt of the arcanium, she had poured over the volumes in Abigail's library, not eating or sleeping, shunning the daylight and losing all notion of time. Each of the tomes led to nothing but frustration until, at last, she found it.

What she discovered stole her breath and sent shivers rippling through her body.

It couldn't be...

No, she had to be certain.

And so, Anna had waited for this very night—on All Hallows' Eve when the Veil was at its thinnest and the powers of the undead were at their highest—to conjure Gideon to do her bidding, to confirm what she believed couldn't be possible.

Now, while she waited for Gideon's return to the Conjuring Chamber, Anna kept vigil over her mother's body and sipped her whiskey, letting its heat warm her. She could no longer see the Guardian, but she could still feel his bone-chilling presence in the cell with her. As the minutes stretched on, her mind travelled back to Burlington and the nightmarish chain of events that had led her to this moment. And after a time, her thoughts drifted to Kitty Hayes.

In the weeks following her return to Boston, Anna had sent a Familiar to Burlington to bring back news of Kitty. While awaiting rescue with the orphans from the destruction on Juniper Island, Kitty had come up with a fantastical but plausible story to explain the night's terrible events. Virgil Stroud and some of the university's other faculty and students had gone on a murderous rampage in pursuit of the town's orphans, whom they intended to imprison and use for macabre experiments in the name of science.

Lucretia must have been their first victim, though her body was never found. Kitty had been visiting the poor farm where she had spent her childhood when the group attacked. A trio of heroic men had come to her aid, only to be overcome and butchered by Stroud and his disciples. Stealing the steamboat may have been a reckless and criminal act, but Kitty had been possessed by a desperate fit of hysteria brought on by her fear for the children's safety.

Jonathan—an ardent and endearing boy when he wanted to be—corroborated Kitty's account, and while the tale seemed flimsy enough, against all expectations, the authorities appeared inclined to believe it. Stroud and the others were nowhere to be found. With no other witnesses, the town constable had no other explanation for the grisly murders on the poor farm that had led a young woman to flee town with a gaggle of orphans on a stolen steamboat.

The mystery of the disappearances of Tabitha Brant, Catherine Abell, and Mary Byrne would never be solved, though many in town now wondered if they too had fallen victim to Stroud's homicidal cabal.

As for the mutilated remains of the men found in the harbor, Constable Lewis was quick to conclude that Jericho Byrne, Dirch Gray, and their villainous friends must have finally picked a fight with a gang more vicious than they.

Kitty had taken on the role of Cassie Byrne's guardian and would continue as such until a legal adoption was formalized. In the meantime, Kitty was also petitioning the town to appoint her to the now-vacant position of overseer of the poor farm. A woman had never held the post, and they would expect her to hire a man to see to the farm work, but there was none in town who could name someone more qualified to care for the downtrodden and needy than Kitty.

As she thought of the young woman now, Anna was

inclined to agree. Had their lives been different, she might have found a good friend in the fiery Irishwoman.

Anna swallowed another gulp of whiskey as a more unpleasant thought crept into her mind: Lucretia and her followers might be dead, but there were more monsters just like them—many more. The Order of the Lupamatri were still out there, biding their time in the shadows, waiting for the right moment to reveal themselves.

Waiting to strike.

The chamber grew even colder, a numbing chill that gnawed at Anna's very bones.

Gideon had returned.

Anna hurried to the black-framed mirror at the western point of the pentagram. Within it, a dense mass of mist was drawing itself together. It shifted and twisted into the ghostly image of a young man who might have been handsome were it not for the hollow holes of his eyes.

"Speak!" Anna demanded, her eyes gleaming. "What have you found?"

'Tis as you suspected, Gideon's undead voice intoned. *In the moments before her death, your mother opened a portal into the Veil.*

Anna's heart quickened in her chest. "For what purpose?"

To escape her transformation from woman to beast.

The crystal glass fell from Anna's nerveless fingers and shattered across the floor. She felt breathless and lightheaded as she stared at the vaporous image of the spirit in the mirror.

Your mother is not dead, Mistress. Her spirit is here with us beyond the Veil where she now awaits.

An icy chill crawled up Anna's spine. "Awaits what?"

For you to bring her back.

A heart-rendering despair gripped Anna as she cast her eyes downward to where her mother's body lay preserved beneath her shroud.

"That's impossible," she lamented. "My mother spent a lifetime searching for a way to return her parents to her. There is no magic that can restore the living once they have moved beyond the Veil."

No, whispered an ancient voice in her head. *There is a way…*

Author's Note

Thank you, dear reader, for the generous gift of your time and attention. If you enjoyed this book and would like to see more, please consider taking a moment to leave a quick review on Amazon and/or Goodreads. A kind word from a reader like you is one of the best ways you can support independent authors and is very much appreciated.

Until next time, look under the bed, close the closet door, and whatever you do, don't turn around…

**She was innocent of witchcraft when they arrested her.
She was guilty when they hanged her.**

A Firebrand of Hell, a short story prequel to the best-selling *Book of Shadows* series, is now available absolutely free!

Set one hundred years before the events of *All Hallows Eve*, find out what drove Rebecca Hale to sell her soul to the devil on the eve of her hanging.

Visit www.michaelpenning.com to download your free copy!

Books by Michael Penning

***Book of Shadows* Series**
Novels:
All Hallows Eve
The Suicide Lake
The Wolf Society

Companion Stories:
The Damnation Chronicles

Standalone Novels:
Solitude

Michael Penning is a bestselling author and award-winning screenwriter of horror and dark fiction. He has been obsessed with all things dark and spooky since before he could finish his own sack of trick-or-treat candy. When he's not coming up with creative ways to scare the hell out of people, he enjoys traveling, photography, and brewing beer. He lives in Montreal with his wife and daughter. For updates and free giveaways, visit www.michaelpenning.com and follow Michael on social media @michaelpenningauthor.

Printed in Great Britain
by Amazon